A LITTLE SOMETHING
TO SHOW YOU HOW I FEEL . . .

She opened the box and, to her amazement, there was a smallish box inside, the kind that might hold a bracelet. If Mike wanted to give her a bracelet, it didn't seem characteristic of him to do it this way. Anticipation had now given way to uneasiness, and she lifted the cover off slowly.

There on a bed of white cotton lay a dead sparrow, its head severed, a long hat pin fastening the head to the body . . .

WHEN A SPARROW FALLS

A shattering novel of one man's passion . . .
and one woman's nightmare.

WHEN A SPARROW FALLS

JEAN FIEDLER

DIAMOND BOOKS, NEW YORK

WHEN A SPARROW FALLS

A Diamond Book / published by arrangement with
the author

PRINTING HISTORY
Diamond edition / March 1992

ISBN: 1-55773-673-1

Diamond Books are published by The Berkley Publishing Group,
200 Madison Avenue, New York, New York 10016.
The name ''DIAMOND'' and its logo are trademarks
belonging to Charter Communications, Inc.

PRINTED IN THE UNITED STATES OF AMERICA

10 9 8 7 6 5 4 3 2 1

ACKNOWLEDGMENTS

My thanks and gratitude must go to the following experts: Detective Ramesh Nyberg, Metro Dade Police Department, Homicide Bureau, Miami, Florida; Detective Thomas Natale, Ballistics Division, New York City Police Department; Officer James DeMaio, Sixth Precinct, Nassau County Police Department, New York; Ms. Chris Keeler, Annoyance Call Bureau, New York Telephone Company; and Mr. Michael Britt of MBI Hunting and Target Club in Mineola, Long Island, New York.

I am deeply grateful, too, to Leo Wollman, M.D., psychiatrist and gynecologist, who first aroused my interest in a type of gender dysphoria that was important to my story; to my friend Susan Dunlap, who took the time to read an early version of this book and whose doing so helped to change its direction; to my agent and friend, Alice Harron Orr, who started the ball rolling; to the members of the Saturday workshop—Lee Alperin, Carla Potash, and Dorothy Mongan—for their continued encouragement; to my dear children, Judy and Mitch Aaron and Joan and Jim Mele; and to my favorite three young people, Richard Mele, Diana Mele, and Alexandra Aaron, who add great joy to my life.

For Hal, with love and appreciation

PROLOGUE

March 6

Torrents of rain beat down on him. On a trash pile near the abandoned railroad tracks he had found a plastic bag and covered his head with it. But now a gust of wind tore it off. The homeless man began to shiver and cough.

When the outline of the shack appeared, he blinked his eyes several times. Mirages were no strangers to him—sooner or later they would vanish. But this mirage was tenacious. In fact the closer he got to it, the more detailed it became.

His heart began to race at the possibility of shelter. How many nights had he slept in the woods? He couldn't remember. His memory, unreliable for a long time now, seemed to have huge holes in it. It was even hard to remember when he had last eaten.

The shack was probably used for storing coal, he thought, judging from its proximity to the railroad tracks. Maybe he could even build a fire and stop shivering.

He ran the last few steps, gasping and coughing as he approached the door of the shack. For a few seconds, as his eyes grew accustomed to the dimness, he thought he was in paradise. He had been right about the coal—there was some in the corner.

Someone had built a fire on the wooden floor. The fire had charred the walls, and the wet burnt wood still smelled smoky.

Even in this dim light, he could see the blackened walls. A Maxwell House coffee can in the corner caught his eye. If he found some kind of container maybe he could even

1

boil himself some coffee. The hot liquid might help his cough. It took a long time to collect rainwater, but he was in no hurry.

He spied an empty pickle jar near the can and walked over slowly, dreading that the can would be empty. But it was not—there was enough left for a weak cup of coffee. The homeless man smiled. This was almost too good to be true. It was time his luck began to change.

Then he became aware of another smell. It reminded him of other shelters he had found where an animal had crept inside to die. His eyes roamed the room, but it was empty. No animal anywhere. When he dropped his wet, ragged bundle on the floor, he saw that the floorboards were loose. The odious smell was strongest here. He started to gag.

Maybe the floorboards were loose for a reason. In the years that he had been homeless he had heard many stories—some of them gruesome. He had always been grateful that he had never stumbled upon any dead body.

Could an animal have found its way here and desperate with hunger, have clawed up the floorboards? He knew that he had to check.

Crouching on his knees, he held his breath and tried to move one of the loose boards. It moved too easily. Directly beneath it lay the remains of a hand. No longer could he hold his breath—the smell overpowered him and forced him, still on his knees, to crawl to the open door where he vomited until there was nothing left to throw up.

He had to tell the police about the dead body under the floor here. If they knew, they would dig it up, and then he might come back and stay here for a while.

Now he was standing, his mouth open to catch the rain that would cleanse his mouth, when he realized that *he* could never tell the police or anybody about this body. The only thing to do was to get the hell out of here as fast as possible.

The homeless man went back inside and got his bundle

of rags. As an afterthought, he picked up the coffee can and the jar and put them in his bag.

His eyes returned to the loose floorboard. The next person who found this refuge would see the body and report it. Maybe a group of boy scouts on a hike . . .

It seemed indecent to leave a body unburied there, but how easy it would be for the police to take him into custody and accuse him of the murder.

"It's not right not to tell," he muttered to himself, wondering now if the body belonged to a man or woman.

But he wasn't going to look.

CHAPTER ONE

March 7

In the terrible months that followed, when she thought about this evening with Mike, Liz remembered it as almost perfect from beginning to end—the last such evening before the horror began.

She had never outgrown her love of surprises, and the fact that the celebration was unexpected made it even better. Liz had been alone in the Teachers' Room during her free period, correcting themes, when the phone rang. Startled, she dropped her pen and made a green streak on Sandra Crawford's paper. "Damn," she said aloud and picked up the receiver. Her "Hello" sounded brusque even to her own ears.

"May I speak to the sexiest English teacher at Glen High?" a familiar voice said.

"Mike! How did you know I was here?"

"I didn't—I hoped. How many places are there to hide when you have a free period? Anyway, I called for a reason."

"Is everything okay?" she asked. "There's nothing wrong with you or Loren?"

"Nothing wrong with anybody, baby. I just realized a little while ago that today is March seventh. Do you know what that date signifies?"

Liz's thoughts darted about, trying to remember something that was obviously worthy of remembering. "It's not your birthday . . . or mine."

4

"Try counting back six months," Mike said, sounding a bit smug, she thought.

"Okay . . . give me a minute . . . September seventh. Oh Mike! It's when we had our first date."

"And they say that women are more sentimental than men," Mike commented. "Well, as soon as I realized what day it was, I knew we had to do something special, even if it meant juggling things around a bit."

"But, Mike, it's Thursday . . . you always have the kids on Thursday."

"So I do, but I've done Barbara favors by taking them when she had something special, and *you* told me you were finally getting to some reading, so I knew you were free. I made a reservation at Leightons on the Lake at seven-thirty sharp. What do you say to that?"

"I say it's marvelous and you are the best, the most thoughtful guy a woman could have!"

"What about handsome?"

"That, too. Oh, how I loved that place when you first took me there! It seemed so elegant, so . . . ." She paused, unable to find the exact word that would do it justice.

"Precisely why we're going back. Okay, love, I'll pick you up at six-thirty. It may take an hour to get there at this time of year."

Liz hung up the receiver, wondering as she often had at her own good fortune in having met Mike, fallen in love with him, and being loved in the way she had always dreamed of being loved. Good fortune? She owed meeting Mike to her twin brother, Loren.

She knew that one of the reasons Loren could tolerate his job as senior math teacher at Grant High School was because Mike Raymond was the head of the math department and because he and Loren had become friends almost from their first meeting. Liz had heard so many glowing stories about Mike that, half-jealous, she was fully prepared—even hoping—to dislike him.

On that evening when Loren had generously invited her

to go along and have dinner with him and his friend at a neighborhood Italian restaurant halfway between Great Neck and Bayside, she had worn a black turtleneck sweater, jeans, little makeup, and a sober demeanor.

And instead of fulfilling any of her disagreeable fantasies, she had fallen in love with him almost as soon as she saw his smile and shook his hand in greeting.

For an instant, the thought of Loren saddened her—if only he could be as happy as she was—but she refused to pursue this train of thought, determined not to allow any sadness to mar this anniversary of hers and Mike's.

Still, she wished that somehow Loren could be part of the celebration. Of course, he could come to dinner with them, but she knew that even if Mike were willing, Loren would not be. Rarely, despite repeated invitations, did he ever join them for anything they suggested.

"No!" she said aloud and forced herself to turn her thoughts back to the evening ahead.

On September 7th she had worn an orchid silk blouse and long matching skirt, her hair pulled up in a low chignon that showed her favorite amethyst earrings. She would wear the same outfit tonight with her white wool Ungaro coat in concession to the frigid March winds. The coat had been a birthday gift from Loren. It was the first designer coat she had ever had.

Mike's brown eyes sparkled with pleasure at the sight of her. "I wasn't sure you'd remember what you wore that night," he said. "And," he added, "I didn't want to remind you."

"You could have," she said, reaching up to pull his head down so that she could kiss him.

"I never thought I'd rate such a beauty," Mike said, holding her close. The tenderness in his voice made her breath catch.

The drive took almost the hour Mike had predicted: the

Hutchinson to the Saw Mill River Parkway and then into Westchester. Finally, there it was—Leightons on the Lake.

It was an old country inn with a fireplace and a small intimate-looking dining room. Most of the tables had a lakeside view, and there were lanterns hung so that although it was dark, one could actually see the lake.

An attractive, dark-haired waitress came over to their table and instead of taking their drink orders, brought over a bottle of Moet, which she proceeded to pour into two long-stemmed glasses.

"Did I miss something?" Liz asked in delight.

"You have before you a suave, sophisticated man who gets across what he wants by a gesture . . . or by giving an order on the telephone six hours in advance." Mike raised his glass and motioned for Liz to do the same. "To us, my darling, for a lifetime of loving, and to you for making my life happy for the first time in years."

They clicked glasses and drank. Then Liz said, raising her glass, "Ditto!" Clicking glasses again and beginning to drink, she paused. "There's another toast we have to drink."

Mike's eyebrows lifted.

"To Loren . . . who was responsible for . . . everything."

"Almost," Mike added with a lascivious wink as he drank deeply.

By now the dining room was almost filled, but to Liz's surprise, their orders were brought promptly, and everything was as delicious as she recalled—the New England clam chowder, the broiled sole with lyonnaise potatoes and fresh broccoli, and the salad of arugula and endive with a dressing she had tried in vain to duplicate for months.

When the waitress brought the dessert menu, Liz laughingly protested, "I can't. One more drop of food, and I'll burst. Just coffee for me, please."

"And two orders of chocolate mousse," Mike said, adding, "Coffee—black for me."

"How can you eat two portions of chocolate mousse?" Liz asked incredulously.

"Wait and see." Mike grinned as if he had a secret. It was a small boy's grin, which Liz found enchanting.

The waitress smiled as she set two dishes in front of him and poured their coffee.

"I've been getting some strange looks from the people at the tables around us," Mike confided in a low voice. "Do you mind if I set one of the dishes in front of you, sweetheart?"

"Of course not. You go right ahead," Liz said innocently. "I don't want strange people looking at you as if you're weird . . . even when you do act that way."

She sipped her coffee and surreptitiously took a spoonful of the mousse. Creamy and richly chocolate, it was not to be resisted.

Not surprisingly, she found that one spoonful demanded another and then another. She glanced up to find Mike looking at her and laughing.

"Talk about shrewd and manipulative," she said, smiling at him, enjoying the smug expression on his face.

Mike lit his pipe, looking as relaxed and happy as Liz had ever seen him. "I want to discuss something with you," he said, "something I've been putting off out of cowardice, I guess."

The mousse suddenly tasted cloying, and she stopped eating, waiting, wondering what this could be. He hadn't brought her here to celebrate their six-month anniversary to tell her he had found someone else. No, of course he hadn't. . . .

"Don't look like that, baby," Mike said tenderly, obviously aware of what she might be thinking. "It's about the kids. It's time you met. I wanted you to meet them after our first date, but every time I set it up, something happened to get in the way, and I knew they weren't ready—especially Donna. The divorce was hardest on her. Jimmy took it much better, but then he's younger. From my experience with kids her age I know that divorce badly rocks them. Thirteen, in the middle of all kinds of changes, and suddenly her father and mother decided to split, and her father left—a father she seems to think is her property and hers alone. Three years later, she's sixteen, but nothing has changed.''

"I've seen it with my students at school too," Liz said. "Maybe it's still too soon, Mike. Maybe we should wait a little longer."

He shook his head. "No, she's not getting better or less possessive. As a matter of fact, she mentioned last weekend that maybe Barbara and I could try again. I don't think I've done her a favor by putting this off, Liz. It's time for you to meet each other—this Sunday, to make it definite— for lunch."

She had wondered when Mike would suggest this meeting. Each time she had suggested it he had put it off. This was the first time he had spoken so openly about Donna. Obviously it was she, not Jimmy, who had been standing in the way.

Liz began slowly, "I think I know a little bit about what Donna must be feeling, and I'm not a teenager. When Mother left—it was three months ago—I felt lost, as if I were five years old. Loren did too, maybe even worse, if that's possible. . . . I still miss her terribly. It's not hard for me to understand her falling in love with Leopold, but why doesn't she want to phone us or have us phone her? How can Leopold have become so important to her that she can let letters be our only contact? And she's so evasive about where they are. I can tell only by the postmarks on her letters. You should see me with my magnifying glass trying to decipher the town.

"I keep wanting to call her, but I don't have a number, and it doesn't seem right to intrude. . . ." Liz stopped. "I've changed the subject, haven't I?" she said wryly. "Getting

back to the subject at hand—maybe if I keep a low profile
and just act natural as I do with my kids at school, Donna
won't find me so hard to take.''

"She'll love you when she comes to her senses, but that
may take a while. She's not an easy kid, Liz, and sometimes her intensity scares me. She loves hard, but she hates
even harder.'' Mike's face had grown sober, and Liz's
heart sank.

But he was continuing. "In any case, I want her to
know—I want both Donna and Jimmy to know—that I've
met the woman I want to marry, if she'll have me.''

Oh, my darling, Liz thought, *if she'll have me.* She
loved Mike. For the first time in her twenty-eight years,
she was sure that this was the man she wanted to live with
for the rest of her life. What if Donna made this impossible? She was just a kid, but it had become clear to Liz
as Mike talked about Donna, that he was afraid of her.

What did he mean by "hates even harder"? The words
continued to repeat themselves in her head, and she realized that she was terrified of the meeting on Sunday.

❦ ❦ ❦

CHAPTER
TWO

March 7

Ken and Caren sat in the waiting room of the hospital—
where relatives of pediatric surgery patients were permit-
ted. Caren looked pale, wan, probably hadn't slept much
the previous night, the night before the tonsillectomy when
the hospital had allowed her to sleep in Ellie's room.

It was hard sometimes for Ken to believe that Ellie was
not a child Caren had given birth to. When Elinor was
killed Ellie had been only six months old, and he had
wanted to die, too. Only the thought of Ellie had kept him
alive—that and his desire for revenge.

A year or so later, he had met Caren one day in the
supermarket. Ellie was sitting in the small seat of the cart,
smiling fetchingly at everyone who passed. Caren had been
unable to resist smiling back, and this was how it had
begun.

He had married her when Ellie was almost two. Two
years later, he realized that he was happier than he had
ever expected to be again. As Ellie had grown older her
resemblance to Elinor increased—the golden hair, the delicate features, the infectious smile. In a way, he had not
completely lost the wife he had worshipped and could more
and more appreciate Caren, who adored Ellie and him.

He glanced over at the dark head leaning back on the
couch cushion and felt a rush of warmth for her. How
many women would be loving enough to take another
woman's child to her heart as Caren had done? He had
once seen her look at Elinor's picture in an old photo al-

bum, but the expression on her face had been one of sadness rather than envy.

The uneasiness he was experiencing was probably due to fatigue. He had slept little the previous night—the house was too empty. Rising and walking over to the couch, he touched her hair gently. "Do you want some coffee, darling?" he asked.

She shook her head. "Ken, why is it taking so long? It's a simple tonsillectomy. It's not even that her tonsils were diseased. They were just enlarged."

He controlled his impatience. "She was getting one cold after another. We took her to two doctors before Dr. Ransome. He said she'd be great after the tonsils came out."

His wife seemed not to be listening. "She looked so little last night. She kept saying, 'Mommy, will it hurt?' Why is it taking so long, Ken! Maybe . . . you could go to the desk and ask."

"We were told to wait right here, Caren. The doctor is supposed to meet us here. Stop worrying, darling. Dr. Ransome is the best there is—that's why we picked him. We were lucky he could fit Ellie into his schedule. He's on the staff of three hospitals. . . ."

Why was he talking so much! The words were coming out almost compulsively. Damn it! Why *was* it taking so long! To cheer Caren, he said, "Maybe they forgot about us and took her straight up to her room."

The slender face brightened. "Do you think so, Ken?"

But just then, he spied a figure in a white coat coming down the hall in their direction. Both Ken and Caren rose spontaneously, beginning to walk towards him. Then Caren stopped. "That's not Dr. Ransome," she said nervously.

The young man in the white coat was headed straight for them. White-faced and stiff, he said in a tone that was barely audible. "Mr. Porter . . . Mrs. Porter . . . I'm Dr. Crown."

"How do you do," Caren said politely. Then, "Where is Ellie? Is it over? Is she all right?"

Dr. Crown stood there dumbly, looking at them. He took Caren's hand in his and held it awkwardly. Finally the words came out. "I have bad news. . . ."

"What are you talking about!" Ken demanded. Caren's face was ashen now, and he put an arm around her shoulders to steady her.

Dr. Crown dropped her hand. He looked sick.

"Is Ellie in the recovery room? Where is Dr. Ransome? Why did he send you?" The questions tumbled out, as if by asking them, he could keep himself from registering the words *I have bad news.* . . .

Sweat ran down Dr. Crown's face, and he looked as if he might faint. He began again, obviously forcing himself to speak. "Mr. Porter . . . Mrs. Porter . . . I'm so sorry . . . there was an emergency. An artery burst . . . we tried everything we could. Her heart stopped. Your little girl didn't . . ." He turned his head away. The word "survive" was a whisper.

Caren screamed, and Ken grabbed the doctor by the lapels of his jacket. "You're lying! Where's her doctor? Where is Dr. Ransome?"

Dr. Crown shook his head. "You can't see him now. He'll be in touch with you later."

An icy calm had come over Ken. This was a nightmare, and what he must do now was to play out the dream. "You say Ellie is dead. I don't believe you. It's some kind of stupid mistake. I want to hear it from Dr. Ransome himself! Where is he!"

Dr. Crown's head kept shaking as if he had some kind of palsy. "You . . . you can't see him now. Please—he will be in touch with you."

By now, interns and nurses had gathered and had given Caren—wildly hysterical now—a sedative. Ken refused one. "Don't touch me," he said fiercely. "I'm waiting for Dr. Ransome!"

But they had not seen Dr. Ransome all that day. They remained in the waiting room all evening, Caren asleep on the couch—the sedative had been a strong one—and Ken waiting for someone to come and tell him that it had been a terrible error. No one approached them, except a nurse to bring him a cup of coffee. He took the coffee and suddenly remembered Dr. Crown. "When does Dr. Crown go off duty?" he asked.

"About eleven—in a few minutes," she said, adding, "I'm so sorry!"

At eleven, Ken stood in the doctor's parking lot, waiting. When Dr. Crown saw Ken, he gasped, "You! What do you want of me?"

The street lamp lit his face. He still looked sick.

"Please . . . tell me what happened! Did he have a stroke, a heart attack? For God's sake, tell me!" Ken saw the flash of terror cross the young man's face. And now he persisted, following his nebulous clue. "What was it? Stroke . . . heart attack . . . You've got to tell me!"

The man shook his head; the palsy-like shaking had returned. "I can't! Jesus Christ, I can't! If it gets out, I'll never be allowed in a hospital again."

Ken was amazed at his own control. "It won't get out. Please tell me!"

"I can't tell you anything. I'll deny I even spoke to you. I was just the lackey sent to tell you. They were all protecting him. Please, Mr. Porter, your little girl died on the operating table. It's a terrible tragedy, but we can't bring her back. Just go home now and wait for Dr. Ransome to call you."

"Hold on! You just said they were all protecting him. What did he do? I promise not to mention your name, ever. Tell me!" he repeated. He could see the muscles in the other man's throat working nervously.

"I can't! I can't! Please leave me alone. I can't tell you any more than I have. I've told you . . . too much." He wrested away from Ken and walked rapidly away.

The bitter taste of bile rose in Ken's throat, and he went into the men's room to throw up his guts.

Mechanically, he went back to the waiting room and half-carried Caren to the car.

The next day Dr. Ransome called. Caren answered the phone and received his condolences.

"But it was a simple operation! You told us yourself!" Her last word ended on a note of hysteria.

Ken grabbed the phone out of her hands. "What happened?" he shouted. "What really happened?"

"Her heart stopped." Dr. Ransome's voice was cultured, smooth, sympathetic. "We did everything we could to save her."

That night, sleepless, Ken had a sense of *déjà vu*. It had all happened before—after the automobile accident when Elinor, barely alive, had been taken to a hospital and died there within minutes. "Your wife . . . is dead, Mr. Porter." Now, he thought, I've lost them both.

And this time the loss was more than he could bear.

Only one thing kept Ken from killing himself that night—the few words that the young resident had inadvertently let slip. "They were all protecting him."

Now it was up to him to find out how Ransome had killed his baby. And he would find out! The vow that somehow Ransome would pay for this murder gave him a reason to go on living.

March 10

Making her debut as a future stepmother wasn't something Liz could rehearse for. In lieu of rehearsal, she had resorted to changing her outfit several times. It was eleven-thirty, and Mike would pick her up in half an hour. Pants and a blazer, skirt and sweater, dress, jeans, skirt and shirt and jacket. Nothing looked just right, and that, she realized was because she, herself, hadn't decided on the image she wanted to present to Mike's children.

First impressions were important—especially important since she hoped to marry Mike and would be seeing a great deal of these two young people.

Chic, modest, interesting, conventional—the adjectives floated through her mind, and for an instant each seemed right until careful scrutiny ruined it for her. She was not normally undecided; usually she spent little time wondering what people were thinking of her. But once again, this was different.

In desperation, she ran across the hall. Loren's door was closed as usual. Resisting the impulse to fling it open, she knocked.

"Come in," came a sleepy response.

Only his head was visible. The covers were pulled tightly up to his neck.

"Did I wake you?"

"It doesn't much matter now, does it? What time is it?"

"Oh God—almost quarter to twelve, and Mike is picking me up in fifteen minutes. Loren, what shall I wear?"

He groaned. "Since when am I your fashion consultant?"

"Please, no questions! The question answered by another question doesn't appeal to me in the best of times. Loren, I am absolutely incapable of deciding what to wear to meet Donna and Jimmy."

"Aha . . . the mist is beginning to clear. Well, let's see. What are the choices?"

She told him, watching him furrow his brow in thought—just as hers did. So often she had the eerie sense of spying on herself when she looked at Loren. Their resemblance was astonishing, but in a psychology course in college she had learned that this kind of likeness did occasionally occur between fraternal twins.

A hand pushed aside the covers. Loren snapped his fingers. "Eureka, I have it! The brown pants and camel velvet jacket. Gold earrings, your chains, tan boots. Chic and glamorous—that's the image you want, Liz. Get as far away from the schoolteacher stereotype as possible."

It made sense. "What would I do without you?" she said gratefully.

"That's a hypothetical question. Do you want another inspired answer?" He yawned and closed his eyes.

"Go back to sleep, then. I'll tell you all about it tonight. Oh, and Loren, would you walk Duke for me if I'm not here for dinner?"

He grunted, and she rushed out of the room, heard him yell—she had forgotten to close the door—ran back to do it and then to her own room to dress.

When Mike pulled up to the curb at 12:05, she was ready, a lightweight camel's hair coat over her shoulders. Her hair, swept back in a ponytail showed her gold hoop earrings. Chic and glamorous! Maybe . . . but did kids *like* chic and glamorous? Suddenly she was unsure again, but the die was cast.

As she approached the car, she was startled to see that

the front seat was occupied. Mike had run down the path to meet her.

"Don't you look beautiful!" he said softly. In a whisper, he added, "Sweetheart, please sit in the back with Jimmy. Donna likes to sit up front with me. It's a carry-over from when she used to get carsick. I hope you don't mind."

She forced herself to smile, and obediently climbed into the back seat beside a dark-haired boy, a young teen with huge dark eyes that were now examining her carefully. The girl's back was rigid. She had not turned around.

"Liz," Mike said, too heartily—Liz could detect an odd nervousness in his voice—"I'd like you to meet the two apples of my eye, Donna and Jimmy. Kids, I want you to meet my . . . friend, Elizabeth Ransome—Liz."

Donna turned her head briefly. She had long brown hair that reached her shoulders and she, too, had her father's brown eyes. Her features were good—she was a pretty girl—might even be beautiful when she smiled. She wore, Liz could see now, a gray turtleneck sweater and faded jeans. She did not smile but murmured something that sounded like "Hi," and then turned her head again.

"What name do you like best?" Jimmy asked, and Liz wondered if he was trying to make up for his sister's rudeness.

"Liz, I suppose," she said slowly. "My mother calls me Lizzie sometimes. Elizabeth sounds very prim and proper. What about you—do you prefer Jim to Jimmy?"

He nodded, an embarrassed smile on his lips. "Just try getting people to remember, though. Some of my friends at school try—when they don't forget. . . ."

"Hey, I'm pretty good. I call you Jim . . . most of the time," his father said.

"Mommy doesn't," came a voice from the front. "I've never heard her call you Jim."

"Yeah, well it doesn't really matter, I guess," Jimmy

said flushing, and again Liz felt sure that he was embarrassed by his sister's hostility.

"We're going to a great place," Mike said, sounding to Liz like a salesman, a rather uncertain salesman.

"Where?" Donna demanded.

"The Jolly Fisherman in Roslyn. You all like fish, and theirs is first-rate. And the desserts . . ." But Donna's exclamation of dismay stopped him. "What's the matter?"

"You promised," she began in a voice that sounded as if she might begin to cry at any moment.

"Promised what?"

"That the next time we'd go to McDonald's."

"I meant . . . when it was just the three of us. We can go to McDonald's any time."

"Any time! That's not until Thursday!"

"It doesn't matter, Mike," Liz said quietly. "McDonald's would be fine with me."

"But I've made reservations," he protested. "You can't even get into that place without a reservation."

"Don't be such a pill, Donna," Jimmy said. "You sound like a spoiled baby. We'll go to McDonald's next week. I don't even like their hamburgers all that much."

"I'm not going to The Jolly Fisherman," Donna said defiantly. "You can all go if you want, and Daddy can take me home."

Once again Liz intervened. "It's easy to call the restaurant, Mike. They'll probably be happy to free a reservation. McDonald's is fine with me, really . . . if it's okay with everybody else."

"I don't care where I eat," Jimmy declared. "This whole thing is stupid."

Mike had slowed down. They were approaching a gas station. "I'll run out and phone," he said tightly.

With Mike there, the atmosphere had been stiff and cold. Now it was positively frigid. This situation was the most ludicrous Liz had ever been in. A teacher who dealt with kids like Donna every day, she was tongue-tied in the presence of this hostile sixteen-year-old who refused even to look at her.

Topic after topic shot through her mind and were as quickly rejected. Finally it was Jimmy who took it upon himself to break the silence. "Uh . . . Liz . . . what do you teach?"

She turned to him gratefully. "English—senior high."

"Wow," he exclaimed, grinning. "Does that mean I have to talk right when you're around?"

Smiling back at him, she said, "I'm only an English teacher at school."

"You have a twin brother too, don't you . . . who teaches with Dad?"

"Yes, and we have a pact. I don't bother him about his English, and he balances my checkbook."

They laughed companionably. There was no movement from the front; not even a faint snicker had escaped Donna's lips. And that was probably as funny as I can get, Liz thought, more disappointed in the girl's lack of response than she wanted to admit even to herself.

When Mike returned, although Liz could still detect his tension, he appeared to have recovered his good humor. "Mission accomplished," he announced. "McDonald's, here we come."

The McDonald's on Northern Boulevard was swarming with children, and the parking lot was filled. They headed for the one near Springfield and although that, too, was crowded, they managed to find a parking spot, and once inside, a table.

"Give me your orders," Mike said, but Jimmy broke in.

"Donna and I'll go, Dad. This was her great idea. Let her stand in line."

"I don't mind," Donna said loftily, still not turning her head. "What does everybody want?"

"Liz?" Mike turned to her, an unspoken apology in his eyes.

"Hamburger and coffee," she said, looking directly at

him, trying to say with *her* eyes, It doesn't matter. Don't you feel bad!

"That's all? Sure you don't want a Big Mac?"

She smiled. "Sure."

"Okay, double the order and add one of french fries. You guys get whatever you want."

They went off. As soon as their backs were turned, Mike took Liz's hand and pressed it to his lips. "Oh baby, I'm so sorry. I couldn't have imagined that my darling little girl could act like such a . . . bitch."

"I guess . . . she just doesn't like me," Liz said, trying but not succeeding in keeping her voice steady.

Mike groaned. "It's not you, darling. It would be anybody. Can't you see? She's green with jealousy. It's a lousy thing to say about your own child, but if she blushed, I swear she'd turn orange." He gave a small, rueful laugh. "Well at least Jimmy has taste. He likes you . . . that's quite obvious."

Liz swallowed hard. "I guess she isn't ready. . . ."

"It's three years for Christ's sake!" he exploded. Then obviously struggling for control, he said more quietly, "She was the one hardest hit by the divorce. We had always been very close . . . and I guess my not being around all the time has been harder on her than I realized."

The mirror on the wall opposite gave Liz a glimpse of herself. Chic and glamorous—oh, yes indeed! Perfect for McDonald's. Damn you, Loren Ransome, she thought miserably. I should have worn my old jeans and T-shirt and messed up my hair. Then maybe she wouldn't have minded me so much.

Liz was sharply aware that Mike had released her hand. She looked up. Jimmy and the Dragon Lady were approaching. Donna's face, animated in conversation, stiffened as she came over to them. "Here's your change," she said handing the money to her father.

Lunch was as difficult as the ride, perhaps more difficult because now they were forced to face each other across a

table. With insufficient forethought, Mike had seated himself next to Liz, and now across from them sat Jimmy,
busily wolfing down his hamburger while Donna, eyes
downcast, concentrated on hers.

What sustained Liz through the meal was the inspiration
that had seized her halfway through the miserable hamburger. And as soon as it was decently possible, when the
hamburgers and fries and apple pie had been eaten and
the Cokes and coffee drunk, she looked at Jimmy and said
as apologetically as she could, "I hope you'll excuse me.
I shouldn't have left my lesson plans for Sunday, but it
seems to me I always do. So . . . Mike"—she turned to
face him—"do you mind dropping me off?"

"You mean now?" He sounded incredulous. "It's not
even two o'clock."

"It's a week's plans. Not all department heads are like
you, my . . ." About to say "darling," she hastily
amended it to "my friend" and continued saying whatever
came to her mind. "Caroline Jordan runs a tight ship. She
wants to know in great detail what I'll be doing next
Thursday at ten-forty A.M. And it had better be to her
liking. It's not something I can just dash off." She was
babbling, rambling on for far too long, lying through her
teeth. He must have been aware of why she was doing
this. Caroline Jordan, as he knew from frequent reports,
was a darling who glanced at lesson plans and said apologetically, "The administration wants this, kids, not me.
It gives them a kind of security."

Liz, without appearing to notice, saw the quickly
masked look of relief that had crossed Donna's face when
she made her announcement.

Jimmy, on the other hand, frowned. "If that's what you
have to do to be an English teacher, cross that one off my
list."

"A good thing too," Donna said, grinning for the first
time that afternoon. "You have to know how to speak
English before you can teach it."

What a pretty thing she is when she smiles, Liz thought, charmed in spite of herself. Slender, beautifully boned face. Magnificent eyes . . .

"Dad," Jimmy said quietly, "since she joined Mensa, she's been worse than ever. She thinks she's smarter than God!"

"You could take the test too if you weren't such a coward," Donna retorted. "It's not a hard test—you might even pass it."

"Yes, I just might." He gave her a long, serious look. "But I don't care, Donna. I'm not like you that way."

"Okay, kids, enough!" Mike raised his hands in the manner of a referee. "There's nothing like letting a guest see the worst of us right off. Then everything that follows is a delightful surprise. I'd like another cup of coffee. How about you, Liz?"

She nodded. As soon as Mike had joined one of the lines, Donna rose too and said to the air, "I'm going to the rest room." She disappeared without looking at either of them.

"I'm sorry she's acting like this," Jimmy said, sounding apologetic.

"It's nice of you to say so."

"She thinks she's so hot! You know, if she wanted to, she could be as sweet as sugar."

"I imagined that. There's no law that says we must like everybody we meet."

"If there was such a law, Ms. Know-It-All would break it." Jimmy looked around and said softly, "If I tell you something, can we keep it between us, Liz? I can't tell anyone else."

"Of course."

"Since she took Driver's Ed, she takes the car when Mom isn't home. And she doesn't even have a license yet. I want to tell Dad, but I'm scared to. She said she'd kill me if I did. I know her and I wouldn't put it past her. Maybe she has to act like a hotshot because of those older guys she hangs out with. She was just sixteen—she's younger than all of them.''

Jimmy, having revealed something that obviously troubled him, continued. "I feel bad because this is so important to Dad. And he's always been great with us.''

His eyes still conveyed the innocence of childhood. Maybe he would never lose it completely. Having met Jimmy, Liz realized now that his father sometimes looked like an older version of him.

"Thanks for listening," Jimmy whispered, and Liz saw that both Mike and Donna were approaching.

As Mike drank his coffee, he gave a sudden grimace and touched his abdomen. "Isn't it too soon for me to have a stomachache from that blasted hamburger?''

"You sound like a real hypochondriac, Daddy," Donna said lightly. "McDonald's makes perfectly good hamburgers, one hundred per cent pure beef. I eat them all the time, and I've never gotten sick, not even once.''

"As a scientist, there's a lot I could say to refute your 'proof,' but I'll refrain." His eyes met Liz's. "You're not drinking your coffee. If you've had enough, let's go!''

On the way to the parking lot, Mike said, "Donna, sit in back with Jimmy. When Liz gets out, you can come in front with me again.''

"Okay," she said, not unpleasantly.

Sure, Liz thought, she's won. The first round is all hers, and she knows it.

The sight of Bayview Avenue was a giant relief. When Mike pulled up in front of the large white Colonial house, he said, "I'll walk you up.''

Liz forced herself to turn back and look directly at Mike's children, first at Jimmy, then at Donna. "I'm glad to have met you," she said.

Donna murmured something without meeting her eyes, and Jimmy smiled a smile that lit up his face. "Same here," he said, adding, "See you again.''

Liz nodded. For an instant a lump had lodged in her

throat, and she felt like crying. Mike took her hand as they walked up the path to the front entrance. "I'm sorry, baby. This was one hell of a fiasco. And don't think I'm not going to give that young woman a piece of my mind."

"No!" The exclamation was so vehement, it startled her as well as him. "Don't make it worse, Mike. Please don't. Let's just leave it for now. I don't want her to hate me more than she already does."

"Okay . . . I see your logic, but I feel so stupid . . . so powerless." He kissed her quickly on the lips. "I'll call you later, love."

As she walked into the house, a thought that would recur many times in the weeks to follow surfaced for the first time. I've made an enemy, and there's no way in the world I can change that except by . . . giving Mike up.

Her heart contracted in a painful spasm. No, I can't. No matter what happens, I won't!

☙☙☙
CHAPTER
FOUR

March 11

The bar was dimly lit, even more so than usual, he thought. It was probably as safe as any place could be. Who would notice him in a small Elmhurst tavern? Who would suspect that the illustrious surgeon, Ralph W. Ransome, would choose to spend his free evenings in a cruddy neighborhood bar?

He had told Liz he was off to a professional meeting. Donelley's Bar was where he usually attended such meetings. He grinned at the thought. How ridiculous it all was. Perhaps most ridiculous was the fact that he chose to continue day after day, barely able to accept the thought of the new day when it did arrive.

"Double Scotch," he told the familiar-looking ginger-haired bartender. When it was slid across the counter, he took the glass and moved to a table in the far corner of the room, the darkest corner where nobody would be likely to discern his features.

For the past two nights he had had an A number one reason for getting drunk. Anyone in his position would be out seeking oblivion. For some reason this made good and comforting sense to him, and he felt justified, as though someone had given him permission to do just what he was doing.

Why, he wondered, as the faintly bitter liquid slid down his throat, was he reacting this way to a perfectly ordinary fatality? How the hell could a physician practice if he reacted to each death as if it were a personal loss! God knew

there had been other deaths over the years. Not too many—
none that could be directly attributed to carelessness on
his part. What puzzled him was the reason for his trau-
matic reaction to this particular death. It wasn't as if he
had known the child. He had seen her exactly twice—once
to confirm the diagnosis and agree to operate, and the
other time on the operating table. A routine, simple tonsillectomy.

Why in God's name had the parents insisted on him!

"We want the best," the child's mother had said earnestly. Porter . . . that was the name.

"It's simple, uncomplicated surgery," he had said.
"Any E.N.T. physician could do it. My schedule is pretty
heavy right now."

"We want you, Dr. Ransome," Mrs. Porter had said.
He remembered her as a pretty, dark-haired young woman
with gray, worried eyes. The blond little girl bore no resemblance to her at all.

He remembered another woman whose worried eyes had
seemed to be constantly focused on him. Thea . . . his
wife of twenty-nine years, now the mistress of a fiddle
player.

Everyone—his colleagues, even his children—had
treated him so gently afterwards. And he had not been
able to admit to anyone that her leaving had been one giant
relief—not to be compelled to hear the countless variations
on the same theme.

"Ralph . . . please don't drink tonight! You're on call.
Ralph, you're operating in the morning. . . . Ralph, don't
drive! You're drunk!"

What a relief not to suffer the humiliation of a limp
prick when she tried to arouse him. But that was a long
time ago . . . two years . . . three? He couldn't remember. He couldn't remember either when he had last known
desire. The longing came rarely now. Actually it was the
memory of longing that returned from time to time.

When he noticed that his glass was empty, he called to

the bartender for a refill. Sometimes, it seemed to him that he had been drinking all his life, but actually he recalled having his first drink at fifteen. When had it picked up and become a daily necessity? He couldn't even remember.

One morning at 3 A.M. he had been jolted awake by a heart that was pounding, his body in a cold sweat. I'm terrified, he thought, waves of panic coursing through him.

He had awakened Thea, who wanted to call an ambulance to rush him to the hospital.

I've got a thyroidectomy at eight was the thought hammering in his head. "Thea, get me a drink," he demanded.

"But Ralph . . . the ambulance . . . let me call first."

"Get me a drink," he had shouted.

Cowed, she had brought the bottle of Scotch to the bed. And it had worked, miraculously. In less than an hour his panic symptoms had disappeared. He was in the O.R. at 7:45, and the operation had begun promptly at 8:15. A first-rate job, he recalled now.

Two hours later, he was still at the table, another empty glass in front of him, one of a succession of empty glasses. When had he last eaten? He knew that he should eat something. Except that the thought of food nauseated him. Each time he had tried in the past two days to put a morsel of food in his mouth, he had smelled blood. So much blood! She was just a baby, but the blood . . . he had been showered with it. For an instant in that room, the little girl on the table had become Lizzie. He had killed his own Lizzie. A low moan had left his throat. Later there were people near him. "Dr. Ransome. Are you all right, sir?"

And some hidden strength had surfaced and erased the image. It was the fine blond hair that was the same. That was all—the fine blond hair.

No, he couldn't eat. What he wanted was another double.

An hour later he remembered that there was a Dunkin' Donuts on Northern Boulevard, near Springfield. He would stop there for coffee and a donut. The thought cheered him as he slowly rose and went to the counter to pay the barman.

The Dunkin' Donuts on Northern was bright, well-lit, cheerful-looking. Best of all, it was open twenty-four hours. Often in the middle of a sleepless night when he knew he had an early morning surgery, he would drive over there. Three o'clock in the morning, four . . . it didn't matter. The coffee was always hot and strong and the donuts fresh.

Now at midnight, the place was almost empty. Two men sat at opposite sides of the counter nearest the door. He chose a seat at the end of the counter. The woman who took his order was not someone he recognized. He was glad of that.

While he was drinking his coffee, the hot liquid as comforting in its way as the booze, he stretched out his hand to take the change the waitress had set down on the Formica counter. Dispassionately he observed his hand. It doesn't shake, he thought, a sudden feeling of triumph racing through him.

It doesn't shake, and I'm still the best goddamn surgeon in New York City. Maybe the entire East Coast!

At this moment he had completely forgotten the name of the child who had died under his knife two days earlier.

March 13

Ken had spent the day following Dr. Ransome. When a death occurred in one's immediate family, the newspaper generously gave its employees a week off.

By programming himself to learn as much about Dr. Ralph W. Ransome as he could, he had made it possible for each day to have a focus. He knew the address of his office, and with some astute phone calls and then the use of the Nassau County directory, he had learned not only where Dr. Ransome resided but also that there were two other members of the family who had phones of their own, an Elizabeth Ransome and a Loren Ransome.

He was exhausted after a day spent trailing the surgeon—from his office to the hospital, then to a fancy restaurant where he had gone with two other men, then back to the office where Ken waited outside until 9 P.M.

He was about to go home and resume tomorrow, when Ransome came out and purposefully got into his car. If he were going home, Ken decided, he would give up for tonight, but no, Dr. Ransome did not turn off at the Lakeville Road exit. Instead he went on, heading west and exiting at Woodhaven Boulevard.

Magically Ken's fatigue lifted. He had been a newspaper man for ten years, and his nose told him when a story was imminent. Now he was interested in something much more significant than a story. Ransome was going to lead him to something. He sensed it.

When the gray Cadillac pulled up on a side street in Elmhurst, Ken's elation subsided. Where was he going in this seedy neighborhood? Did he have a mistress he kept hidden? Ransome walked down the street and turned to his right.

Ken parked his car and followed. Two stores from the corner was a tavern. Ransome didn't hesitate at the doorway. He walked in as if this place were familiar to him. Ken waited outdoors for ten minutes, the chill March winds making him shiver. Then he walked in and sat down at the bar. There were only two other men at the opposite end.

A faintness had overtaken Ken as he entered the tavern, the boozy smell nauseating him and bringing back memories that he detested. His father had spent a lifetime at bars, had ruined his law practice and his reputation, and had spent his last years drinking almost as fast as the cirrhosis was destroying his liver.

His father, too, had chosen taverns in seedy neighborhoods where nobody would know him. And progressively he could hold more and more, so that although he professed to be sober and might even have seemed so to some clients, he was drunk all the time.

"Yeah?" the red-haired bartender asked, taking him out of his memories.

"Miller's," Ken said, adding, "Oh, where's the john?"

The man pointed. Ken left his drink, put down a five-dollar bill, and walked in the direction indicated. There were tables, and at one of them sat his quarry, with a double whiskey in front of him. He was staring straight ahead.

Ken opened the door leading to the men's room, and when he came out, he averted his head. It wasn't likely that Ransome would recognize him, but it was better not to trust to luck. He returned to the bar, drank his beer slowly, and waited.

After an hour or so, he ordered another beer, and an hour after that, still another.

The next time he went to the john, Ransome had a double on the table in front of him, and his eyes were closed as he drank.

Was this it? Ken wondered. Was the eminent Dr. Ransome a drunk? In fairness, it was too soon to conclude anything. He must keep watching—night after night until he learned more.

It took Ken three nights to learn Dr. Ransome's ugly secret.

On the third night as Ken sat nursing his beer, he heard a beeping sound from the other side of the room. The next thing he saw was a groggy Ransome making his way to the bar. He threw some bills down on the bar and left, his raincoat over his arm.

Ken had followed, had watched him try to unlock the car door with his keys for a few minutes before he succeeded, and had seen him drive off. He was behind him on the Long Island Expressway and got off at the Community Drive exit where, after two or three blocks, Dr. Ransome drove up the winding hospital entrance reserved for staff, and got out of the car.

Obviously he was going to operate—drunk!—as he probably had on the day of Ellie's tonsillectomy.

Finally, Dr. Crown's words made sense. "They were all trying to protect him." The words rang in Ken's head. Now he knew. Dr. Ransome was a murderer whose colleagues covered for him.

I could wait for him and follow him and kill him, he thought dispassionately. But this seemed too easy an end for the murderer of his child. No, Ellie's murderer must suffer the same kind of loss that he and Caren were suffering.

The names of the two other Ransomes came to him. "If Ransome has a child . . ." he said aloud, but he finished the thought in his mind.

☙ ☙ ☙
CHAPTER
FIVE

March 14

For the first week or so after her mother left, Liz had tried to keep the household together by stocking the larder and preparing attractive and balanced dinners. After dining in solitary splendor for five nights out of the seven, she was forced to realize that her father had drastically changed his routine and that Loren's dinners at home were even more sporadic than usual.

Dinners with Mike during the week didn't often work out because he taught math at Hofstra on Monday, Tuesday, and Wednesday—for the additional income, he said, and because it was a pleasant change for him from highschool kids. Then, on Thursday, he was always with his own children.

This Thursday evening, Liz checked the freezer; it was full, but nothing appealed to her. Pizza, she thought. If Loren came home, there would be enough for him. If her father appeared. . . . her instinctive thought was, I can stick it in the freezer. This was followed by, Idiot! You are twenty-eight years old, old enough to eat whatever you damn please. Pizza was anathema to him.

As she headed for the door, Duke raised his head expectantly. She patted his coat. "Sorry, boy, not this time. I'll be right back. I'll give you some of my crust, okay?"

Duke was too civilized and mature to complain, but as Liz opened the door to go out she felt guilty. Duke was a Briard, her mother's gift to her and Loren when they were twenty-one, but from the beginning he had been *her* dog.

She fed him and walked him and loved to play with him. From a lively, frisky puppy who barked ferociously whenever any stranger came to the door, he had matured into a much quieter dog who was more discriminating about whom he barked at.

Liz would never forget the day he attacked the postman. Her father had been furious and had threatened to get rid of Duke, but Liz had begged, promising to send him to Obedience School. Her father's capitulation had been ungracious. "For the time being," he had said.

And now, years later, Duke was a model dog—his puppy days over, he was devoted to the entire family, but especially to Liz.

Joe's Pizzeria was crowded as usual. Liz wished that she had had the forethought to phone in her order. As she joined the line, she heard a familiar voice call out, "Hey, Ms. R.!"

She turned to see Doug Williams, all six feet of him. A second glance shocked her into the awareness that he had changed drastically since the previous year when he had been in her English class. Now he was pale and thin, but the most disturbing thing about him was the glazed look in his eyes.

Liz had seen enough kids on drugs to know that Doug had become one of them.

Reaching out a hand to shake his, she said, "It's good to see you, Doug. How are you?"

His handshake was awkward, and his pale face flushed. "Okay, Ms. R., fine. Say, I'm with a . . . friend. Would you . . . I mean, we saw you come in, and he'd like to meet you."

Liz hesitated, and Doug obviously spotted her hesitation. "Please, Ms. Ransome. I'd really appreciate it."

There was an urgency in his voice that communicated itself to her. She liked Doug—they had had a special relationship since she had volunteered to tutor him last year after he fractured his foot. "Okay," she said.

The relief on his face was visible. He smiled, and for an instant the old familiar Doug emerged.

"How is school this year?" Liz asked.

"Boring. Mr. Ross—he's okay, I guess, but you spoiled me."

Liz laughed. "I never thought you were an apple polisher, Doug."

"I'm not. It's the honest-to-God truth."

The smile had left his face, and now they approached the last booth, where a tall, dark-haired young man was standing.

This was no close friend of Doug's, Liz surmised. He was attractive in a rather dramatic sort of way, and when he smiled, his smile was an engaging one.

Uneasily Doug performed the introductions. "Hoke, this is Ms. Elizabeth Ransome. Ms. R., this is my . . . friend Hoke."

"I'm happy to meet you," the young man said, moving so that he could usher Liz into the booth. His voice was low, his speech cultured.

Liz accepted his direction somewhat unwillingly. Normally, she would have somehow sidestepped this invitation, but she recalled Doug's urgency and decided to learn more about what was going on—if she could.

Doug sat down beside her, and Hoke, still standing, said, "What are you having, Ms. Ransome? They have good veal and peppers here." He sounded as if she had suddenly become his guest.

"I'm just going to order a small pie. I can't stay."

An annoyed look crossed the young man's face, but it quickly disappeared. Then he snapped his fingers as if having suddenly come to a decision. "Doug, order Ms. Ransome her small pie."

The Doug of Liz's memory would have said, "Go do it yourself!" This new Doug, flushing again, said only, "Right," and rose quickly. *To do his master's bidding* was the phrase that came to Liz's mind.

The young man leaned across the table and looked directly into Liz's eyes. "I've seen you lots of times when I pick Doug up after school. He told me how nice you were to him last year after he broke his ankle. He said you tutored him at home on your own time. The first time I saw you, I told him, 'She could tutor me any old time.' So before Doug gets back, would you have dinner with me one evening?"

Disconcerted by his aggressiveness, Liz shook her head. "That would be impossible . . ." It must have been apparent that she was loath to use his name. The word stuck in her throat.

"Hoke is the name, Ms. Ransome. Why would it be impossible? Is it because Doug introduced us?"

"That's not it at all." Liz was aware that her face felt hot and that his pushing was strangely upsetting.

"Then what? Because I'm friends with Doug? Since his dad died, he's alone a great deal. I feel sorry for him. His mother works. I guess you know that."

There was nothing wrong with the words, but there was something else, an assurance, a sense of being in control, which she found disturbing and which made her distrust him.

"I don't want to seem rude, but I don't owe you an explanation," she said, attempting to sound cool. Abruptly she rose from the booth. "I'd better go up front and wait for my pie."

Not waiting for a response, she moved quickly to the counter where Doug was standing, looking uncomfortable.

"Doug," Liz said quietly, "please stop and see me after school tomorrow. We haven't talked for a long time. I want to know how your mother is doing, and I want to catch up with you. Okay?" she added, since he had said nothing and his expression had turned blank. He seemed hardly to have heard her.

"I don't know, Ms. Ransome," he said finally.

"If you can't make it tomorrow, any day after school is fine with me. You're not just another student to me, Doug. You must know that. I feel bad at not having kept in touch after the year ended, but there's been . . . trouble in my own family. Anyway, I do want to talk to you."

Not meeting her eyes, Doug mumbled, "I'm not sure about this week."

"You're in trouble, aren't you?" she said gently.

"No, no, I'm fine, really. Look, I've got to get back. Our food is ready—so is your pie. See, it's coming up."

Doug got a tray for his order, paid for the food, and stood poised for flight as the man put a large pie and two salads on the tray.

When Liz turned to take out her money to pay for her order, Doug had disappeared.

On her way home, she thought, He's afraid to talk to me . . . afraid I'll learn about something he doesn't want me to find out. This brought with it another thought. If Doug is on drugs—and I could swear he is— where is he getting the money to buy the stuff? What kind of trade-off is he making?

The memory of the imperious tone Hoke had used to dispatch Doug to the counter struck her vividly. Now she was almost certain of the identity of Doug's supplier.

March 18

A week had passed since the funeral. The first days were devoted to friends come to pay their condolences. And then there were people who had learned to anticipate Ellie's smile and wave as they passed her in the neighborhood, riding her bike, going to the store with Caren, playing on the front steps of their house. They came, too, these people Ken had never seen before.

He had returned to work after a few days because it was easier to be in the office, where there were fewer memories of her. He did what he was supposed to do, operating on a kind of automatic pilot. Ellie, baby that she was, had somehow restored Elinor to him in a way that had enabled him to deal with his grief. Now he had lost them both, forever.

Caren wept much of the time. Her eyes were always red-rimmed now. When he came home at night, he was aware that she tried to control the tears, but in the midst of a sentence her voice would break, and she would run out of the room weeping. He had known that she loved Ellie, but he hadn't quite realized that Ellie was the focal point of her life as she had been of his.

Ken did not weep. In order to retain his sanity, he planned carefully the course of action he had decided to follow.

He opened his address book to the *R* page and found what he was looking for: Loren Ransome, 1322 Bayview Avenue, Great Neck. Telephone: 182-4210. Elizabeth Ransome, same address, with a different number.

He left work early and picked up his car near the station. From Douglaston, he drove to Bayview Avenue in Great Neck. There, on the tree-lined street, a short distance from the large white Colonial house, he waited, hidden by a large fir tree, binoculars in hand.

About four-thirty, a small yellow Honda drove up. A young woman parked the car in the driveway and walked up the path to the house. She carried a small suitcase in one hand, a briefcase in the other. Setting the suitcase on the top step, she turned for a moment so that he could see her face.

This, then, must be Elizabeth Ransome. He was aware that his heart was beating too rapidly. For some reason, he had not attempted to visualize her, and her beauty startled him. Of medium height—5'6'' or so—with darkish blond hair that touched her shoulders, swept aside so that her large gold hoop earrings were visible, she had unusual eyes—were they violet blue? In spite of the strong lens, he couldn't be sure. She moved easily, lithely, like an athlete or a dancer.

Probably the apple of her father's eye, Ken thought with

bitter detachment. It was obvious to him that she must be the one, and although he was shaken by her beauty, he reminded himself that her father had murdered his child and that the only way he could survive without going crazy was to retaliate with direct retribution. His beautiful little girl would never live to be a beautiful young woman.

She ran into the house, and less than ten minutes later, another car drove up, this one a red Fiat. A young man got out, but instead of walking to the house, he stood near the car, facing the street and looking up at the sky. Ken was stunned to see a young man who looked almost exactly like the young woman who had just entered the house. Had his hair been longer and had he worn earrings and feminine clothing, Ken was certain that he could not have told the two apart.

Twins, he thought. Of course, that was it. Twins, but obviously they were fraternal—male and female twins could never be identical, and yet here they were. He wondered if his eyes were the same color as hers.

This must be Loren, Ken decided. He wondered what kind of work he and his sister did that freed them so early in the afternoon. They could be teachers, he guessed, judging from the briefcases they carried, or freelance consultants, or . . .

As Loren walked up the driveway and rummaged in his pocket for a key, he turned again, this time looking out at the street. Ken was struck by the expression on his face— a profound sadness, as though all the misery in the world had been heaped on his shoulders.

He knew an instant of empathy. Loren Ransome was clearly miserable, and it was equally apparent that Elizabeth Ransome was not. Had he seen the twins three weeks ago, when Ellie was alive and he, himself, was content and fulfilled, the physical similarity would probably have been all he spotted.

CHAPTER
SIX

March 19

Liz had stopped at a Mobil station on her way home, to put air in her tires. She had just completed the operation and was back in her car, fastening her seat belt and about to release the emergency brake when she became aware of a knock on her window.

To her dismay, Hoke was leaning against the door.

With a reluctance she didn't bother to hide, she pressed the button that lowered the window.

He was smiling at her, and at the same time she sensed that he was appraising her keenly.

"Do you have a minute?" he asked.

"Not really. I'm running late." What was he doing here? she wondered.

"I'll make it short, then. Look, I want to get to know you better. I like the way you look and the way you speak. You are a beautiful woman. And I want to take you to dinner, any place you choose—not like that cruddy pizza place." He sounded disdainful.

So she was right. She had not misinterpreted his interest. Trying to sound as civil as possible, she said, "Thank you. But it would be impossible."

"Why? You must have one free evening."

His persistence had begun to irk her. "We've just met, and I don't think I need to explain. Can't we just leave it at that?"

"Oh, I see!"

She had expected him to step back, but instead he moved

closer, leaning into the open window. His smile was gone, replaced by a mask. "It's really that you think I'm not in your class. Isn't that the unadorned truth? After all, you're a teacher *and* a doctor's daughter, and I'm just . . ."

Suddenly his tone changed to a more mollifying one. "Look, I'm willing to stick my neck out. I'll ask you again. Women sometimes change their minds. Maybe not right now—not tonight or tomorrow—but will you ever go out with me? Next week, maybe. Next month?"

For an instant she felt remorseful for the way she had spoken, but abruptly she recalled Doug's glassy eyes and heard again the contempt in Hoke's voice when he gave him orders.

"No," she said as evenly as she could. "Not now, not ever." Something made her add, "In any case, I'm engaged to be married. Please . . . please let me shut my window."

This time he did move away. His face wore a strange, enigmatic smile. "I don't believe you're engaged, Ms. Ransome. It's something you just thought up. For some reason, you've decided I'm not a suitable catch. But you're wrong. You're dead wrong."

Quickly she rolled up the window, released the emergency brake, and started the car. Why hadn't she been able to handle this as she had planned—coolly, maturely? Why hadn't she said she was engaged the first time he asked her. If she had, maybe he would have believed her.

She had made an enemy. . . . Another enemy.

❦❦❦
CHAPTER
SEVEN

March 21

The nightmare began for Liz on a cold, wet March night. It had rained all day, but at school she was hardly aware of weather. Home now, at eight o'clock, the monotony of the drops against the window had begun to make her vaguely uneasy. Later, she would wonder whether the uneasiness had been precognition.

She was alone, a state she liked and in the past had often longed for, but tonight something was wrong, subtly different. Her skin prickled, and she thought with mild amusement that Loren would call this last a feline characteristic—probably a vestige of some former existence. Even Duke was restless. Certain changes in the weather affected him, and now he was pacing back and forth.

Moving rapidly through the house, Duke at her heels, she closed doors and windows, making sure that the storm doors were locked.

The Ransomes had moved into this large white Colonial house when Liz was eight. She had loved it at first sight— the spaciousness of the rooms, the nooks and crannies where she could hide and not be found for a long time. She had felt like a movie star, having her own bathroom with orchid tile and an orchid bathtub. Any shade of purple was her favorite, and her bedroom had pale orchid walls with wallpaper that had lilac sprigs on a white background. Her bed had a real canopy; the spread was orchid and white eyelet, and as she grew older, she could pretend that she lived in the time of Jane Austen and would dream of one day meeting her Mr. Darcy.

Flawing her happiness was Loren's misery—both with the house and with his room. The house was too big for him, too scary. He didn't like being all the way down the hall from Liz's room. And he hated his own room. His bathroom had maroon tiles and a maroon tub. Maroon was a color he loathed. His room was a "real boy's room," according to his father. The wallpaper depicted fishermen, skiers, ball players, and rugged mountain scenes.

Loren could not imagine that his mother would have done this to him, and one day she had confessed that his father had actually showed some interest in his room by saying it was the kind of room he would have loved as a boy.

Loren's light-ash bed had a gray and maroon plaid spread that slipped neatly over the mattress. He detested the room and the furnishings and spent more time in Liz's room than in his own. He sat at her desk when they did homework, and she sat on her window seat.

Old memories tend to appear when one is alone, she thought as she approached her father's room. Here the window was wide open, and rain had already spattered the sill and was seeping down onto the rug.

Of course Loren's windows were tightly shut, his room as neat and methodically organized as he was. A quick glance at herself in the mirror startled her. If I didn't know I was me, I'd swear I was Loren, she thought.

The oddness of their physical similarity was something she accepted but had never fully understood. "Genetic freaks" was the name Loren had given them.

The telephone rang three times. Racing from the linen closet, she picked it up, her "Hello" a breathless one.

There was no answer. "Hello," she repeated and was discomfited to hear a click.

Damn! It was probably one of her students. Maybe someone whose sense of humor manifested itself in calling a teacher. Or maybe . . . someone whom she had unwittingly offended—as teachers tend to offend students.

Several names came to mind, but it was fruitless to pursue this. All teachers get anonymous phone calls, she knew, and popularity among the students did not make one immune. Still, she was aware that she had a reputation for fairness and she cherished this reputation.

The house seemed unusually still. How different she thought, from this time only a few months ago—before her mother's departure. *Defection* was the way Loren spoke of it—only half facetiously, she had noted. Although she missed her mother desperately at times, Liz knew that she had had no choice. It was clear that she no longer loved her husband, and her son and daughter were adults who could do without her. Because of their closeness, though, the decision to leave was not one her mother could have made easily.

Her lover was a famous violinist who had met Thea Ransome in a Master class he occasionally chose to teach. Six months later she had gone off with him, leaving notes, three individual ones for the members of her family, all neatly typed on the small typewriter she used for correspondence. She had even taken the typewriter with her.

Liz knew hers by heart—the important parts—"Please try to understand, Lizzie, why I'm leaving. It's time for me to take what Leopold offers me. I'll be traveling with him most of the time but will send you a post office box number where I can pick up my mail.

"Your father will manage as long as he has his bottle. That's all Ralph has wanted for longer than I can bear to remember.

"I don't ask you to take over the running of the household. But I do ask you to be there for your father and Loren. Please try to understand, Lizzie, my darling, lovely girl."

Even now, when she thought about the letter, Liz wanted to weep. Her mother couldn't have known that her leaving had taken the spirit out of their home. Now it was just a house. Sometimes, Liz was overcome by the guilty knowledge that her being there for her father and Loren would never be enough.

But fierce loyalty to her father made her unable to acknowledge fully her mother's accusation of his drinking. How could anyone call him a drunk! Maybe he drank too much at times, but he was one of the most respected surgeons in New York City. Her mother had needed a reason—maybe her father had drunk more than he should have at a number of parties, and this was what her mother was referring to. . . .

She shook her head, trying to clear it of the cobwebs that seemed to have invaded her brain.

Loren had withdrawn even more than usual in the past few months. Outwardly he was the same, taught his math classes during the day, met friends for dinner when he chose to. Sometimes she suspected that he was seeing a woman, but any questions she asked were skillfully evaded. He treated her relationship with Mike with a pleasant disinterest, but with a lack of curiosity that often pained her. She wanted to talk to him about this first really serious relationship in her life, but although he listened when she began to talk, his lack of interest was so obvious, it stopped her. She had always been more curious than he. Maybe men were different, she told herself, even a fraternal twin.

The shrill ring of the phone invaded her thoughts. Glancing down at her watch, she saw that exactly half an hour had passed since the last call.

Her "Hello" was hesitant, and there was no dialogue on the other end—just silence and finally a shrill giggle that preceded the click this time.

"Damn those kids!" she said aloud, but abruptly the thought came to her that it might be someone else—not one of her students at all.

It was too easy to blame a student, but who else could it be?

Unwilling to pursue this train of thought, she drifted back to Loren.

Before Mike, she and Loren had spent most of their free time together. Sometimes she had joked about their closeness. "I can see us at seventy . . . Mr. and Ms. Ransome, looking more and more alike as the years pass, both of us bald as turnips, neither of us having married because we're so used to living together, it would be too hard to start with someone new."

She realized that she hadn't said that for quite a while—not since she had met Mike and fallen in love with him.

A week ago Sunday she had met his two children for the first time. The meeting had been a disaster, but as Mike had said—and it was something she desperately wanted to believe—it was just the first time. "They're sure to love you when they get to know you," he had said more than once, clearly trying to comfort her.

Maybe they would, Liz thought somberly. But Donna had hardly spoken to her, just stared at her with hostile brown eyes as if she could see all the flaws her father seemed to have missed.

At nine o'clock the phone rang again, as if the caller were on some kind of self-imposed schedule. This time there was an expressionless voice that delivered a message of a sort. "I'll be calling you again, Elizabeth."

This kind of scene in a movie had always filled her with a delicious sense of growing terror. Those thoughts—aborted after the second phone call—ran rampant now. Could it have been Donna? Yes, of course, it could have been. Donna's hatred had been unconcealed. Or was it Hoke? She assumed that he felt rejected and frustrated.

Two enemies, she thought, disquieted.

As if in sympathetic agreement, Duke emitted a long, low howl. She knelt beside him and rested her head on his tawny, shaggy fur.

❈ ❈ ❈

CHAPTER
EIGHT

March 21

The phone continued to ring at twenty-minute intervals. Each time Liz heard the sound of breathing, sometimes a giggle, and then the sharp click of a disconnection. There had been no message of any sort beyond the statement that she would be called again. Maybe it was a stupid joke after all. . . .

This was a stereotypical situation, she thought, one people laugh at, one she'd laughed at. The heavy breather, ha, ha. But she didn't feel like laughing now. What she felt was fear—fear that wrapped itself around her and made her feel impotent.

When the phone rang again, she picked up the receiver and screamed into the mouthpiece, "Goddamn you! Why don't you leave me alone!"

In the instant before she replaced the receiver, she heard an incredulous, "Liz! Is that you?"

"Oh, my God! Mike . . . I'm sorry! I thought . . ."

"I can't imagine what you thought or, rather, who you thought it was."

She told him quickly, adding, "I'm sorry, darling. I guess it was getting to me."

"Lizzie, sweetheart"—he sounded patient and almost fatherly—"phone calls like that are part of our profession. We've all had them. Did you flunk anybody last report period?"

"Only three kids, but there was no way they could have gotten better grades, no way at all, and they all knew it."

"Still, it may have been one of them. Don't confront

them just yet, though. Wait a while . . . see if it happens again. They're just kids, Liz, and your caller will probably get bored very quickly.''

''You make me feel a little better,'' she said.

''That's what I'm for, love . . . that and a few other things.'' He laughed.

She loved his laugh. Almost as much as she loved his body—long and lean and muscular. A sudden desire ran through her own body, and she realized that she hadn't heard what he had been saying.

''Liz?''

''Sorry, I was having lascivious thoughts.''

''About me?''

''No, about the mailman.'' Suddenly she remembered why they were not together right now. ''How was your visit with the kids? Did they like the idea of our taking them to the museum next Sunday?''

''One question at a time.'' His tone was still light, but now there was an undercurrent that made her vaguely uneasy. ''The visit was fine. I took them out for spaghetti and meatballs. That always goes over big. Now . . .'' He hesitated. ''About Sunday, I'm not sure.''

''You're not sure or they don't want to go?'' She hadn't meant to speak so sharply.

''Okay . . . now, Liz, try not to let this bother you. Whatever we do is fine with Jimmy, but Donna is another story. I tried to prepare you for that. She wasn't ready to meet you last week. It's my fault. . . . I was so eager for you and the kids to get to know each other. But when I suggested our taking them to the museum, she got hysterical. I'm afraid she's kind of possessive right now.''

''I see,'' Liz said slowly, the hurt in her so strong that it was hard to get the words out. ''It is possible, Mike, that she just doesn't like *me*.''

''No, it isn't! She wouldn't like any woman I love, right at this moment. She's sixteen, Liz. It's a tough age for a girl. You should know that better than I.''

His use of the words "woman I love" acted as a balm, and now she could attempt to be gentle and tolerant and understanding. "I do know, Mike. I really do, and it's much better not to push right now."

"That's what I think." His relief was audible. "We'll just have to go along with her for a while and see what happens."

Abruptly Liz had an unsettling thought. "Mike . . . what time did you take the kids home?"

"Mmm . . . about two hours ago. I had to stop at the library to take some notes for an article I'm writing. I just got home a few minutes ago. Why? Is something else wrong?"

She could not share her sudden suspicion with him. The first call had come an hour and a half earlier. Unfortunately, it did make sense. . . .

A feeling of dejection seized her, dejection that could not be eased even by the love and concern in his voice.

Finally after all these years, she thought, I've found someone I love, and his daughter hates my guts. She recalled Donna's cool, appraising stare that didn't seem in the least childish. It was rather the look of a woman who has come face to face with her rival.

That's what we are, Liz thought somberly, we're rivals for Mike.

"Mike," she said abruptly, "may I come over?"

"Tonight?" He sounded surprised.

"I want to be with you." She heard the longing in her own voice.

"Of course, sweetheart. I'll make some tea. Drive carefully, love."

"I promise."

Amazingly, her depression was lifting. It was possible that she was exaggerating the importance of the calls. Maybe she could view it as a nuisance that would soon be over. Maybe this person would never call again.

CHAPTER
NINE

March 21

The apartment was really only one room with a tiny Pullman kitchen and a small bathroom, sans tub—just shower, sink, and john. But it more than met Loren's needs. Needs—desires—he wasn't sure which was more accurate, but this place of his own was something he had yearned for, perhaps as long as he could remember.

He had never liked Great Neck. Middle Neck Road, Great Neck's main drag, especially repelled him—the expensive, cutesy boutiques, the gourmet food shops, the restaurants that catered to patrons who didn't blanch at twenty-dollar entrees. Most of all, he detested the fashionably trim women—young, middle-aged, and old, all in their pastel designer jogging outfits, their hair carefully coiffed or arranged in carefully calculated disarray by someone named Ramon or José or Michel.

Fortunately Bayview Avenue was removed from Middle Neck Road. Here there were trees and grass and individual-looking homes—Colonials, Tudors, Victorians, discreetly set apart from each other, with an individuality the people on Middle Neck Road seemed to lack. He liked the luxury that the white Colonial house offered him, but he could never forget that the house belonged to Dr. Ralph W. Ransome.

The apartment, this cruddy little apartment, was *his*.

Most weeks, he spent several days there after school. Occasionally, he stayed the night—as he would this evening. But the fact that it existed gave him a kind of comfort that sustained him.

His love for elegance had of necessity been forfeited. Apartments in Manhattan ran high, and even this tiny rental on Twenty-third Street and Eighth Avenue ran over six hundred a month. But even if a more luxurious apartment in a fashionable location were something he could afford, he knew that it was better for him to be in a building with no doorman, many apartments, and no chance for gossipy neighbors to become suspicious of him.

He had leased the apartment six months earlier, and already it had taken on an importance that he had not foreseen. It was only here that he could face what he wanted to be, where the desire appeared almost reasonable. It was only here that he could indulge himself in acting out his fantasy,

Over six hundred a month for an apartment without a closet. He smiled with only a trace of cynicism. Fortunately there was no rent on the house in Great Neck. On his salary, he could not have managed two rents. Why had he ever become a teacher? he sometimes wondered. Liz had dreamed of being a teacher since early childhood; it had been easier for him to follow her lead in the choice of careers than it would have been to branch out independently. And, once he actually became a teacher, he found that he liked it—his teaching role, some of his students, and being looked up to. He had actually taught many of those kids how to think mathematically.

At times he was aware of pride in both himself and Liz for teaching in public high schools. True, both of the schools were in exclusive areas, but their students were a heterogeneous group, and the atmosphere was not a rarefied one as in the private schools he and Liz had attended. Loren walked over to the fiberboard wardrobe he had purchased and opened it.

A sensuous, musky fragrance permeated the clothes inside. He buried his face in a silky mauve dress that hung nearest the door. A groan left his throat. The dress, a beige skirt and black jersey top, a long beige coat-sweater, a pair of sandals, nylon pantyhose, a slip and a bra—this was his wardrobe, hanging in an almost empty closet.

One visit to Lord & Taylor had been sufficient. The shoe salesman had raised an eyebrow when Loren asked for the beige sandals in size 8 ½.

"It would really be better for your wife to try them on," he said in that superior way affected by some salespeople. "You know, lasts vary even if the size is right."

"No, thank you. I want to surprise her," Loren had said as calmly as he could, although his heart was pounding so furiously he was sure it was audible.

"It's your funeral," was the salesman's inelegant rejoinder.

And to himself Loren had said, How right you are, you dumb fuck! How right you are!

Arms filled with packages, he had entered the apartment, thrown everything on the studio couch, and then proceeded with a pleasure that was strongly sensuous to open each box slowly, to handle its contents lovingly as he drew out first the skirt and then the top.

He had spent two hours there that night, trying everything on, his fingers clumsy with the delicate hooks of the bra, a roughness on his thumb catching on the nylon pantyhose and snagging one leg.

Not until he had gone to the bathroom, applied lipstick and mascara, and combed his hair without a side part, did he dare to look in the mirror above the sink.

He gave a long, low whistle. Even knowing what he did, the image in the mirror stunned him.

If only . . . he thought.

The end of that thought was familiar to him. It had been horrifying at first, but now the horror was dissipated. Each day, it seemed to grow less intense.

As Loren walked through the doorway, he tripped over a small suitcase someone had left at the entrance.

Someone, he thought, annoyed. Only Liz would do something so careless. "Liz," he shouted up the stairwell, "are you crazy!"

She ran out on the landing and peered down. "What did I do now?"

"I almost broke my neck on your damn bag. Don't you ever think before you leave your junk around?"

"I'm sorry, Lor! I really am. The phone was ringing, and I ran to get it, and then . . . I forgot."

"Mike, I suppose." He was walking up the stairs now, her bag in his hand.

"It stopped before I got to it. I think it was one of those . . ."

"Your anonymous caller?"

Her face had lost its smile. "I suppose so." She took the suitcase from him. "Thanks . . . I'm really sorry."

"When I break my neck on something you've left lying around, you'll make amends by taking care of me in my wheelchair for the rest of my life."

"You sound as if you'd like that," she said accusingly.

"Right! I can't think of anything I'd like better. I especially love it when you become psychoanalytical."

"Okay, okay, let's stop bickering. I get uneasy when the phone rings. I was trying to convince myself that it wouldn't happen again." She flashed him a conciliatory smile. "Let's sit down in my room for a second. I've hardly seen you in days. How long is it since we heard from Mother?"

Loren shrugged. She must know that he did not want to discuss their mother.

Her bed was made for a change, he noticed. This meant that she hadn't slept in it last night. Odd for a Thursday.

He sat down on her desk chair while she perched on a hassock opposite him. "What's on your mind?" he asked.

"The damn phone calls! The voice doesn't say more than a word or two. The past couple of days, it ends with 'I'll be calling you again, Elizabeth.' "

"Have you contacted the police?"

"Of course I have—after the third one—and the police officer I spoke to told me to come down to the Sixth Precinct. But when I got there, he explained that in order to make out a report I had to be willing for the person to be arrested. How could I do that if it's one of my students or . . . Donna? Maybe it was to make me feel better, but the cop thought it could be a goof. Most of the time, he said, the calls stop. But that's not all—" She seemed about to continue and then hesitated.

"There's something else?" he said. "Go on."

"Well . . . I'm worried about Doug—you remember the student I was tutoring? I saw him at the pizza place last week, and he looked awful. He acted oddly too, and there was somebody with him. . . ." Pausing she seemed suddenly aware that he was hardly listening.

He hated this kind of discussion. He did not want to think about her annoying telephone calls. Her concern for this stranger—her student—irked him. A sharp pain in his right temple made him rub his head vigorously as if that would make it go away. Of course he knew that she wanted his help, his counsel, and he wished he could give it, but she couldn't know that his own life was pure hell, each day more difficult than the last. There was little left for anyone else.

"Why don't you say something?"

It sounded like a demand to him, but if he said, "For God's sake, Liz, don't torment me!" she would gaze at him in hurt surprise. What he did say was, "I've got a headache . . . I'd better go take some aspirin."

"Maybe it's a sinus headache. Take a couple of Sinu-tabs. That makes the sinuses drain."

"Thanks, Doc. Why didn't you consider medicine as a career?"

"Why didn't you?" she returned. "You were supposed to be the doctor, remember?"

"Oh yes." Inwardly Loren winced at the memory. "I remember very clearly. I think our father stopped talking to me for a couple of months when I refused to go into the pre-med program he had set up for me. I don't think he's taken me seriously since . . . if he ever did."

"Poor Dad." Liz sighed. Then in a change of subject and mood that was so typical of her, she said, "Do you remember how fascinated we were when we first read *A Thousand and One Nights*?"

The memory made Loren grin. "We both read 'Open Sesame' as 'Open See Same.' Whose idea was the code word anyway?"

"I'm not sure, but I think you thought of it. You loved the idea of a secret code word we could use if we were in danger. 'Trouble' is more like it, but 'danger' seemed more dramatic. Do you remember the day we got our hair cut exactly the same way? I think we were eight. What a day! I can remember Mother telling Dad about it. 'Lizzie got an A in math! And Loren got a commendation on his English essay. Can you imagine that!' "

" 'Frankly no' is what I believe our revered father said. Of course, by then he had caught on. No television for a week or something brilliant like that." He heard the sudden harshness in his own voice when he referred to their father. "But he couldn't take it away from us."

"Why would he want to?"

"Because he hated our closeness, Liz. He couldn't control it. He couldn't make you share his contempt for me."

"Oh, Loren, you still think that. You still feel it?"

"It doesn't matter, Liz. He didn't succeed. And See Same is still our code word!"

"Do you ever think about how he must feel now? He

doesn't talk about Mother, but that can't have been easy to take.''

Loren snorted. ''I guess you've been able to forget what her life must have been like. Don't you remember when we were in college? She was alone almost all the time. He was either out drinking or on call at the hospital or at one of his meetings. That's when she went back to those Master classes. . . .''

Why was he finding excuses for her? Just thinking about his mother made his head pound.

''You look so pale, Lor. I'm sorry . . . I shouldn't have mentioned . . .'' Liz sounded uncertain and stopped.

No, he thought, but you always do. You got double your share of everything, including strength. When she left, you took it in stride, and I fell apart inside. I sound as if she deserted me when I was five years old. I was twenty-eight, old enough to be married myself.

A sudden nausea made him retch, and he ran into Liz's bathroom. Afterwards she made him lie down on her bed, put a wet towel on his forehead, and covered him with a blanket. He was surprised to see tears in her eyes.

''Our family isn't a real family anymore. If it weren't for Mike . . .''

''But Mike *is* here,'' he said quietly.

''It seems unfair, Lor.''

''What does?''

''That I've got Mike, and you don't have anybody.''

''Wait a minute. Whatever gave you the idea that I have nobody?''

''You didn't let me finish. I meant anybody you care about, really care about—the way I do Mike.''

''Liz,'' he said gently, ''lay off, will you?''

He knew that he had hurt her. She moved away from him swiftly and began to pick up things that had been strewn around the room. She seemed to be under the impression that they were sixteen again and were still sharing all their thoughts and dreams with each other.

It wasn't her fault that she was the lucky one, more whole than either he or their father. Their mother was whole too, but he didn't want to think about her now. A wave of remorse came over him. He sat up in bed. "Liz, I'm sorry. I guess I should tell you. I do have somebody, but it's not a relationship like yours and Mike's. There are complications."

She was dying to ask more, he could tell. He knew that she wondered if he were gay, and was inwardly amused that she had never dared to ask. Perhaps she sensed that he had told her as much as he would ever tell her.

CHAPTER TEN

March 25

The package was on the front hall table with the rest of the mail. As soon as Liz opened the front door, the smells of Lemon Pledge and pine solution reminded her that this had been one of Bertha's days. Now the house would be really clean for a couple of days at least.

Wrapped in brown paper, the package was addressed to Ms. Elizabeth Ransome, and she knew an instant of pure childish glee at the idea of a surprise. She was startled that the reaction came so spontaneously. The little girl, Lizzie, seemed to emerge at odd times. Sometimes Mike spotted her and was indulgently amused. When Loren caught a glimpse of her, he seemed delighted at times and annoyed at others.

There wasn't much Loren didn't know about her, and until the last year or so, she had felt confident that she knew all the important things about him too. In the last year, though, she had detected changes. Never as spontaneous as she, he had grown even more reclusive. She attributed this to their mother's leaving. Ridiculous perhaps, a grown man missing his mother in that way, but Loren and his mother had always been unusually close. Often Liz had felt jealous of this closeness—just as she knew Loren was of her relationship with her father.

The feeling of sadness that came over her now made her impatient.

Why do I always do this to myself? she thought. I've got a lovely present to open—it's not my birthday or

Christmas—and I'm moping about something completely out of my control.

She picked up the package. It was oblong, like a box of candy. Of course it was from Mike. Last week they had gone walking in town and passed a chocolate shop. She had flattened her nose against the window and stared at the display of chocolates. Chocolate-covered fruit and nuts of all kinds, truffles, caramels, fudge, bark chocolate, both light and dark, mocha, orange . . .

"Oh God," she had breathed.

"You poor little kid. You look like an updated version of the little match girl," Mike had teased her, laughing. "Come on, baby, I'll buy you a chocolate something."

She had drawn back. "No! If I start, that's it—I'll be off to the races, and then my allergy takes over, and I'll begin to sneeze. I haven't eaten chocolate in ages. One piece, and I'm a goner. I appreciate it, but no thanks."

"Liz! You should have seen your face. You were positively drooling. A couple of pieces of chocolate aren't going to make you eat the whole box."

"No, no, really," she had said. "Not now . . . my willpower isn't in very good shape. Another time . . . maybe."

Apparently he had taken her at her word and decided that now was the time.

She glanced through the rest of the mail. Most of it was for her father, a few advertisements for her, and a letter from her mother. Good! She hoped she'd answer some of the questions she had asked in her last letter. Carrying her briefcase in one hand, the package in the other, she climbed the stairs to her room.

Here, too, were the combined smells of lemon and pine and a new fragrance, lavender. Recently, Bertha had began to spray some lavender air freshener in her room before she left. Sniffing with pleasure, Liz took in the neatly made bed, the cleared dresser surface, the general appearance of neatness and order. She loved the idea of neatness, but it was so hard to remind herself to put things away, hang clothes in the closet, collect her earrings and chains and store them in her jewel box. Loren got the neatness gene, she thought. And Bertha wouldn't enjoy cleaning her room nearly as much if everything was in its place.

The rationalization made her smile, but secretly she had often wondered what Bertha actually did in Loren's room. There never seemed to be anything to do except vacuum.

Getting out of her skirt and sweater, she conscientiously hung up the skirt in her closet, then folded the sweater and laid it away in a drawer. She pulled on a pair of jeans and a T-shirt, and then approached the package.

Funny, the writing didn't look like Mike's, but then it was really more printing than writing. Carefully she pulled off the string and undid the package. A box of candy as she had suspected. Russell Stover. No question but that he had taste. She smiled at her own pun. Lifting the box, she noticed its lightness and was for an instant disappointed.

Regardless of the allergy, she was looking forward to chocolates, and chocolates were heavy. Could Mike have taken her at her word and got jelly or marmalade squares?

She opened the box and, to her amazement, there was a smallish box inside, the kind that might hold a bracelet. If Mike wanted to give her a bracelet, it didn't seem characteristic of him to do it this way. Anticipation had now given way to uneasiness, and she lifted the cover off slowly.

There on a bed of white cotton lay a dead sparrow, its head severed, a long hat pin fastening the head to the body.

Revulsion churned her stomach, and for an instant she thought she would be sick. A cold chill permeated her body. The telephone calls, more frequent of late, were increasingly frightening in their persistence. And now this!

She shivered, and her teeth began to chatter. Someone hated her with a desperation that was becoming more and more evident.

CHAPTER ELEVEN

March 26

Liz had never thought of her home as cold and unfriendly—until the calls had begun to accelerate. Now, she could not stop shivering, and after turning up the thermostat, decided to take a hot bath.

Just as she was taking a towel from the linen closet, the phone rang. She froze, hoping that it would stop, half afraid that it would before she got there. She reached it after the third ring, and heart thudding, said, "Hello."

An unfamiliar voice, husky, the diction somewhat crude, said, "Is this the doctor's house? Dr. Ralph W. Ransome?"

Her relief was so great that she curbed her impulse to thank him for calling and tried to compose herself. "I'll give you his office number," she began, prepared to rattle it off. "His service can give you an appointment."

"No, miss . . . you don't understand. Are you a relative of the doctor's?"

Cautiously she said, "I'm his daughter. Is something the matter?" Then sudden fear seizing her, she cried, "Has something happened to my father?"

"No, no accident, nothing like that, miss. It's just . . . My name is Barney Donnelley, and I have a bar and grill over in Elmhurst. Your dad is here. He passed out . . . I didn't know what to do so I went through his wallet and found this number."

"You've made a mistake," Liz said, sounding, she realized, more certain than she felt. "My father is Dr. Ralph Ransome, and he's at a medical meeting."

"The man with his head on one of my tables has cards in his wallet with the same name. I would of called the cops, miss, but your dad is an important-looking gentleman, well-dressed, talks good . . . comes in three, four times a week."

"I don't understand, Mr . . . Donnelley. My father is at a medical meeting. Someone may have stolen his wallet. That's the only explanation I can think of."

"Miss Ransome, please . . . if he's not your father, I'll call the cops, but I think you should come down here and check it out."

Something made her resist the impulse to tell him to call the police. If her father's wallet had been picked by the man who was out cold at the bar, she had better go down and retrieve the wallet. She could almost hear her father's, "Good girl, Lizzie! I didn't even know it was missing."

"I'll come down, Mr. Donnelley. Where are you located?"

She listened to his directions for a few minutes but nothing registered. "Wait," she said, "I'll write it down."

Even with the written directions, she found herself driving erratically—going through two stop signs and one red light. Elmhurst was unfamiliar, full of one-way streets. She hadn't realized how tense her body was until she saw the tremor in her right hand on the wheel. How ludicrous this entire episode was, she thought. The explanation, when she finally found it, would probably be a simple one, and later she and her father would laugh over it together.

As she pulled up behind the large gray Cadillac, her heart began to thump in rapid, irregular beats. It was her father's car, complete with M.D. and familiar license number. *No!* she cried out silently. Cars can be stolen as easily as wallets. Maybe her father was lying somewhere, hurt. . . .

She was shaking as she crossed the street to the bar. Her legs felt like cardboard.

Donnelley's Bar & Grill looked shoddy and uninviting. This, for some reason, cheered her up. Her elegant, discerning father would never set a foot into a place like this.

Then, as she opened the door and walked in, a wave of terror seized her. What if this was some kind of ugly scheme to get her down here and . . .

A burly man with a fringe of red hair on his balding head, stood behind the bar washing glasses. Her heels clicked on the wooden floor, and he glanced up, an exclamation of relief on his lips.

"Barney Donnelley, Miss Ransome," he said. "I was beginning to get worried. Your . . . the doctor is at a table in the back."

She followed him, wondering if her legs would continue to propel her forward, and then at the last table, she saw a tall figure slumped over, his head on the table.

It was his jacket, the dark tweed jacket. She pressed her hand against her mouth to keep from crying aloud, amazed that she could contain herself.

Closer now—the slender handsome head, dark hair just beginning to gray—the reek of alcohol nauseating her.

Barney Donnelley was watching. His eyes were enigmatic, but his voice was gentle. "It happens, miss . . . to the best of them. Tonight all he ordered was doubles—straight doubles. I don't even know how much he put away."

Incapable of any action now, she allowed the bartender to take over. Dimly she heard his instructions. "I'll need a hand to get him to the car, miss. It's better if you drive the Caddie—this isn't the best neighborhood—and then maybe you can bring someone back with you for your car."

Somehow she helped Donnelley move her father to the car, watched as he settled him in the front seat and fastened his seat belt, heard him say, "Be careful, miss. I

know you got a pretty bad shock there. . . ." His words
died away.

Though she could barely swallow—her throat was constricted, her mouth dry—she managed to say, "Thank you,
Mr. Donnelley." There was more she wanted to get out,
but the words refused to come.

"Don't mention it," he said quietly. Then, as she was
about to close the door, he added, "Don't be shocked if
he don't remember anything about tonight. He's in a
blackout. I've seen plenty of them."

She nodded, accepting the strange fact even as her mind
continued to reject it. Of course he would remember, and
his explanation would cast light on this . . . this horror.

The large car was awkward to maneuver, and she drove
home slowly—even on the Long Island Expressway she
was below the speed limit. Her attention focused on the
simple mechanics of driving until she turned off the expressway to Lakeville Road, which became Middle Neck
in Great Neck.

Please God, she thought, let Loren be home! There was
no way she could get her father into the house without
Loren's help. As she approached the driveway and saw her
brother's red Fiat, the tension in her body relaxed.

An hour later she sat in a tub of hot water and wondered
how she would face her father tomorrow morning. Loren
had been better than she could have expected. In dealing
with the crisis—getting her father into the house, undress-
ing him, and putting him to bed—he had shown none of
the shock she had experienced.

When he'd emerged from their father's room and shut
the door, Loren had said, "Come on down to the kitchen.
I'll make you a cup of hot chocolate. You look almost as
bad as he does."

Later, facing each other across the snack bar at one end
of the kitchen, she said, "Loren, you knew, didn't you?"

"That he's a drunk?"

The word was gross, as gross as the shoddy Elmhurst

bar. "That he drank . . . too much," she said, hearing the note of reproach in her voice.

Loren ignored it. He seemed to consider for a while before replying. "We've given each other a wide berth for a long time now, Liz. He doesn't respect me, and I reciprocate—in spades!"

"He probably started to drink more heavily when Mother . . . left." She knew that she was being disloyal to her mother, but loyalty to her father seemed more important now.

Anger flashed in the violet blue eyes so like her own. "Don't lay that on her, for Pete's sake! Don't you realize that his drinking was one of the things that made her decide to go in the first place!"

"I don't want to talk about that," she had flung back automatically.

"No, you wouldn't. The King of Creation can do no wrong. How the hell are you going to come to terms with finding him dead drunk in a bar! I'm really interested in how you're going to pull that off."

Now in the tub, she wondered, too, how she was going to manage it. Surely, though, her father would have an explanation. They were close enough for him to confide in her. Probably the only reason he had not until now was that he had wanted to spare her the pain.

Love and pity made tears come to her eyes. Loren's taunt hurt doubly now because she wanted so badly to rationalize what had happened and was unable to. It was as if in exposing her father to Loren's scorn she had betrayed him.

On the trip back to Elmhurst to pick up her car, Liz was silent except for reading the directions to Loren. When they got to the yellow Honda, she said, "Thanks. I appreciate your bringing me."

"Think nothing of it. I'm sure you'd do the same for me." He spoke like a polite stranger and waited until she had unlocked the door to her car and was safely inside. Then he drove away quickly.

She hated it when anger made Loren withdraw. Most of their arguments from childhood on had stemmed from something that had to do with their father. Would she ever learn to stop putting herself in the middle? she wondered.

❦ ❦ ❦
CHAPTER
TWELVE

March 28

For three days now, Liz had had a new phone number, and—as she had hoped—the anonymous calls stopped. Except for Mike, occasionally Loren, and a couple of colleagues she had sworn to secrecy, her phone did not ring.

What she had not anticipated was that her anonymous caller would substitute her father's number for hers. This was a phone that could not be taken off the hook nor left unanswered. Her father had been adamant about that. He had always said, "Even if it's used for an emergency call only once in ten years, that emergency call must go through."

The policeman on duty, Officer James, advised Liz to take the package with the dead sparrow to the post office. "They'll want a report, and we don't have one. Until you're ready for an arrest, Ms. Ransome, there's nothing we can proceed with." Then, in an obvious attempt to comfort her, he added, "Nothing has really happened. This is kid stuff. If it is one of your students, he or she will probably get tired of this kind of prank."

The young Asian woman at the post office accepted the package and took Liz into a small office so that she could supply the necessary information. "If you get anything more through the mail, bring it in immediately," the young woman said.

And the phone calls persisted.

CHAPTER THIRTEEN

March 29

During the first week or so, the homeless man had thought of little else. Wandering in the woods as he did, he never came upon a phone. It was impossible to call 911 without a phone, he reasoned. But although plausible, this excuse did not satisfy him.

In a philosophical moment, he argued the pros and cons of forcing himself to get into a town and notify the authorities.

For the dead person, it was all over. Lucky stiff, he thought, for an instant amused at his play on words. But following this, came the thought of the dead person's relatives. Maybe they thought he was just missing and would one day reappear or be found. At least if they knew the person was dead, they could stop hoping and end a terrible chapter in their lives.

There was nobody in this world who cared anything about him. Occasionally at a shelter he met someone who was kind to him, who spoke to him courteously. Someone who could look beyond his ragged clothes and the foul odor of his body, and remind him of a time when he had been a respected member of society.

That was a long time ago, he told himself. A long long time ago. The next time he hit a town, he would pick up a phone and dial 911.

If he could gather up the courage.

CHAPTER
FOURTEEN

March 29

In the cubicle, Loren reached for the phone, wondering what he was doing here. The strong rock beat of the music seemed to pulsate throughout the place. Curiosity had finally overcome his inhibitions, but now he was feeling uneasy and embarrassed.

On the other side of the glass partition, the young woman in the red T-shirt and black shorts frowned. She had been moving her long slim legs to the rock beat in a kind of dance. It was certainly visible to her that he was not responding.

"What do you want me to do?" she demanded, looking annoyed. "Show me what you got."

He didn't bother to respond. Having hoped that she would act like a sexy woman, that he would learn something from her about what turns a man on, he realized that all she seemed interested in was the cigarette in the ashtray that she eyed from time to time. She reminded him of a bored animal in captivity.

How different the reality was from his fantasy of a soft, seductive female body in a silken chemise or teddy.

"So what *do* you want?" Her dark eyes met his in a challenge.

"I guess . . . nothing."

Her face was a mask, concealing any feelings she might be experiencing. She picked up her cigarette and inhaled, then sat down on the bench and crossed those long beau-

tiful legs. Cigarette at the side of her mouth, she began to
file her nails.

Now it was she who was staring at him, as though it
were she who had paid five dollars to look at him through
a glass curtain. She raised the phone to her mouth. "Why
did you come? Hah!" Then she added, "Why the fuck
are you here?"

Loren stiffened. It was none of her business why he had
chosen to spend a few minutes at a peep show. Why had
he? He felt ashamed and somehow soiled.

She must have sensed his withdrawal because suddenly
she lifted the ugly T-shirt to reveal pendulous breasts with
large brown areolas. He was shocked—he had envisioned
delicate pink ones.

She leaned forward, her breasts almost touching the
glass. He realized that she was young, maybe twenty, slender, well-formed, but her face was without expression.
And, he realized, she looked tired—much more worn than
the twenty-year-olds in his world. Only eight years younger
than Liz, but a century apart from her.

With no preamble she said, "Some guys, they use up
ten bucks. I can't figure you out. You a priest or something?"

He smiled, genuinely amused. "No."

"You sound educated like . . . a lawyer or something."
Her own speech was slovenly. Still leaning forward, she
snapped her fingers. "I know. You just wanted to look."

She would not have been familiar with the word "vo-
yeur". And it wasn't even the right word. He had *not* been
sexually aroused. Sudden disgust at his feeling of superi-
ority filled him.

Abruptly his time was up. An opaque screen covered
the glass of the partition separating them.

He walked out with the smell of the place still in his
nostrils, a mixture of semen, smoke, and disinfectant.

Moving rapidly, he walked down Forty-second Street
without looking to the right or left. He had heard it was

safer to walk fast and act as if you knew just where you were going. He had worn shabby jeans and an old jacket and had only ten dollars on him.

Nobody bothered him, and he walked swiftly downtown to Penn Station where he had a ten-minute wait for the 9:20 to Great Neck.

They were in bed when the thought came to Liz after lovemaking—a time when she felt closest to him. "Mike," she said softly, her head on his shoulder, one hand gently playing with the hair on his chest.

"Mmm?"

"You're sleeping."

"Not guilty . . . I'm wide awake." He yawned even as he was protesting, and they both laughed.

"I was thinking about Loren," she said slowly.

"In bed with me, thinking about Loren. We'll have no incestuous thoughts in this here bedroom, my love." The mock severity of his tone was tempered by another yawn.

She smiled, loving him. "I feel so damn guilty at times about Loren . . . and you."

"Loren and me? We never had a thing going, honest."

"Be serious for a moment, darling, and listen to me. You and Loren were such good friends, and then I came along and if Loren hadn't introduced us, we might never have met. And how do I repay him? By taking you away so that you hardly see each other anymore."

"We do . . . in school. We eat lunch together a few times a week." Mike sounded defensive.

"I know, but that's not what I mean. You used to have dinner together, when there was time to really talk. And"—she took a deep breath—"I'd like you to start doing that again."

He tilted her face upwards and kissed her lips. "You really would, wouldn't you? You must care about that guy an awful lot. I'm not sure I'm not jealous."

"He's part of me," she said simply. "It's not like hav-

ing an ordinary brother and sister. Being a twin is peculiar
. . . at least in our case.''

He raised his head and looked down at her. A half smile
played on his lips, but she sensed that he was at least
partially serious. ''I'll give you a problem,'' he said.

''A math problem? Right after you've had your way with
me! That's not worthy of you, Michael Raymond.''

''A life problem . . . If you had twenty-four hours to
live, who would you want with you?''

Her response was swift. ''You and Loren and my father
and my mother and . . . Duke.''

''No other relatives? Maybe a few distant cousins? Liz,
sweetheart, you want it all. The problem I'm giving you
is much harder. Twenty-four hours to live and one person,
just one.''

She wanted desperately to say what she knew he was
waiting to hear, but she had never lied to him.

There were sudden tears in her eyes. ''I can't, Mike. I
can't. I'm crazy about you—you know I am—but if I knew
I had to die in twenty-four hours and Loren wasn't with
me, the last twenty-four hours wouldn't mean anything,
and I'd be dying that much sooner.''

He stroked her hair gently. She saw that his own eyes
were misty. ''I started out being funny, and then I don't
know what the hell came over me. Anyway, if you're crazy
about me, I'll be satisfied with that, but only . . .'' He
grinned.

''A condition?''

''That you spend the twenty-four hours before the last
twenty-four with me. Is it a deal?''

''Yes! And you're my darling idiot!''

''That's a fine thing to call the chairman of a math department! Let's see if you're ticklish.''

''No, Mike, please. It's not fair! You *know* I'm ticklish!'' She moved away from him, and snatching a pillow,
held it in front of her.

"That's right, I remember now. *You're* the ticklish one!"

He grabbed her, disposing of the pillow with little effort, but instead of tickling, he began to kiss her.

They made love again, and afterwards, replete and pleasantly drowsy just before she dozed off, she said, "You will see Loren again without me, darling?"

"Mmm," was all he said, but this time it was enough.

❦ ❦ ❦

CHAPTER
FIFTEEN

April 5

"Have a nice weekend, Ms. Ransome," a boy's cheerful voice called from the doorway.

Liz looked up from the papers she was grading. "Oh, Dan, thank you. Same to you."

Dan Richards had been one of her brightest students. She had known him since his freshman days, and now that he was a senior and no longer one of her students, he often dropped by to talk after school. She was aware that some of his friends teased him about his obvious interest in her, but he continued to stop in after school just to talk.

She was surprised by his sudden, "You okay, Ms. R?"

"Sure . . . Why do you ask? Don't I look okay?" She was startled at his perception, and looking up, saw that his eyes were intently searching her face.

"That's not what I meant. You . . . you've been acting different, as if something is wrong. You're not sick, are you?"

The look of concern on his handsome young face touched her. She longed to confide in him but knew that she dared not. If he mentioned her phone calls to only one other person, the entire school would know about it within days. At times she wished that her caller was indeed one of her students, but it had begun to seem less and less likely.

"No, Dan, I'm not sick, and it's sweet of you to ask. I'm . . . having some family problems."

He was tactful enough not to go on, and to sense that

74

she didn't want to talk anymore. "Well . . . I didn't mean to interrupt your marking papers. I guess if you get finished, you don't have homework to do. Right?"

"Right. Dan, thanks for stopping by, and please don't mind my wanting to finish these up. I'll see you next week."

"Sure. Well . . . Have a nice weekend. . . ." His voice had tapered off on an odd note, and he had moved over to to the door, waved, and in an instant was gone.

Liz had a sudden memory of the telephone voice, and to her horror, she thought, What if it's Dan? Why was he asking me questions about how I am and if there's anything wrong?

Oh my God! No wonder the police looked at me the way they did. They probably thought I was nuts. Maybe I am! How could anyone in her right mind suspect Dan of making those calls!

On Fridays, the school cleared out earlier than usual. She had stayed later than she normally did, and suddenly the building seemed inhospitable and lonely. Sweeping the papers into her briefcase, she went to the closet and got her coat.

When she drove up to the house she saw Bertha near the door, hat and coat on, preparing to lock up. She called to her, "Come on, get in, I'll give you a lift to the train."

"You don't have to do that," Bertha protested.

"Neither do you have to do some of the nice things you do for me," Liz said, suddenly cheered by the sight of her old friend. "Get in, please."

Heavily, Bertha climbed in next to her, depositing her tote bag on the floor near her feet. She was a stocky woman of fifty or so, with gray hair and a pleasant dark face. She had been housekeeping for the Ransomes since Liz was a baby. Once the children were grown, she had preferred to live in her own home and come in three or four times a week. But after Thea Ransome left, she had taken to doing extra things, little things to help Liz, like ironing her blouses, although this was not one of her duties. Sometimes she stopped at the market for a chicken and cooked it so that all Liz had to do was warm it and prepare a vegetable.

"You tired, Lizzie?" she asked.

"I guess . . . a little. How are your feet? Did you go to the podiatrist?"

"Not yet. They're not hurting so bad now, anyway." She laughed, and Liz joined her, knowing that it was no use to nag.

They chatted companionably until they reached the station, and just as she was getting out, Bertha said, "I almost forgot. There is a big beautiful package came for you this afternoon. The delivery truck brought it a little while ago."

The breeze that came through the open window chilled Liz. There were more questions she wanted to ask, but she could hear the sounds of the 4:30 train pulling into the station.

"Hurry, Bertha. See you on Tuesday if I get home early enough."

"Bye, honey. Thank you for the buggy ride."

A big beautiful package. Who would be sending her a big beautiful package? Maybe Mike . . . to make up for the other package that had arrived exactly eleven days ago?

The box was large and beautifully wrapped. The paper was expensive and heavy, the ribbon, red satin, tied in a large bow. The turmoil in Liz eased and she began to breathe more normally. It was obvious that this package had been lovingly wrapped.

With a sense of anticipation, she unwrapped it carefully, making sure not to tear the paper. There were mounds of tissue paper covering up whatever it was.

Slowly, she removed the top layer and found herself staring at the grinning mouth of a plastic skull.

CHAPTER SIXTEEN

April 11

There was a pile of mail on the hall table. Bertha always made a habit of separating the piles. Today, they were uneven—a big one for her father, a medium-sized one for Loren, and "a wee one for Baby Bear," Liz said aloud.

Taking the solitary envelope and opening it, she withdrew a single sheet of paper. Four words leaped out at her—four words made up of letters cut out of magazines.

Her heart began to pound as the message seemed to imprint itself on her brain.

D E A T H   K N O W S   Y O U R   N U M B E R !

Years ago, vacationing at Cape Cod, Liz had swum too far out. She could still remember the paralyzing fear that had penetrated her body and made it impossible to move.

The sensation was the same now. But relaxing her body and trying to breathe deeply would not save her life this time.

CHAPTER
SEVENTEEN

April 11

All day Loren had been aware of a sharp sense of anticipation. He had been more than usually tolerant of his students, even those in Period Four, his nemesis, and he had known with a secret guilty pleasure why. His excitement stemmed from the knowledge that Mike had invited only him for dinner this evening, not as a favor to Liz, but simply because he wanted to be alone with him as in the old days.

This morning, he recalled, she had seemed wistful. "I'm glad you're finally going to see each other without me, but I'll miss you . . . both."

He felt compelled to say, "I'm sure if you want to come too," but she had cut him off. "No, absolutely, not! In the first place I've cooked dinner for me and Dad if he isn't at a meeting. In the second, I'm doing my nails, and in the third . . . what if my caller phones?"

Abruptly her face had shadowed. "No, I thought I could try to laugh about it, but I can't. I'm still petrified whenever I pick up the phone. You can't imagine how ghastly it is—first the skull and then that message."

Now he was sitting in the Teachers' Lounge, drinking a cup of coffee. He liked having the last period free, even if it meant having classes back to back for most of the day.

At 3 P.M. the sharp peal of the dismissal bell pierced his reverie. Mike ran in an instant later—his room was two doors away—appearing harassed.

"Loren, I'll be with you in a minute. I got a message from Barbara to phone her back."

There was a small enclosed phone booth in the rear of the room. Mike closeted himself, murmuring, "I'll just be a few minutes."

Ten minutes later he was still in the booth, and Loren had the uneasy feeling that somehow their evening was in jeopardy. When Mike did come out, his face was flushed, his irritation visible. "She is so damned self-indulgent!"

"Trouble?" Loren asked, trying to sound detached.

"She wants me to take the kids tonight. She's got a sudden date. Some emergency. Damn . . . I've been looking forward to this time with you. We see each other every day, but we never have a real chance to talk. Hey, wait a minute." Mike's face lit up, then sobered again. "I'm not sure you'd want to . . ."

Loren was well aware that his own disappointment was much keener than the occasion warranted. His eager reply was much too eager, he realized. "Sure, I would . . . try me."

Mike laughed. "Well, I thought maybe you wouldn't mind going home with me and having dinner with the three of us. I'll cook up some spaghetti and meatballs— the kids expect it—you remember what a good cook I am. Then, after we eat, the kids can watch TV or do homework while we catch up."

"Sounds fine to me," Loren said as laconically as he could manage. His heart was beating wildly.

"Great! Let's figure out the logistics. You follow me home. Barbara will drop the kids off about five. Give us time for a drink while I'm fixing the food."

In the car Loren wondered what it would be like to meet Mike's children. They had spent last winter in Florida with Barbara's parents, and the opportunity to meet had never come about.

Liz still blanched when she spoke of Donna. She had even told him in strictest confidence that one of the people she suspected of being her mysterious frightening caller was Donna. "She's a very bright kid, and she loathes me!"

"Have you told Mike?" he had asked.

"Of course not! Can you imagine what he would think of me for even suspecting her? I just hope . . . as time goes on and she gets to know me better, that she'll stop hating me."

Liz had faltered over the last words. She was not accustomed to being hated, and obviously it was shattering.

Loathing, especially self-loathing was nothing new to Loren, but this was no time to indulge in so unprofitable an activity. If the last shrink had accomplished anything, it was probably getting him to accept the premise that one is responsible for one's own thoughts and can change them. He had done that, and found it worked.

Loren followed Mike's conservative beige Plymouth and parked in front of a six story apartment on Sherwood Street in Roslyn. A few miles away was the elegant spacious split level that Mike had once pointed out to him as they drove past.

"It doesn't seem quite fair, does it?" he had said more philosophically than bitterly.

"You mean that Barbara still lives in the house?"

"Mmm. I had a study and a basement and a darkroom setup for my photography. But . . . hell, I guess it's only fair that I be the one to give up my home since I was the one who wanted out. What bothers me most, I guess, is that my salary by ordinary standards is perfectly decent, but most of the time I feel like a pauper. I'm not sure Liz can understand that. I guess you two were brought up without ever thinking about money."

"I guess we were." Loren longed to tell him about the apartment on Twenty-third Street which ate into his own salary, but he stifled the impulse. There was so much he would have liked to be able to tell Mike. Somehow, it would be easier and more natural than to tell it to the shrink. But he didn't dare. He forced the thought away and got out of the car.

There was nothing distinctive about Mike's apartment, but Loren had always felt comfortable there. The colors were subdued—mostly beiges and browns—actually not Loren's colors at all, but he liked being there, and as soon as he stepped through the doorway, he was conscious of a sharp sense of loss. He had not been here in months. In the old days, before Liz, he and Mike would come back to this apartment two and three times a week.

"What are you drinking?" Mike asked now.

"Better tell me what you have."

"Sir, are you suggesting that my wine cellar may not be able to accommodate your patrician tastes?"

Loren laughed. Suddenly he felt very happy. More than ever it felt like old times again. "Vodka and tonic. Does your wine cellar go that far?"

"Would you settle for gin?" Mike was grinning.

"Actually, I'd prefer gin."

"That's what I call a scholar and a gentleman. Your sister would have made a big fuss."

"Like . . . 'Why can't you ever remember to get vodka?' " Loren mimicked her so perfectly that both men broke into laughter.

"Does she do you as well?" Mike asked, still laughing.

Loren shook his head. "Not quite. Her voice isn't low enough, but she tries. We used to do it all the time when we were kids, especially at the dinner table. It drove my mother crazy. 'More potatoes, please,' I'd mimic Liz. Most of the time my mother wasn't paying any attention, and she'd pass the plate to Liz, who'd look surprised. 'I didn't ask for more potatoes.' " He mimicked her again perfectly. "Then the old man would wake up and send one or the other of us away from the table."

"Usually you, I bet," Mike said.

Loren nodded. "Usually."

Mike got their drinks, lit a pipe, and settled himself in

his leather sling chair. Loren sat on the rocking chair, lit a cigarette, and drew on it sharply.

"I thought you had quit smoking." Mike sounded surprised.

"I did quit, but there are times like now when I want one."

"Does Liz hound you about it?"

"She's been threatening me with lung cancer for years."

"Me, too," Mike said.

They both laughed companionably. Loren felt his body relax as he sipped his drink and took slow drags on his cigarette.

The shrill ring of the doorbell was an intrusion. Sighing, Mike rose. "That'll be the kids. Leave it to Barbara to be an hour early when she drops them off."

Donna came in first, eagerly, swinging her book bag with abandon, even prettier than the pictures of her that Loren had seen. She stopped in confusion when she saw him. Behind her, a slim boy with Mike's dark hair and eyes let out a howl. "You stepped on my foot with those clogs of yours!" He turned to Mike. "Dad, I may need a doctor."

"You're lucky it isn't Wednesday. You can't find a doctor on Wednesday."

"Before we expose our guest to the worst of us, I'd better introduce you," Mike broke in. "Loren, these two are Donna and Jimmy"—and, turning to them—"my friend and colleague, Loren Ransome."

"Hi," Jimmy said.

Donna smiled at Loren. Without missing a beat, she said, "Isn't your father off on Wednesdays?"

Loren grinned. "Right. Always has been. I think Wednesday is some kind of holy day for M.D.'s."

Donna flashed him another smile. So she wasn't going to hold his sister against him. He was relieved. Liz had prepared him for her beauty, but he had expected a sullen, rather nasty adolescent. This girl was charming.

"I feel that you really know each other. I've talked about all of you often enough," Mike said. "By the way, kids, you're early. I haven't started dinner yet."

From Liz's account, Loren expected that Donna would suggest going to McDonald's. Instead she said, "We can all help, Daddy. Just tell us what you want us to do." She turned to Loren rather shyly. "Do you like to cook Mr . . . ?"

"Loren," he supplied. "Please."

Flushing prettily, she said, "Thanks, Loren. Anyway, do you?"

"Like to cook?" Loren considered briefly. "So so. I'm not the kind of cook your father is. I'm good for things like chopping celery . . . even onions if you twist my arm."

She smiled at him. "Okay, that's your job then. Daddy, Loren and I are going to chop vegetables for the sauce."

Jimmy went into a mock faint. "She's sick, I swear, Dad. Get the thermometer. The great lady here is actually going to soil her hands!"

Donna flashed him a murderous glance, but her tone was lofty and reserved as she said, "Don't be absurd. You sound absolutely puerile."

Loren concealed a smile. Puerile indeed. But it succeeded in muzzling her brother. Jimmy shrugged and went into the kitchen.

Two hours later they were seated around the table in the dinette, eating spaghetti and meatballs, salad, crusty Italian bread, and drinking Chianti. Donna and Jimmy had been given a taste and then appeared satisfied with their Cokes.

At one point during the meal Mike casually mentioned Liz. Donna turned to Loren with a serious adult expression on her lovely face. "I know that you and your sister are twins, but you're absolutely nothing like her."

"How do you know?" Jimmy burst out. "You didn't say two words to her. All you did was act obnoxious."

Donna's color rose, and it was apparent that she was controlling her temper with difficulty. "He's got a crush on her," she said to nobody in particular.

"Okay, you two. That's enough!" Mike said firmly. "Who's for Sara Lee cherry cheese cake?"

That cleared the air, and for the moment at least, their running dispute was shelved.

Loren drank espresso, complete with lemon peel, puffed slowly on another cigarette, and felt more content than he had in months. Donna, the thorn in Liz's side, actually liked him, and although Jimmy had obviously succumbed to Liz's charms, he appeared equally willing to like her brother. He became aware that Donna was staring at him with shining eyes. He smiled at her, bringing a blush to her cheeks. He could have kissed her for what she said next.

"Daddy," she said earnestly, "this was such fun—all of us having dinner together. Let's do it again soon on one of our Thursdays or maybe a Sunday."

Reaching across the table and tousling her hair, Mike said affectionately, "That sounds like a great idea."

"We could do it like . . . once a week," Donna said eagerly. "It could become a tradition."

"Boy, you're pretty sure of yourself," Jimmy said. "How do you know Loren wants to see us that often?"

"Easy, kids," Mike broke in, but Donna, her color high, once again interrupted. "Let's just ask him. Then we'll know for sure." Her eyes met Loren's and held them. "Would you?" she asked shyly.

She was a beautiful, appealing kid all right, and at this moment he adored her. He hoped that his own excitement was not visible; the erratic beat of his heart sounded in his ears like a drum. "I like traditions," he said, trying to sound cool, measured, composed. "I've never been in on the making of one, though."

It was exactly the right thing to have said. They beamed at him—all three of them, their smiles very similar. Mike had bequeathed one of his best features to both his children.

Now Loren was experiencing an unfamiliar euphoria; his heartbeat was no longer erratic, and his chest seemed to be expanding with joy. Then it struck him. My God, he thought, My God!

He stole a quick glance at Donna. She was still staring at him, too young to dissemble, too young to conceal what she was feeling.

She's falling in love with me, he thought, his momentary dismay dissipating as his mind leaped ahead.

🦋🦋🦋

CHAPTER
EIGHTEEN

April 12

Having been awake for most of the previous night, Liz now faced her class, the faces in front of her swimming and merging.

The night after the message appeared in the mail, she had gone to a movie alone and sat through it twice, hardly following the plot. It was after twelve when she got home. The phone was silent.

But as if to make up for it, two nights later the voice said, almost casually, "You know I am going to kill you, Elizabeth Ransome."

The phone had dropped out of her hand, and the voice said no more until at last there was the final click.

She forced herself to focus on Martin Bocci, a boy in the last row.

"Take ten minutes to go over the section on sentence fragments," she said.

There was a loud groan. How, she often wondered, had they learned to groan in unison.

"I know," she said, "you dislike mechanics, but I've been getting too many papers with incomplete sentences. Page one thirty-six, please."

A ten-minute respite for her, but flooding her mind was the conversation with Carol Skinner, who had seemed very unhappy about her last report card. She had come up to her desk before class to protest.

"It's not fair, Ms. Ransome. I deserved more than a C." Her round pink face had been flushed with indignation.

Trying to appear calm, Liz had taken out her roll book and held it up for Carol to see. "Look, Carol," she had said patiently, "each zero is for undone homework. If your class work weren't so good, you would have failed this quarter."

She might have been speaking Hindustani. Carol looked at her blankly and said, "I don't care. Bonnie Wilks got a B. She never says a word in class."

"No, but she does all her homework and gets A's on most of my tests."

Carol tossed her head. She moved towards her seat, muttering sullenly, "It's still not fair!"

The ten minutes were up. She saw them looking at their watches. But she could not concentrate. One of them out there in this innocuous classroom could be the one.

What if I asked them point blank? she thought. Who is doing this to me? And why? If it started as a joke to get Ms. R's goat, you've succeeded, but it's enough now. If you don't like your grade, I'll change it. Tell me what it is you want, and I'll do it!

The words screamed loudly in her head, but she had not said them aloud. No, nobody was staring at her curiously. The noise level was high as always this last period of the day when everybody waited with unconcealed impatience for the bell.

Now she forced herself to separate the images in front of her and to consider them individually. Adam Miller . . . Jenny Black, Tim Boyle, Alex Grossman . . . As rapidly as she considered them, she was forced to reject them one by one and by the time she had gone through the twenty-five students in the room, she had rejected them all.

If she was any judge of kids, nobody here would have sent her a gift of a dead bird in a candy box or a hideous plastic skull.

Maybe if she did this with all her classes, the three other English classes, she might hit on someone.

Actually she didn't dare confide in them en masse, she realized. If one of her students was the mysterious caller, some smart aleck might be stimulated by the idea and then she would have two callers or three or . . . Oh damn! What was she doing anyway, focusing on her students! There were other more likely suspects—Hoke . . . and even . . . Donna. No matter how many times she tried to convince herself that it could not be Donna, she kept coming back to the girl who drove without a license when her mother was out.

She found it hard to admit even to herself how hurt she was at Loren's ready acceptance into Mike's ménage. Mike had told her with so much pleasure on the phone last night about that first dinner when Loren had met Donna and Jimmy and how easily they had taken to each other.

Sensitive, perceptive Mike—he hadn't even realized the implications of what he was saying. "And Donna wants to make it a weekly event," he had finished, laughing.

Her mouth had felt stiff. Unable to stop herself, she had said, "And are you planning to?"

He hadn't even caught the edge in her voice. Still laughing, he had said, "What did Loren ever do to me to deserve a fate like that? I think that much togetherness might be a bit excessive."

"Is that why you haven't suggested . . . our getting together again?"

Damn the quiver in her voice! And why had she asked a question so potentially dangerous?

The laughter was gone. Mike's tone had been controlled and almost too patient. "I think I've explained to you, Liz, a number of times, actually, that Donna took the divorce very hard. We were very close . . . we still are, and she must see you as taking something she regards as hers."

"That's crazy! I don't want to come between you and Donna. What you and I have has nothing to do with her!

Can't you make her see that!" A shrill note had come into her voice, and she had winced, afraid of what he might say.

"Christ, Liz, the kid is sixteen years old. You know what sixteen-year-old girls are like even better than I do. Remember yourself at that age . . . hypersensitive, moody, laughing, crying almost at the same time. If I force you down her throat now, it may ultimately wreck us!"

"Oh, Mike!" She had shut her eyes in horror, and somehow what she was feeling must have communicated itself to him.

"Sweetheart, be patient! Please be patient." He sounded gentle and loving once more.

It was all right for now, but she had taken a risk she dared not take again.

The sharp peal of the bell pierced her reverie. "Hey, Ms. R., did you call the roll?" someone in the back of the room demanded.

Damn! She had not, and unless she did it right now, people would be marked absent who were here and all hell would break out in the office. "I'm doing it right now," she said to a chorus of "But the bell rang!"

"Quiet," she shouted and over their protests began to call out their names.

The room had emptied and she had spent ten minutes gathering up her papers. Now she was preparing to lock her door, when her phone rang. It was Dotty, the office manager. "Liz, Steve Rosner wants to see you in his office."

"Now?" Liz asked. It was rare that she received a summons from the principal.

"Right now, please." Dotty's voice sounded serious.

All the possible reasons for a call to the administrative office ran through her mind. Complaints from students, parents, an accident to a member of her family or even Mike. Oh no, God, please, not that!

Within five minutes she was knocking on Steve Rosner's door. "Come in," he called.

A slim, serious-faced man with a keen sense of humor and compassion for teachers and students alike, he was someone with whom Liz had always felt comfortable. Now he rose to greet her, but there was no smile on his lips. "How are you, Liz?" he asked.

"Me? I'm fine. What's the matter, Steve?"

"Sit down, Liz." He pointed to the chair facing his desk and sat down opposite her. "You're not looking your usual cheerful self, and you've lost weight. Is there some health problem you're not telling us about."

"Of course not. I'm fine." She heard the defensiveness in her own voice. "Has someone been complaining?"

"No, of course not, no real complaints. But I've had visits from some of your students who say that you are not acting like yourself—absent-minded, not really interested in what is going on in class."

"What is that supposed to mean?" she said sharply.

"I don't know. That's what I hoped you might tell me. Is anything troubling you at home?"

How could she tell him, I'm getting threatening calls at home, and they're beginning to drive me crazy! I think one of my students may be sending me gifts of dead birds and skulls.

No, it was out of the question.

"There is something, isn't there?"

"Please, Steve. I'm okay. My good students are all do- ing well, the mediocre ones about what I expect from them. Believe me, it's . . . it's not a school problem."

The principal rose and stepped around the desk to pat her shoulder. "I'll take your word for it, Liz. You're one of our best teachers, and I don't want that good teaching jeopardized. You know our parents—they want their kids to get into the best colleges, and if they have any suspicion that you're not up to par, I'll be getting delegations here in my office."

"What do you want me to do?" she asked, realizing that she sounded more challenging than she meant to.

"Nothing now, but if you are not feeling well and if there are more student questions, I may have to ask you to take some sick leave. I don't expect this to happen, Liz, so relax and don't act so defensive.''

Tears came to her eyes, and she turned away so that Steve wouldn't see them. When she had her voice under what she hoped was control, she said, ''I'm sorry, Steve,'' and because she was afraid that she would burst into tears, she left the office quickly.

Darting into the Teachers' Room, Liz was relieved that the place was empty. While Steve Rosner's words continued to disturb her, they were replaced by the deadlier words, ''You know I am going to kill you . . . .''

She knew that she had to do something and realized that she had procrastinated long enough. There was only one logical place to go. She would return to the police department, but first she must steel herself to drive home for the other package and the letter.

At the police precinct, she was relieved to see that Officer James was on duty. A tall, slim man, probably in his forties, he greeted her politely. ''What's happening, Ms. Ransome? I was hoping things had settled down for you.''

He listened intently, examined the contents of the package with care, and took notes on a lined yellow pad.

Liz spoke haltingly, wanting to sound convincing but afraid that she sounded more like the paranoid kooks whom the police saw too often to take seriously.

''There were no identifying marks on the package?'' he asked.

She shook her head. ''None that I could see. I hate even touching the box.''

The officer gave a slight smile. ''Hardened criminals don't usually go in for this kind of thing. Plastic skulls such as the one you brought in are bought in gag stores for Halloween parties. I know that's no comfort to you, though.''

He gave her a long slow look, and his expression grew serious. ''But this last phone call is one that deserves some attention. The other stuff—the packages, the letter seem more in the nature of annoying pranks. Has anything similar ever happened to you before this series of incidents?''

Liz shook her head. "Just an occasional phone call—the usual heavy breathing, whispering, and hanging up, that kind of thing. Every few months or so something like this happens—it does to almost all of us at the school—but nobody has ever threatened to kill me!''

"Of course, the threat to kill you may be part of the whole scare campaign—someone out there doesn't like you—that's clear," Officer James said soberly, adding, "What I'm picking up is that with all the threats, nothing tangible has injured you physically. That's the outstanding fact. Your box with the dead bird and the skull were unpleasant, I admit, and the letter was obviously meant to scare you, but real criminals don't usually act in the manner you're describing. The facts seem to be that despite the threats, nothing has actually happened to you. That's puzzling. But now another wrinkle has been added—the threat to kill you. If there is anyone you suspect, now may be the time to file a report and give us a name.''

Liz was quickly losing whatever calmness she had come in with. The image of Hoke's face abruptly rose before her.

"The calls started right after I refused to go out with someone I had met very recently. He goes by the name of Hoke, and I think he's a drug dealer, but I don't know his last name. Is that enough to go on?''

"If you give us a physical description and tell us as much about him as you know. Your signature gives us the power to arrest him if we think he's guilty. If you're willing to go for the report, I'll introduce you to one of our detectives, and he'll take down what's necessary.''

He smiled encouragingly, but she could not return the smile. "One more thing. I'm going to call the Annoyance Call Bureau at the phone company and have them put a tracer on your father's phone immediately. Normally, with annoying calls, one may have to wait a number of months, but your life has been threatened, and that gets immediate priority. However," he continued, "if a pay phone is being used, the trace won't work."

Forty-five minutes after meeting Detective Levin in his office and giving him her report and signature, as well as her father's phone number, Liz left the Sixth Precinct drained and uneasy.

On her way home, Liz recalled that her father had bought a gun a couple of years ago when a neighbor was murdered during a robbery attempt.

He had knocked on her door one evening, sounding mysterious. "There is something I want to show you," he had said gravely.

"What is it? Where are we going?" He was motioning for her to follow him. They were headed for his study.

Once in the study, he closed the door and said, "I've bought a gun, Lizzie, a Beretta 22 semi automatic pistol. The owner of the gun store in Mineola recommended this particular make. I'm telling you about it because I don't trust either your mother or brother to keep their heads if there is an emergency. I do trust you."

She had been proud and terrified at the same time. A gun, a real gun in their own home! When he showed it to her, a small, flat gun, the kind one could put in a pocket or purse, she asked, trying to keep her voice steady, "Is it loaded?"

"No, but I'm going to show you how to load it and then how to unload it. It's something I learned in the Army. And I'm going to teach you how to clean it. You've always had good coordination, Lizzie. Remember when you were an archery champ? You always hit the bull's-eye."

"I remember, but Dad . . . I've never used a gun . . . I'd hate to shoot anybody."

"Good. That's the way I always felt. I was in a medical unit in the Army. My job was to help save lives, and I was always grateful that I never had to use my gun." He had smiled and ruffled her hair. "I bought this so that we can defend ourselves if it becomes necessary. A gun is something for any sane person to be wary of. Let's hope, darling, that you never have to use it."

In a few hours one evening she had learned how to load the gun, how to unload it, and then to clean it. Her father had arranged that they get gun permits and join a gun club on Long Island, where they spent several hours a couple of times a week, practicing.

Liz had been surprised at her own eagerness to learn and even went to the range without her father when he was busy. Her deftness did not escape the notice of the instructors, who urged her to work at becoming a sharpshooter. She still recalled how much she had enjoyed the exhilaration of her first target hit. It was a secret between her and her father, and she had felt proud that he trusted her with his gun.

The hardest part had been not telling her mother or Loren where they were going when they practiced on a Saturday. Often they had left the house separately, even taking two cars—Liz, ostensibly going shopping in Garden City or Manhasset, and her father to the hospital. It was easier when she went to the range after school.

Now she opened the study door, feeling like an intruder. The heavy medical books on the bookshelves, the stacks of medical magazines, the faint aromatic smell of tobacco that still clung to the room even though he had given up his pipe two years ago—all these smells made her wish she could go to her father and tell him what she was doing, but she sensed that it was better not to trouble him with her problems now. If he looked for the gun and found it missing, she would tell him then.

Liz took the gun out of the desk drawer and loaded it. Then she slipped it into her bag. She planned to carry it with her wherever she went, with her permit.

Although she had not visited the gun club for a while, there was no reason why she could not go back to practice. Tomorrow, after school, she decided.

Just the thought of the gun made her feel less powerless.

CHAPTER NINETEEN

April 18

He knew that it was time to phone his service—actually long past time—but his thoughts continued to wander, and when his hospital patients came to mind, they quickly disappeared again.

His beeper needed batteries, and he had deliberately neglected to replace them. He hated the feeling of having the hospital dictate his every move. At the same time, he was uneasy, as if there were something he had forgotten.

At this moment—he had been drinking now for at least two hours—he felt comfortably insulated. The paralyzing fear that increasingly seized him when he knew that he had an early morning surgery had abated, and he could think with reasonable clarity, even detachment. But now the recurrent thoughts of his answering service began to annoy him. If he phoned in now, he could forget about it for another couple of hours, he decided.

Rising slowly and carefully from his chair, he pushed away from the table and headed a bit unsteadily for the phone at the rear of the tavern. It was not a place he knew well. He had decided that he would never again frequent any one bar.

He rang his number, and after what seemed like a long time, his service answered. No wonder his patients complained, he thought, as he gave his box number and waited for the messages.

The operator was back on the line more quickly than usual, and her ordinarily mechanical voice was filled with excitement. "It's an emergency, Doctor. The hospital phoned—Mr. Cowan. They said you operated on him this morning. He's very bad."

"Thank you," he said curtly and hung up.

The next hour was a nightmare. The hospital resident who spoke to him sounded distraught. "We've been trying to get in touch with you for hours. There are signs of internal bleeding, and it looks as if you may have to open the incision."

"I'll be there as quickly as I can. I've been with a patient all this time." His excuse didn't sound credible even to him.

He was well aware that he was in no condition to drive. Two cups of black coffee cleared his head somewhat, but his driving was erratic, and he would have almost welcomed an accident. To operate on a dangerously ill man required all a surgeon's skill.

Sweat poured off him—his shirt felt clammy and wet although the car was cool—and his hands shook as they gripped the wheel.

His arrival at the hospital caused a furor. In a consultation before his arrival it had been decided that surgery was probably the patient's only hope. Someone got Dr. Ransome into his green gown. Automatically he scrubbed up and entered the operating room.

A nurse handed him an instrument. He took it from her, staring at it wildly. It was red, dripping red with fresh blood. "How dare you!" he shouted at her, waving the instrument in front of her nose.

The ringing in his ears obliterated the sounds around him. He was dimly aware that someone took the knife from him and then, over his protests, forcibly led him out of the room.

Liz knew that she would always be grateful to Bill Reiser, her father's best friend, for taking over as he had. He was the one who had found the sanitarium for her father and persuaded him to accept the inevitable.

Up most of that night—a night she would never forget—still shaken from her narrow escape, thanking God that Duke had been with her, Liz dreaded what the morning would bring. She had called the school at six, leaving a message on the tape to say she wouldn't be in, and to request a substitute. Then at eight, Bill Reiser had phoned her. "I'm coming over now, Liz, and I'm taking him to North Meadows. Is he up yet?"

"I don't know. Bill . . . do you think he'll accept it?"

"Let's hope so. I'll be right over."

True to his word, he had appeared less than an hour later and had gone directly up to his old friend's room.

Unable to concentrate on anything, Liz made coffee, toasted some muffins, and set the dining room table, an untouched cup of coffee in front of her. For the first time she could remember she was relieved that Loren had not come home last night.

After some time, Bill Reiser came down, his face sober. "He's on his way . . . in a few minutes. He looks rotten, Liz, and he's bitterly ashamed."

"Will he go?"

"He's fighting it."

Then she heard her father's steps on the stairs and looked towards the doorway. His face, unshaven, looked gray; his eyes were bloodshot. The corner of his mouth twitched.

He sat down at his accustomed place, heavily, and not looking at anyone, proceeded to stare straight ahead.

"Coffee, Dad?" Liz asked tentatively.

He gave a short nod, and when she placed the cup in front of him, he managed to gulp some of it down, still not looking at either of them.

Then suddenly he pounded his fist on the table and shouted, "Goddammit! There's nothing wrong with me. What happened could have happened to any surgeon!"

"But it didn't, Ralph," Bill Reiser said quietly. "The man almost died, and if the rest of the staff wasn't so skilled, he damn well would have. And . . . the little girl, Ralph, she did die. I saw her parents in the waiting room." He paused, and Liz saw her father's face blanch and his hand begin to tremble.

"Dad," she began, overwhelmed with pity for him. But now he turned on her.

"No, Liz, please. This is between Bill and me. I would appreciate your leaving us alone."

She walked out, feeling like a child who had been unjustly reprimanded.

The two men were closeted in her father's study for at least two hours. Then Bill came out and walked stiffly into the living room, where Liz had been sitting almost without moving. He looked exhausted, but there was a faint smile on his lips.

"Okay . . . he's willing, but only on one condition."

"And that is?"

"That his family stay out of this. He doesn't want visitors or letters or cards. He'll go to the sanitarium and stay there until his problem is licked, but he's terribly ashamed, and seeing you seems to underscore the horror of what he did."

"He doesn't even want to see *me*," Liz said slowly, the words sticking in her throat like a pill that refuses to be swallowed.

"You especially . . . I'm sorry, Liz. I think it's best to get him away from here as soon as possible—today in fact. I'll drive him out. The place is on the North Shore, beyond Nesconsit."

"How long will he be there?" Liz asked, adding quickly, "I'm sorry . . . that was a stupid question."

"It's a natural question and one I wish I could answer,

but I can't. When he's ready to see you, he knows where you are. For some reason, he's allowing me to take charge. We're very old friends, but I'm not a member of his immediate family. To him there's a crucial difference. Take heart, Liz.'' He put a gentle hand on her shoulder. ''Dr. Aaron is excellent—low-key, intelligent. I feel sure he'll help bring Ralph out of this.''

''Thank you . . . for everything,'' Liz said softly. ''I can pack for him. He might not mind that.''

Bill Reiser nodded. ''Go ahead—pack whatever seems necessary. I'll stop by from time to time for anything else he wants.''

When she had filled one suitcase and a tote bag for his toiletries, she brought them downstairs, and Bill Reiser carried them out to his car.

Through her bedroom window she saw her father and his best friend get in the car and drive away. One remark of Bill Reiser's kept repeating itself in her head. ''The little girl—she did die.''

She wished that she had asked him, but perhaps . . . it was better not to know.

CHAPTER TWENTY

April 22

Liz stood on the steps of the school, waiting for a glimpse of Mike's car. He had said on the phone that he was picking her up right after her last class. Their only contact for the past three days had been by phone. When he heard about the sanitarium, he had said, "I don't want you to be alone now, but I'll be getting the kids for the entire weekend, starting with Friday. Barbara's away until Monday morning."

"It's okay," she had said, hearing the stiffness in her voice but unable to do anything about it. "I probably wouldn't be good company. . . ."

Mike's groan had been audible over the wire. "Baby, please, we're beyond that. I wish sometimes that you and I were in a strange city where nobody knew us and where nobody depended on us. But while I'm wishing . . . never mind, Liz. This is just one weekend. I'll pick you up right after your last class on Monday, and we can wing it from there."

Liz recalled her father's attitude towards Mike—coolly friendly. It had been evident to Mike that a schoolteacher was not what Dr. Ransome had in mind for his favorite child. Mike, however, had always accepted the snubs gracefully, even able to excuse her father. "I know that I'll give Donna's boyfriends a hard time—even if I don't mean to. Nobody will ever be worthy of her . . . in my eyes."

Before her meeting with Donna—that disastrous lunch—

Liz had loved to hear anecdotes of when Donna was a little girl. In addition to being beautiful, she was an unusually bright child, and Liz was able to share some of Mike's pride and pleasure in her. She's too old to be my daughter, she had often thought, but she can be the sister I never had.

And then came the meeting, and all the love that Liz had stored up for her had been pushed back in her face. It was hard to love someone who hated you . . . might even wish you were dead.

Mike's strong, tender voice on the phone had nurtured her, and soon he would be with her. What would I do without him? she thought, feeling more vulnerable now than ever before in her life.

Lost in thought, she became aware of the car only when it stopped and Mike opened the door for her. "Hi, sweetheart," he said, reaching over to kiss her. "You look as if everyone has forsaken you. Are things that bad?"

She nodded. "Seeing my father like that—it was like watching a mountain crumble before my eyes."

"How about some cappuccino at that new little café in Port Washington?" Mike asked, obviously trying to distract her. "You've lost weight, baby. Maybe a cappuccino with ice cream. Lizzie, darling, I hate to see you like this."

"I know. . . . What I've got to keep telling myself is that Dad will be fine. It's just that I feel . . . as if I've lost him." Tears came to her eyes, which she didn't bother to brush away.

Mike's hand reached over to grasp hers. The warmth began to spread through her body. "I love you," she said.

"That's why I'm taking you to that new little café." He grinned, and she smiled through her tears.

The Café Italia faced the water, the sparkling white tables and curved back metal chairs giving it an ambiance that seemed to combine the charm of an old-fashioned ice cream parlor and a Greenwich Village coffee house. Two men were playing chess in a corner, and aside from a couple of women drinking coffee and eating pastries, the place was empty.

A Tiffany lamp hung in the center of the room, accentuating the old-fashioned atmosphere. Behind a long counter stood a dark-haired man near the cappuccino machine. He gestured to Mike and Liz. "Sit anywhere. Gina will take your order in a moment. Gina," he called, "up front."

They found a table that looked out at the harbor. The water was gentle today, a soft aquamarine in spots and dark green in others.

"It's beautiful," Liz said. "It reminds me of Leightons on the Lake. I can hardly believe I'm the same person who was with you that night, thinking that my whole world was so wonderful . . . that nothing bad could touch me."

"You are the same person," Mike said gently. "A little thinner maybe—not so much of you to hold—and some bad things have happened to shake you."

"The spoiled little rich girl is getting it in the neck!"

"Don't call yourself that, baby." Mike's voice was tender. "You're not being fair to yourself."

"Mike." Liz turned away from the view of the water to face him. "Someone wants to kill me."

"That's the message someone has been giving you, but the entire thing is ludicrous. Every teacher I know has experienced crank calls. All kinds of threats . . . One of the fellows in my department got a midnight call last year— the voice threatened to cut off his balls. Bud is alive and well with all his organs intact. He never did find out who made the call."

A sudden flash of anger made Liz say, "That was one call, Mike. I've had dozens, and they are accelerating. I've gone over the list of students who may hate me for one reason or another, but there's not one who fits the bill. Even the police officer thought it was time to file a report."

"I thought you did that a while ago."

"I couldn't." The words came out before she could stop herself.

"Why?"

"I would have had to give them a name and agree that if the cops found that person guilty they could arrest him . . . or her. And I couldn't do that, but it's different now. I don't think it's one of my students at all."

"Okay." There was an edge to Mike's voice now. "Who do you think it could be?"

"One person is that . . . that Hoke, who has some kind of hold over Doug—my student. I refused to have dinner with him twice. . . . There's something strange about him—he scares me. I'm almost sure he's the one, and I gave his name to the police."

"I guess that's possible, but you said 'almost.' Who is the other? And if there are two people, why didn't you give the cops two names?"

Liz was silent. Her eyes were on the napkin in front of her. She had already said too much.

Slowly a look of comprehension came over Mike's face, and with it an almost imperceptible drawing away from her. "You've asked me some questions in the past month or so about where my kids were at certain times. Do you think it could have been one of them?"

"I don't want to talk about it," Liz said quietly.

"Well, I *do*! You certainly don't think it's Jimmy."

"No, of course I don't."

"Well then, by the process of elimination, it has to be Donna. Liz, are you actually accusing my sixteen-year-old daughter of something so diabolical?"

"No, I'm not! At first I thought maybe she was making the calls. But I don't see her sending me a dead sparrow. The skull is something a kid might buy—the police officer I spoke to said as much. A kid could think it was funny to threaten someone she doesn't like . . . they see so much of that kind of thing on TV."

She looked up at him. His face was cold and still. His sudden remoteness triggered the avalanche of words that poured out against her will.

"She hates me, Mike. You saw the way she acted that day. She could hardly bear to look at me, and she knows we love each other, so I'm not likely just to disappear. You even said that at times she scares *you*. You're the one who said that when she hates . . ."

The disappointment in Mike's eyes made Liz's heart lurch.

"I warned you it wouldn't be easy, but I thought you were adult enough and rational enough to wait it out. How can you accuse my child of something so vicious and still pretend to love me!"

"No, Mike, please, you don't understand. I'm at my wits' end. Everything seems to be falling apart. I never wanted to think it might be Donna, but the calls started so soon after that Sunday."

"And that's enough to hang her," Mike said with a sarcasm she'd never heard before.

"Listen to me for a moment!" Her voice had risen, and she was conscious of looks in their direction from the women at the other table. "You're not even trying to see this thing from my point of view. I haven't accused Donna of anything. . . . I'm just trying to figure things out. Can't we just leave things alone? I've told you I don't think it's Donna. I've made a police report that has nothing to do with her. She's not implicated at all. Isn't that enough?"

It took all her restraint not to cry out, I couldn't even trust myself to tell you about the car that came at me from nowhere the same night my father had his emergency. The lights blinded me. I was sure I was going to be killed. Your daughter drives without a license whenever her mother isn't around! But she knew that she could never reveal this to him.

There was a long silence. The stern expression on his face almost prepared her for what he said next.

"I'm afraid it isn't enough, Liz. I've heard all I care to. I think it's time we . . . cooled it . . . for a while."

I'm not going to beg, she thought. I'm losing him, but I can't beg. She rose, but he was already standing. "Whatever you say," she said in almost a whisper.

She was glad that he couldn't know her heart was breaking.

꠲ ꠲ ꠲

CHAPTER
TWENTY-ONE

April 25

The worst aspect of the work he did was the fact that it forced so much of the real Howard O. Kent to remain hidden. And now, since circumstances had made it impossible for him ever to resume his Howard role, he was compelled to be more secretive than he had ever envisioned. Of course, he had taken a new name, but when he had moved to the East Coast, far away from his roots and family, he resumed using his nickname. No last names for him made things much safer, and using "Hoke" insured that when called he would respond. Confident of his reactions, he nevertheless preferred to be safe.

Howard Oscar Kent—Hoke, his friends in third grade had named him, and the name had stuck until his senior year in college when he decided that although he liked the name (it sounded strong and vigorous, and even his parents had forgotten their dislike of it and often called him Hoke), it was not a suitable name for someone who was going to be a physician—a top physician. Kent was what he had answered to until the repercussions from the incident some time later.

It was still painful to recall his plans for himself. He knew that his parents' disappointment over his failure to get into medical school was as strong as his own. They were aware that he was unusually intelligent—his grades had always been straight A's.

Why? they kept asking him and themselves, until even they realized that there was no answer. For a while they thought he did some kind of lab research, but they rarely asked about his work, and he chose to see less and less of them.

Before he left for good he had told them he was doing some secret government work and that he would be traveling all over the world for a while. Their only contact could be on the phone, and this would be rare. By then, they must have realized that they had lost him, that the Howie they knew and loved was irrevocably gone. They wouldn't know me if they saw me in the street, he thought cynically.

After the incident, in their junior year the other three guys had acted as if he did not exist, passing him in the halls as if he were invisible. Of course, he had been the leader of the group, and sheep that they were, they had followed his lead and then blamed him.

Every so often, even now, he would have liked to be in contact with them, but it was impossible. He had made only one mistake, but it had been the biggest one in his life.

Of all the cunts to pick, he had hit on Trisha Masters, who worked part time in the Registrar's Office. She was shy and plain-looking, but he still remembered the succulent body that seemed to have no connection to her face and manner. He had only understood the significant ramifications of her job much later, long after all the rejections from the medical schools he had applied to.

"Gang rape," the judge had called it, but because all four were excellent students and none had ever been in any kind of trouble before, they were reprimanded and fined but not jailed.

It had not gone on their college record. "But," the judge had said, "let this be a warning to you. If any one of you *ever* gets into trouble like this again, I'll see to it that you're put away for a long, long time."

When the last rejection came in from a small school in Missouri, he remembered thinking, Someone must be out to get me. Later he wondered how he could have forgotten—maybe because what had happened had meant little to him at the time. Memory can play cute tricks, he thought philosophically, long after he had been graduated, when there was no chance of confronting the little bitch and making her pay for what she had done to him.

The catalyst was a newspaper item about Jeff Dillon, who had been indicted for securities fraud. There was a brief bio. He had gone to Stanford, was graduated at the right time, and then had become a stockbroker. The Jeff Dillon Hoke remembered had been a serious pre-law student. His dream was to get into the Foreign Service. What had happened to him?

Then in an alumni directory, Hoke had found Brad Ritchy's name. Ritchy, who had majored in anthropology, now lived in Salinas, California. What the hell was he doing in Salinas? He came from Wyoming. His dream after graduate school and a Ph.D. had been to go to Mexico—to retrace Oscar Lewis' path and study Mexicans in the areas that Lewis had covered sixty years earlier.

When Hoke finally reached him and identified himself, there was a long silence. "Damn you, Kent!" were Brad's first words. "Haven't you done enough? Stop hounding me!"

"Take it easy. I just wanted to know what you're up to. What's an anthropologist doing in Salinas?"

"Rub it in. Enjoy yourself—you always were a sadistic bastard. I'm not an anthropologist—as if you didn't know. But just for the record, I got turned down by every goddamn grad school I applied to. What I am now is a fucking drunk. Now get lost!"

"Wait a minute," Hoke began, but the line was dead.

It took him time to figure it out. Three brilliant students who could not complete their educations. There was a fourth—Larry Rucker from New York—but there was no reason to suppose that he had been luckier than the others.

The one link among them was Trisha Masters, who had

worked in the Registrar's office. She would have been the one to handle all their transcripts. She would have known to which graduate schools they were applying. She had been a sophomore when they were juniors, and she would still have been in school for an entire year after they were graduated.

It was then that the pieces of the puzzle began to come together—not all of them but enough to get Hoke started.

He would never forget those couple of months when he had tried desperately to track her down; that was how he had learned about her father and the wide influence he could exert. Trisha, herself, seemed to have disappeared. He had phoned the family home in Texas but was given short shrift—no information at all.

When he began to make big money, he had hired a detective, who had been successful in finding her. Oh, he had been so careful, so discreet, and finally he had made her pay. "Make her pay"—he was aware of the euphemism and of his too long repressed desire to kill her for what she had done to him. What good was superior intelligence if you couldn't make it work for you?

Because of Trisha Masters, Howard O. Kent had left Colorado, had changed his name and his appearance. Even his eyes were a different color. Sometimes, when he looked in the mirror, he was shocked at not seeing the face he had lived with for twenty-three years. Contact lenses were magical.

He had carefully chosen his new base of operations—a big city where he could develop a new clientele. Preferably a wealthy clientele. Choosing Long Island had been a stroke of good fortune. No, a judicious use of his unusual intelligence, he preferred to think.

One element in the puzzle he had worked out so skillfully continued to plague him. What had happened to Larry Rucker?

Larry had loved New York, had said that after graduate school, he'd move back and live there forever. On a hunch,

Hoke had checked the Alumni Directory and looked him
up. Then he checked the Manhattan directory. There he
was—Lawrence Rucker.

When he got Larry at home, he was aware of an instant
of shocked surprise. Of course, Larry had recognized him
the moment he spoke. Then after a long pause, a hard
voice asked coldly, "Where are you and what do you
want?"

Why had he asked where he was? "I'm calling from
overseas." He didn't care whether Larry believed him or
not. But before he could ask his next question, Larry said,
"Don't you know the police were looking for you?"

"I haven't been in the country for a while. Why the hell
would they be looking for me?"

Now Larry sounded puzzled. "About a year ago the
cops got to me and the other guys. Trisha Masters was
missing, and they were probably put on our trail by her
father. They kept asking for you—when any of us had last
seen you. They must have been in touch with your folks—
Didn't they tell you?"

"My parents were in an automobile accident a couple
of years ago," Hoke had said, spacing his words so that
the effect was halting and pained. "My dad was killed
immediately—my mother lingered for a week or so."

Even with the way he obviously felt about him, Larry Rucker
was such a nice guy, he started to say, "I'm sorry—"

But Hoke cut him off. "Thanks. What happened to you?
Did you become a physicist?" He still remembered the
tension building in his body as he waited for the answer.

"When no grad school in the country will accept you,
you don't go to grad school. The same thing happened to
all of us."

"I know. What are you doing, then?"

"I'm in my father's business." Larry's voice was hostile.

"That's four of us all screwed up."

"Right. Are you satisfied, Kent? Now you know everything I'm going to tell you. The cops think you had something to do with Trisha's disappearance. Did you?''

He knew what he had called to find out. There was no need to continue talking. About to hang up, he heard the crash of the phone reverberate against his eardrum.

Four out of four, Hoke thought, conscious of the shallowness of his breathing. The little bitch in the Registrar's Office got us all, and whatever she didn't get to, her father with his wide network of contacts and influence, accomplished for her.

Now that he knew what had happened to Rucker, Hoke could relax and begin to enjoy his prosperity. He had no friends. But there was plenty of money for clothes and cars and travel. Women were impressed by his good looks, his obvious intelligence, his refined speech, and his freedom with money. There were many numbers in his little red book.

Being a physician would have given Hoke real power, but selling kids drugs also gave him power, and money, plenty of money. Armani suits, Calvin Klein shirts, Gucci shoes . . . There was nothing he wanted that he couldn't buy. And then he had met Elizabeth Ransome.

Doug had given him a great deal of information, most of it unwittingly. A few days ago it had slipped out that the authorities were looking for him. A detective had come to school and was asking questions, but Doug assured Hoke that nobody had told him anything. It didn't matter. Hoke had not appeared in the school parking lot for weeks. He used only rented cars under several assumed names. It was easy to get any number of Visa cards issued to different names when you had the money. And he met his ''clients'' in many different places. Poor Doug had even told him about the Ransome family cabin in the Schunemonk Mountains. It was something to remember, he had decided as he jotted it down in his red book. When the kid was high, he talked, and later he hardly remembered what he had said.

Ironic that *her* father should be a physician and that the kid wanted to be one—or had. Now he didn't seem to want much of anything except the drugs that Hoke could provide.

Wanting someone he couldn't have galled him. For some reason, Elizabeth Ransome had decided to make herself unattainable. Perhaps it was this—this princesslike manner of hers—that had at first intrigued him. And each rejection had only deepened his obsession with her, and his determination.

He was as intelligent as Elizabeth Ransome, as cultured, and as rich. She was no match for him. And he would get her!

❦ ❦ ❦

CHAPTER
TWENTY-TWO

April 28

The phone calls came more frequently now. Any ringing sound was enough to make her heartbeat accelerate. When a phone rang on TV, Liz tensed, her adrenaline beginning to flow.

After the written message and the phone call that said coldly and clearly, "I am going to kill you," her flash of intuition had terrified her. How could she have ever thought this was a goof! This was real and had been from the beginning, and the knowledge that someone hated her enough to kill her made her feel physically ill each time she thought of it.

She had never experienced murderous hate—either her own or anybody else's. She had not suffered during adolescence, had not gone through a parent-hating period.

"My golden girl" was what her father called her in private. She knew that she was his favorite—he had never troubled to conceal it, and she was sure that her father had no idea of how hurt she was when he showed his contempt for Loren.

This was probably the only thing that had made her actively unhappy as she was growing up. Maybe she should have confronted him, but once when she tried, her father dismissed the subject by kissing her on the top of her head and saying, "You're very loyal, sweetheart. I hope he deserves it."

Liz thought Loren did—more than deserved it. His unhappiness disturbed and unsettled her, especially when he withdrew and shut her out. How many times had she wanted to tell him, It's fine with me if you're gay. I just want you to be happy.

But each time the subject crossed her mind, he seemed to sense what was coming and either remembered something important he had to do or erected an invisible barrier that she was powerless to penetrate. After their mother left, the barriers seemed to have solidified.

Liz had been unhappy when her mother went off with Leopold Chernik, but it had not come as a complete surprise. Over the years her mother's gaiety and *joie de vivre* had been diminishing.

And then she began to play the violin again and had enrolled in Leopold Chernik's Master class. The change had become apparent to Liz almost immediately. Her mother had gone to Bergdorf's and gotten a short, fashionable haircut. Her interest in clothes had returned, but most of all, she played, for hours, going over and over an intricate passage until it was perfectly executed.

Sometimes, Liz had asked if she could listen, and her mother appearing somewhat embarrassed had said, "Of course, if you want to, but it's not real playing. It's just practice. I'm trying to get back what I once had."

Liz had studied the piano for years and found herself enjoying her mother's practice sessions more and more. Once, shortly before her mother's departure, she had summoned up the courage to say, "Would you ever want to play duets . . . if I do some practicing first?"

Her mother's eyes had grown moist. "I'd love that," she said simply.

Why is she so sad? Liz had wondered, and only afterwards realized that the offer to play duets had come too late. Her mother had known that her leaving was imminent.

A week earlier Liz had been surprised when her mother said, "The class will be small today—just three of us, and we're meeting here instead of in Leopold's . . . Mr. Chernik's studio. Would you like to meet him . . . them? We'll be finishing up about the time you get home." Her mother had looked eager, youthfully vulnerable.

"Oh yes! I'll scoot out of school as fast as I can. Maybe I can even hear you guys play."

Her mother had embraced her, and once again, her eyes were wet.

As it turned out, she couldn't scoot—she was delayed by the principal just long enough so that she pulled into the driveway as the front door opened and two men and one woman stepped out.

Liz recognized Leopold Chernik from newspaper photographs and from the times she had heard him in concerts. He was a tall, lean man with a long, sensitive face and unusual blue eyes.

Her mother looked flushed and happy as she called, "Liz, I want you to meet my friends."

Liz had smiled and shaken hands with the man and woman whose names she heard and promptly forgot. Her attention was focused on Leopold Chernik, who took both her hands in his, slightly bowing his head as he said in faintly accented English, "I am delighted. Your mother has told us of her lovely daughter, and she does not exaggerate. She tells us that you enjoy to hear her practice. Perhaps one day you will accompany her to my studio."

"It would be an honor," Liz said, unconsciously emulating his formal speech. "I've admired your playing for a long time."

To her surprise, he blushed and murmured, "Thank you," almost inaudibly. Then he took her mother's hand, touched his lips to it, raised his hand in a brief wave, and joined the others who were already in the car.

Liz stole a look at her mother's face, and in that instant she knew.

Later she wondered why they had not talked about Leopold and his obvious feeling for her mother. Perhaps loyalty to husband and father precluded any such discussion.

And this may have been why her mother's leave-taking had to be so sudden, with only letters to the family she had left behind.

How she wished that she could confide in her mother now, but she refused to succumb to the temptation. Her mother sounded content in her letters, and Liz could not begrudge her the happiness.

For some reason, though, her mother did not respond to any of the questions she asked, and she had requested that Liz not try to phone her. "I miss you," she had written, "and hearing your voice would make me want to come right back. Leopold wouldn't understand that. He is very possessive. In any case, we are traveling all the time."

No, it wasn't fair to involve her mother.

She reminded herself that many years had passed since her mother had been able to comfort her or assure her after a bad dream that everything was going to be all right. The calls often reminded Liz of bad dreams she struggled to awaken from.

But these calls were very real. And she was wide-awake.

❧ ❧ ❧

CHAPTER
TWENTY-THREE

May 1

As Liz approached her car, she opened her bag and reached into a zippered compartment for her keys. It was empty. But that was where she always kept her car keys—always!

Could she have absent-mindedly stuck them in her coat or jacket pocket? A quick search revealed nothing.

Anxiety churning inside her, she went to the back of the car and emptied everything in her bag out on the trunk. The last thing to come out was the key chain.

She gathered the contents of her purse and slipped the various items in haphazardly. Holding one hand with the other to steady it, she was able to get the car key in the lock. Then she stood still, trying to quiet the panic that had flooded her body.

Why the panic? she asked herself, striving desperately for control. Wasn't it likely, creature of habit though she was, that she had thrown her keys in the bottom of the bag instead of the zippered compartment? More than likely, this must be the explanation. Had she been rushing to her first period class? Yes, she had. Traffic had been heavy this morning and she had darted into English 11A just two minutes before the bell rang.

The panic was subsiding. She had worked out an explanation that relieved her anxiety. At the same time, she was aware that she had been frantically eager to accept that explanation—as if further exploration were too dangerous even to contemplate.

May 7

A police siren invaded the quiet of the Teachers' Room. Liz was in the midst of marking papers when she realized that the sound, instead of becoming fainter, was growing louder. It seemed almost to be entering the room.

"Sounds like trouble," Mitch Allen commented.

"If it were a fire, our alarm would have gone off," Joyce Bayer remarked.

Liz ran over to the window that overlooked the front of the building. "The fire engine is going around the side."

As if by common agreement the three teachers raced down the stairs and into the front office.

Dotty, the receptionist at the front desk, waved them away. "The building is not on fire," she said.

"Then what is it?" Mitch asked impatiently.

"A car in the lot—that's all I know. Hey," she added as they turned to leave, "the bell's going to ring in five minutes."

Liz and the others ran to the side entrance. At the far side of the lot firemen were directing hoses at a car, its color unrecognizable. It looked like a scene out of a movie. Liz was conscious of an odd sort of disquiet that propelled her forward.

My God! she thought. She had parked at the north end today because, for a change, she had been early. As she ran, she realized that she was heading for *her car*—and the firemen.

By the time she reached the blackened ruin of her once

yellow Honda, she realized that in spite of the horror she felt, she was not surprised.

"Get back, miss," one fireman shouted. "It's dangerous for you to be so close."

"It's my car," she cried, feeling a tearing emptiness inside her as the car continued to disintegrate.

Another fireman came over to her. "Let's go back to the school. It's nippy out here. Somebody will be in to take your statement in a few minutes."

Liz had not known how cold she was until she was back in the warmth of the building. Then her teeth began to chatter uncontrollably.

"Are you okay, miss?" the fireman asked, but she was unable to answer.

Now they were back in the office, and Dotty's keen eyes must have assessed the situation. She pulled off her own black cardigan and came out from behind the desk to drape it around Liz. "Here, honey," she said. "Sit down on the bench there, and I'll bring you a nice hot cup of tea."

Within two minutes she was back, but Liz's hand was shaking so furiously, it was impossible to hold the cup.

"Are you the owner of the yellow Honda?" an unfamiliar voice asked.

Liz looked up. Two police officers had come into the office. One, a gray-haired man, held a pad and seemed prepared to take down information.

At the end of the brief questioning, she had given her name, address, and make of the car, as well as the name of her insurance company. The dark-haired officer who had been standing next to his partner spoke for the first time. "Do you have any idea who could have done this?"

Liz looked around the office. Dotty was talking on the telephone. In a whisper she said, "Someone has been threatening to kill me. I get phone calls . . . a voice says, 'I'm going to kill you!' " Liz swallowed hard to quell incipient hysteria.

"Have you reported this?" The officer's voice was low.

She nodded. "I've notified the police in the Sixth Precinct. Detective Levin has the report. And my phone is being monitored."

"We'll check and bring them up to date about this. I assume there's someone you suspect?"

Dotty was off the phone and at the filing cabinet now, filing or pretending to file. It was her boast that she knew everything that went on at the school.

Liz stood. "Let's step out in the hall." Taking off the cardigan, she walked over and handed it to Dotty. "Thank you. It was a lifesaver."

The two officers and fireman followed her out.

Once in the hall, Liz said, "There is someone I suspect."

In the Teachers' Room at Grant High, Loren sat in a strange inner turmoil, hearing again the panic in Liz's voice as she'd recounted over the telephone what had happened.

"Do the police have any idea of who could have done it?" he'd asked.

"No. They wanted to know if there was anyone I suspected. I gave them Hoke's name, but that's on the report Detective Levin turned in. I suspect him, but I can't be sure he's the one. Loren, it's getting closer. I feel as if something terrible is going to happen."

"Take it easy, Liz. It was a rotten thing for you to go through, but maybe the person who did it got the wrong car."

"Is that possible?" she had asked, a faint glimmer of hope in her voice.

"I'm sure it is. People make mistakes, even criminals. The first thing to do is rent you a car. That will give us a little time for you to decide what you want. I'll drive over to pick you up during my last period. Is that okay?"

"It's better than okay. One of the teachers was going to drive me home, but I'd much rather it be you."

"Great. I'll arrange for the rental to be delivered to the house tomorrow afternoon."

"Thanks, Loren. Really, thanks!"

She had sounded on the verge of tears. Her terror and pain communicated itself to him. Sitting with his head in his hands, he closed his eyes, not opening them until Mike's voice said, "What's the matter, buddy? Trouble?"

Loren told him about the fire, and immediately Mike's concern was for Liz—after all this time of not seeing her, of no contact at all.

"Should I get over there?" he asked, his voice tense.

Loren hesitated. "You've got a class, but my last period is free. I was going to dash over to her school and drive her home. But I'll take your class instead if you'd rather."

Mike's brow furrowed. "Better not," he said slowly, his voice sad but resigned. "Nothing has really changed. If you're going, that's good enough. Are you doing anything about a car rental."

"That's next on the agenda."

"You're way ahead of me. I'm not sure *you* shouldn't be head of the math department."

I love you, Mike.

Startled, Loren looked up, but the expression on Mike's face had not altered. Providence had been kind. He had not said those words aloud.

He sensed that Mike seemed relieved that he was taking over.

His narrow escape had left him shaken. Sometimes he felt as if he were on a moving belt, headed for certain destruction. What if . . . What would Mike have said if his thought had been put into spoken words!

May 18

She took the receiver off the hook and proceeded to dial. With two digits to go, she stopped, pressed the button for the dial tone, and hung up. What would they say to each other? "How are you, Mike?" "Fine, Liz, and you?"

She had called once since that last afternoon, and it had been painful—she couldn't bear remembering. The memory of his voice, strained, distant, made her wince even now.

"Let's take it easy for a while . . . you've been under a lot of strain. . . ."

"Mike, I didn't mean," she had begun and stopped. But she had forced herself to go on. "I was terribly wrong, stupid, to even consider it might be Donna."

But to her horror, he seemed hardly to have heard her. "Maybe it's better this way."

Her lips had felt stiff and swollen, and now each word had become an effort. "If that's the way you want it . . ."

"I don't think we have any choice."

"Goodbye, Mike." She had hung up before he could reply.

How craven she had sounded. And now she realized that apologizing for suspecting Donna would never be enough. She had created this schism. There seemed to be no way to bridge it.

Loren came in as she was staring at the phone. His color

was high, and there was something about him that conveyed barely concealed excitement.

For some reason, she felt as if they were on opposite sides of a seesaw. "Will you be home for dinner?" she asked.

"Nope. Sorry." He didn't look the least bit sorry.

"Are you going out?"

He gave her a strange look, half embarrassed, half something she couldn't fathom.

"It's Thursday," he said.

"So . . . ?" She waited.

"It's the night the kids come over."

The kids? It took an instant before she understood. Slowly, painfully, she said, "Mike's kids?"

Loren's fair skin grew rosier. "We all had dinner together a few weeks ago by accident. Barbara had a date or something that night. Anyway, the kids enjoyed it." He shrugged. "So we've just kept it up." He was obviously uncomfortable. "Liz, what's really wrong between you two?"

"Hasn't he told you?"

"We don't talk about you."

"Loren," she said, forcing herself to ask the question. "What do you think of Donna?"

"Donna? She's a beautiful kid . . . very bright but kind of mixed up. According to Mike, her moods go up and down. Probably typical sixteen-year-old personality."

"She hates me," Liz said quietly.

"So Donna's the whole reason?"

She nodded. "I told you about the car that almost ran over me right before Dad's awful surgery incident. Then a couple of days after that, Mike picked me up at school. I didn't actually accuse Donna of anything, but I tried to make him understand why I suspected her. And then Mike exploded."

"Why would you connect Donna with a car? I know she's taking Driver's Ed, but she can't drive without someone else in the car. Do you know something I don't know?''

She had promised Jimmy that she would never reveal what he had confided to her. "I don't want to talk about it, Loren. Forget what I said."

"I can't make you tell me, but what else are you thinking about?"

"At that abysmal lunch—the only time we ever met— Donna certainly looked at me as if she wished I were dead."

"And if you were out of the way, Donna could marry Mike," Loren said in a pleasant conversational tone.

At any other time she would have laughed—it was unlike her not to respond to Loren's efforts to cheer her up. "It sounds so stupid when you put it like that."

"I know from Mike that Donna has always been the difficult one," Loren said, serious now. "She hasn't given her parents an easy time of it."

"Then you don't think I'm crazy! You think there is a remote possibility that she may be the one?" She looked at him hopefully.

"I didn't say that either. . . ." He paused, reluctant to go on.

"Loren, you know something. Tell me!"

He hesitated, appearing uncomfortable. "Okay, but Mike told me this in strictest confidence. You can't ever tell Mike you know this about Donna. This is between you and me."

A pang of jealousy shot through Liz, but she said quietly, "I know how to keep a secret."

"Okay, well . . ." Loren took a deep breath. "When Jimmy was an infant, Donna tried to smother him with a pillow. She couldn't have been doing a very good job of it, and the baby began to cry. Barbara ran up and grabbed Jimmy away from her. Of course, Donna was only about three at the time, but until she was older, Mike and Barbara both took care never to leave her alone with Jimmy again. Then a couple of years ago, after the divorce, Donna began to "act up" again, as Mike put it. She began smoking grass, and Barbara found some Quaaludes and sleeping pills in her drawer. That's when Donna began to see a shrink. Mike says she's fine now—off drugs and generally okay.''

"Well, whoever's calling me is threatening to kill me. I'm not exactly an infant Donna can smother with a pillow.''

"Don't be ridiculous. I told you about the incident to explain why Mike might have been so angry. He may have been furious with you for suspecting her and then maybe angry with himself for recalling the incident about Donna. Maybe you put a tiny doubt in his mind. I had a double major—Psych and Math—remember?'' He laughed at the obvious absurdity of what he had just said.

"It can't be Donna,'' Liz said, emphasizing each word, wishing that Loren had kept this particular secret to himself. Then she was struck by another disquieting thought, recalling what Jimmy had said about the "big boys" Donna hung out with.

Almost to herself, she said, "She could have hired someone to firebomb my car—maybe a friend.''

"Not impossible,'' Loren agreed. "According to Mike, she's ingenious in lots of ways.''

He slipped an arm around her shoulder. "I'm sorry, kid. Forget I said anything. Okay?''

Without waiting for a response, he added, "I'm running late. I've got to shower. I'll see you tonight when I get back.''

Why can't you stay? she thought in despair, but she would never utter the words aloud.

When Loren, freshly showered and changed into jeans and a red turtleneck, had left, Liz went up to her room and lay on the bed, staring up at the ceiling.

Duke approached the bed, making the low, growling sound that told her it was time to take him out. She rose, slipped on her jacket, and attached his leash. He stood quietly, obediently, the only reliable element left in her life.

In the last weeks, she had lost her mother, her father, and Mike. Much of the time even Loren was distracted, remote. The talk today had been a rare one. Swiftly, a pang of remorse shot through her. She wasn't being fair to him, reminding herself that when her car had been firebombed Loren was the one who had arranged for the rental, who had left school and rushed to her so that he could take her home.

Stop indulging in all this self-pity! she told herself sternly.

She took some old newspapers and walked down the street, holding Duke's leash. The days were getting longer, and Duke was acting frisky, as if he were enjoying the spring evening.

She dawdled, walking slowly, unwilling to return to the empty, still house, dreading the moment when she must enter it. As she approached, she could hear the phone ringing.

ꪧ ꪧ ꪧ
CHAPTER
TWENTY-SIX

May 20

The homeless man had put off going to a shelter for days. Even when his cough grew more and more raucous and his chest was racked with stabs of burning pain, he refused to take that step. Instead, he found shelter in one kind of doorway or other.

But for the cop, he would have wandered on. This one seemed solicitous—he approached him during one of his coughing spells and said, "Look, man, if you don't go on your own, I'll call a squad car to take you to a shelter. There's one not far from here—Fifth Street, a block from Main.

That's why he was here now, lying on a cot, covered by a blanket, with a meal filling his belly. The trouble with sleeping in the shelter was the dreaming.

As soon as he slept for even a few minutes, he dreamed that he was back in the shack. The smell rose to his nostrils, and he grew nauseated. Each time the specter of the decaying hand appeared, he screamed.

On awakening, he often wondered if he had screamed aloud. Only last night, a portly, middle-aged woman in a uniform gave him the answer. When she came over to his bed, she had said, sympathetically, "You must have had a hard night. Did you know you were screaming?"

He had turned his head away, ashamed, determined to get out of the shelter as soon as the coast was clear.

Time was passing—so fast that he often had no idea

which day of which month it was. There might be little time left for him, but there was one thing he had to do.

In the middle of the night he forced himself to gather his few possessions and leave the shelter. As soon as daylight enabled him to read the numbers on a telephone, he dialed 911.

CHAPTER TWENTY-SEVEN

May 20

"Ken . . . aren't you coming to bed?"

Was he imagining the urgency in her voice, the unspoken demand? Maybe he was, but as hard as he tried to control it, his own impatience was audible to him—and probably to her.

"Soon, Caren . . . I'm working."

He glanced down at the blank sheet in his typewriter. She must know that he was lying. He had written almost nothing for weeks—since Ellie's death. The novel, half finished, meant as little to him now as his life.

Three months ago—before—had anyone asked him what Ellie meant to him, he might have replied, "She's my pussycat. I'm mad about her." And that would have been the grossest understatement he had ever made.

He closed his eyes and saw the little blond head that rested on his shoulder when she was sleepy, the wide blue eyes that crinkled with laughter when he twisted his face into the funny contortions that made her shriek with delight. The feel of the small hot body, flushed with fever, which he would sponge with alcohol, was real, even now.

Once, only a few months ago when she had a bout of tonsillitis, he had spent the entire night beside her bed, sponging the hot little body. In the morning he had gone off to his job with maybe an hour of sleep and hadn't minded at all. Her fever had gone down; she had smiled weakly at him as he kissed her cooled forehead, and he was jubilant. She was going to be okay, and soon, when

129

the damned tonsils were out, she'd be rid of the recurrent infections once and for all.

He closed his eyes, hot tears forming behind the shut lids. I'm finished, he thought. It's all over. A little kid who's only been part of my life for four years dies, and I'm destroyed. There's nothing I want. . . .

Abruptly the thought struck him that there was one thing, and that this one thing was what was keeping him alive.

Retribution . . . the only thing that had enabled him to survive after Elinor was killed by the drunken driver. Never religious, hardly familiar with the Bible, he was surprised that the phrase had lodged itself into his head that day of Elinor's funeral and had remained there, to be ruminated over, to occupy more and more of his waking thoughts, and when he slept, to enter his dreams. And on the day of Ellie's funeral, the thought had returned. Until Elinor's murder, he had never thought he could kill anyone.

"Ken!" Caren sounded plaintive now. Once again she was reminding him.

Did she really think he needed the reminder? That conversation he had had a month ago with Joe Berlin, the family doctor whom he had known for years and who had even come to the funeral, automatically repeated itself over and over like a pulse beat in his head.

"Caren needs to get pregnant right away, Ken. She's lost over fifteen pounds, and she's beginning to look like a concentration camp victim—she's not even getting her period. The only solution is for her to have another baby to take . . ." He had stopped, flushed with pained embarrassment and said, "No, not that, of course, but to be a mother again. We don't want to lose Caren too, Ken!"

There had been no answer to that; he hadn't even bothered to reply, because Joe Berlin had also informed Caren of his prescribed remedy, a remedy that only her husband could administer . . . no, in his prick—that limp appendage that hung there, as lifeless now as Ellie's corpse in her small grave.

And Caren expected him to go into the bedroom and perform. A painful memory seized him, one he hated to recall. Only once—a month after Ellie's death—half asleep, he had mounted Caren, who at first must have thought she was dreaming. Afterwards, horrified at what he had done, he apologized, and by unspoken mutual consent, they never referred to it again.

Since then there had been nothing. By now she must have realized that there could be no performance because the star performer, too, was dead.

Soon, if he remained at his typewriter, staring at the blank page, she would finally cry herself to sleep, and another night would mercifully be over.

May 24

He had taken to leaving when Caren was still asleep. She slept badly at night, awakening after an hour or two, and then towards morning, finally resorting to a sleeping pill. She looked ill—her face drawn and white—and at times when she could hold no food, Ken feared that she was wasting away from some pernicious disease. And so she was—from grief, loneliness, hopelessness.

The one thing that might save her, he was unable to give. He was dead. No longer a father, he could no longer function as a husband either. She didn't reproach him— that was not her way—but they spoke to each other less and less as one dismal day followed another. Ellie had been dead for over two months now.

What seemed to be keeping Ken moving and functioning after a fashion were his daily visits to Bayview Avenue.

In the beginning, he had arrived at 6 A.M., in time to see the daughter appear in her purple jogging suit. She started out slowly, and as she passed his car, her eyes focused on the road in front of her, he had caught a whiff of gardenia perfume.

One morning he had arrived in his jogging garb and was running too, hoping to get a glimpse of Elizabeth, when he passed the brother and caught the scent of musk. It was strong and seemed to remain in his nostrils for a long time.

His routine varied in order not to arouse suspicion. This morning, he had arrived at 7:20. He was seated in his car across from the Ransome residence, his car obscured from the girl's vision by a giant old fir tree. She—Elizabeth Ransome—wouldn't have noticed him anyway, he thought.

By now, he had formed many impressions of her. At least three days out of five she ran back into the house, presumably for something she had forgotten. Rarely did she give her engine time enough to warm up, and most days the car, a blue one now—stalled several times before she finally drove it out of the driveway.

The brother, her twin, was often gone by the time Ken arrived.

The brother seemed to be much more methodical and orderly, and it was fortunate that he left earlier. One day, he might have spotted the car and demanded to know what Ken was doing there.

"What *am* I doing?" Ken often asked himself. "Planning," was the answer. He had a sense of *déjà-vu*—the breakdown after Elinor's death and then the planning for retribution. It didn't matter that this was not the first time. Was it easier this time? At first he had thought it must be. Now he was not so sure.

His heart quickened, and he raised his binoculars. She was coming out of the house.

Was it his imagination that she had grown thinner? Her silken legs moving beneath the hem of her fashionable loose print skirt looked fragile, vulnerable, as she tripped along in her high-heeled sandals. She looked like a model, but she was too thin, and there were dark circles under her eyes. His high-powered lens showed this to him, almost too clearly.

There was one striking similarity, he realized suddenly, between Elizabeth Ransome and Caren Porter. They both looked desperately unhappy, but in Elizabeth Ransome's case, there was something more. Her eyes had a haunted look.

Did she perceive with some hidden sense that her life would soon be over?

Now she had turned in his direction and seemed to be staring directly at him, her large beautiful eyes luminous with tears. His heart lurched, and at the same moment, a warmth spread through his groin. For the first time in weeks, the swelling between his legs strained against the cloth of his trousers.

A feeling of despair cut into his excitement. I'm going mad, he thought, but before the madness takes over, I've got to act! Dr. Ransome, great, illustrious Dr. Ransome, you'll get yours, and then after your child is shoveled into the earth, you can drink yourself to death!

Liz had started the engine, reversed it, and stalled.

He was startled that his erect penis still throbbed against his thigh.

Waiting until her car was out of his view, he turned around and drove home. That morning for the second time since Ellie's death, he made love to Caren.

CHAPTER
TWENTY-EIGHT

May 24

Each time Liz had tried to make an appointment with Doug, he had broken it. His attendance at school was erratic, but whenever she did catch sight of him in the halls it was obvious to her that he was trying to avoid her. Although his glazed eyes continued to haunt her, she had been swept up in her own troubles, putting off a visit to Edith Pierce, the vice-principal and guidance counselor, who would surely have been aware of Doug's problems.

Today, though, there had been a message for her from Edith asking if she and Liz could lunch together in her office.

At lunch time, Liz knocked on the closed door; then responding to Edith's "Come in," she opened the door halfway, checking to see if anyone else were there. The office was empty except for a slim, middle-aged woman with short ash-blond hair. She was surrounded by piles of papers and folders. On the side of a small table near the window were two trays with chicken salad, rolls, and coffee.

"Not elegant, but probably edible," Edith said, smiling. Then, quickly sobering, she said, "I'm so sorry about your car, my dear. Are there any leads?"

"None so far." Liz shook her head. On the verge of telling Edith about the calls, she stopped herself. "If there are any, the police aren't telling me."

Edith Pierce was a perceptive woman and must have caught something that made her decide to go on with the subject at hand. "Have you any idea of why I asked you to cut into your lunch hour today?"

"You're not cutting into my lunch hour, Edie. I'm glad that you have time for me. Actually, after you tell me what you wanted to talk about, I have something to discuss with you too."

"Good. I know how friendly you and Doug Williams were. What I don't know is whether you still see him occasionally."

"Are you a mind reader too?"

"Pardon me. You've lost me somewhere."

"I've been worried about Doug since I met him in a pizza place with an older fellow a few weeks ago. He looked awful—his eyes were glassy, and I was sure he was on drugs. I asked him to come and see me the next day, but he hedged. It's obvious he doesn't want to talk to me. If I'm at the other end of the hall and he happens to spot me, the next instant he's gone. The man he was with seems to control him. Without any more evidence than that, I'm sure he's selling him drugs."

Edith was nodding. "So am I, and of course, we've notified the police a number of times. They have had undercover people here in the school, but somehow this young man gets wind of it and lies low for weeks on end."

"Has something new happened?" Liz asked. "What made you think of me?"

Edith sighed. "I'll answer the first question first. Not exactly. But things have gotten worse. I've been consulting with all Doug's teachers. He's either failing everything or close to failing. All his teachers are heartsick about it. We all remember the Doug we knew—the Doug *you* knew. And that brings me to *you.*"

"You think I may be able to do something if I can catch him long enough to talk to him?"

"Maybe I'm being optimistic, but we've got to try."

"Okay . . . of course, I'll try."

"That's all you can do, but I appreciate it, and I can't thank you enough."

"Doug and I were friends, Edie. And something happened to him after his father died. Maybe I can find out what kind of hold that Hoke has over him."

"Tell me more about this man, Liz, and anything else you know about Doug that might help. Let's drink our coffee on the couch, in a civilized manner." She placed the two cups on a table in front of the leather couch and set a plate of chocolate chip cookies beside it. Then she locked the door and sat down on the couch, facing Liz.

"Well—" Liz took a deep breath. "You know I tutored him last year when he broke his ankle—for about two months—and we got friendly. His father died shortly after that, and I know his mother started to work. I didn't have him this year, and I never see him. Then a few weeks ago, I met him and some one he introduced as a friend in the pizza place on Middle Neck Road."

Liz recounted the meeting with Doug and Hoke and mentioned Doug's uneasiness and her own feeling that something was very wrong.

Edith listened, nodding occasionally. When Liz had stopped, she said, "The friend . . . tall and thin, dark hair, good-looking, in his mid-twenties, maybe?"

Liz nodded. "Hoke is what Doug called him. Who is this guy?"

"I suspect—but it's not a suspicion I can confirm—that he is Doug's supplier, as well, of course, as some of the other kids'."

"Does Doug admit he's on drugs?" Liz asked.

"He doesn't have to. His entire pattern tells me he is. Frequent absences, grades slipping. It's rare that his eyes aren't foggy."

"Have you talked to Mrs. Williams? She's an intelligent woman, and she adores Doug."

Edith nodded. "All of that, but she refuses to believe

it. She has all kinds of plausible explanations for why Doug has changed so much.''

"His father's death?"

"Right."

"What about the other kids? Do they admit to knowing Hoke?'' Liz was struck by the feeling of aversion she had to saying his name.

"A few kids have, but nobody admits to knowing his last name or where he lives, and of course, nobody admits to buying drugs from him."

"Can't the police do anything?"

"I've spoken about the situation to the captain of the precinct, but there's no case. You can't arrest someone, let alone prosecute, without good hard evidence. You know that, Liz. Don't you watch the police procedurals on TV?'' She smiled, adding, "That was facetious."

"I know. I do watch them occasionally, though. So we're supposed to let this, this . . . creep just go on destroying kids like Doug! Oh, I'm sorry, Edie, I'm not implying you're doing that."

Edith was eyeing her thoughtfully. "That's where you come in. Doug always liked you, Liz. I suspect he had a crush on you. Maybe you can talk to him and learn something. Sort of off the cuff—you're not a vice-principal. The title makes kids clam up until they get to know me."

"I'll try." Abruptly Liz recalled Hoke's self-assurance, what she thought of as his *hubris* in approaching her. "Edie, he actually thought he could buy me dinner. It was as though he were setting up a date and poor Doug was a kind of servant who was following instructions."

A serious look crossed Edith's face. "Be careful, Liz. I have an instinctive feeling about him. I think he could be dangerous if you cross him."

"I can't help crossing him. I'm never going out with him!"

"Of course not, but try not to antagonize him. Tell him you're engaged to be married . . . or anything you like that will dissuade him. You certainly needn't be honest with him.''

"I did tell him I was engaged, but too late. He didn't believe me." Just saying the word "engaged" gave Liz a pang. She wished she could tell Edith that she and Mike were no longer together, but the thought of him made her want to burst into tears. No, not now. She forced herself to listen to Edith, who was continuing.

"Talk to Doug, Liz, but leave this . . . Hoke out of it. Drug dealers are out of our realm. I don't think either of us is tough enough or experienced enough to deal with him.''

"I'll start with Doug," Liz said. But she had a strong inner sense that Hoke, having so strangely entered her life, would not quickly disappear from it. She realized, too, that she was frightened of him.

❦ ❦ ❦
CHAPTER
TWENTY-NINE

May 25

Loren both hated the apartment and loved it. It was ugly—but it was his. His, the way no other place had ever been. It was here that he could remove the façade that he wore in every other facet of his life.

Thank God for thrift shops! They had provided him with a sofa that opened into a bed, a dresser, a mirror, a hot plate, and a small bookcase that held the collection of books which had finally confirmed what he was, and had shed light on what he could do about it.

It was almost time to dispose of the books about gays. There was little in any of them that was of any use to him. He was not gay, and although he had hoped, when he was younger, that the love he could feel for a man was a sign of homosexuality, he had known for some time now that this easy solution was not for him.

At first—several years earlier—when he had begun to read about the transsexual, he had read blindly, eagerly. Finally, after years of thinking he was crazy, he had come across a book that not only corroborated his sexual preference but provided a solution that seemed possible.

Now, his growing sophistication enabled him to tell exactly which book was sensational trash and which might be of some use to him.

There were doctors he could see in New York, but he had decided on Mexico—for the hormone therapy and finally for the operation. He grinned at the thought of appearing in school with his breasts mysteriously growing like a pubescent girl's.

No, if his plan proceeded on schedule, when Loren Ransome quit his job at Grant High School and disappeared, he would never be seen again. Who would miss him? he wondered, surprised at his vague feeling of sadness.

How he wished he could tell Liz about this. Sometimes he couldn't resist giving her a hint. Was it only a week ago that he had said to her when they were gulping coffee in the morning, "Don't be surprised if I disappear one day without a clue."

At any other time, she would have laughed. She looked dreadful these days—hardly ever smiled—but she did give him a trace of a grin. "Without a clue? Not even a postcard?"

"Maybe."

"Where would you go?"

"As far away as I can get."

Some of the bitterness he felt had crept into his voice, and she had appeared startled. Then she said an odd thing. "Take me with you."

He had smiled at her, fully in control once more. "Maybe . . . I just might."

The memory of this gave him an unsettled feeling. She seemed so damned vulnerable. But then she had never been forced to build up the protective covering that surrounded him and served as insulation.

Suddenly he couldn't wait to get out of the ugly little apartment. But there was nowhere to go, and he did not want to go home yet. He hated to be in the house alone, and Liz had said something about going shopping. Her clothes were hanging on her.

He forced himself to breathe deeply and close his eyes for five minutes. Then he got up, crossed to the Pullman kitchen, and poured himself a stiff Scotch. This relaxed him enough so that he could take a book from the shelf and begin to read at the page on which a silver bookmark rested.

❦ ❦ ❦
CHAPTER THIRTY

May 27

Doug knew that Ms. R. wanted to talk to him, and he knew about what. But he had no intention of stopping to see her after school as she had suggested. How many weeks ago had it been that she mentioned it at the pizza place? He couldn't remember. Weeks sometimes became days to him, and days, weeks.

He wished that Ms. Pierce would stop sending for him and saying the same things over and over, asking the same questions. He was grateful that Mr. Lee was talking about the Constitution and he could drift off. But Ms. R. kept intruding.

Ms. R. was okay. She had been good to him, treated him like an equal, acted as if she really liked him. For a while there, he had a real crush on her, but then his world came apart, and Hoke was right there waiting for him.

At first he had considered Hoke his savior—anyone who could give him what he needed to stop thinking about his dad for a while was a savior. Then his money ran out, and Hoke was willing to give him credit. He had made it so damn easy. All he asked was for Doug to do him a favor now and then. This was where Doug's memory turned blank. God, how he hated himself! But Hoke had some new stuff, and as soon as he swallowed the pill, it was easy to stop thinking.

Now he owed him six hundred dollars. Where the hell was he going to find that much money? If only . . . if only he could get off the stuff! He had had a job at McDonald's after school, but then Hoke had appeared, and after not showing up twice, he was fired. There was Burger King's . . . Wendy's . . . Maybe if he quit drugs, he could find a job in one of them.

The bell rang, startling him. When he saw Ms. R. waiting at the door of the classroom, he wished he could disappear.

"Doug," she said, sounding a little nervous but nice—as nice as she always had—"I let my class out two minutes early so I could scoot over here and get to you. Let me buy you a Coke or whatever you want. I want to talk to you."

He nodded. There was no way he could refuse. She had gone out of her way for him many times. Even now, at sporadic intervals, he still had flashes of feeling when he wanted to act human.

When they got to the parking lot he was relieved that Hoke had stopped coming around to the school to take him home. Now he met him in many different places—the park, a luncheonette, a diner, sometimes a pizza place. But sometimes he spied on him. Doug hated that. His eyes darted around, from the parking lot to the street beyond. Only when he was in Ms. R.'s car would he feel safe.

Ms. R. unlocked a blue car and motioned for him to get in.

"I thought you had a yellow Honda," he said, startled.

"It was firebombed."

"That was your car?"

She nodded.

"Gee, I'm sorry," he said, hearing how uncomfortable he sounded—as if he had somehow been instrumental in what happened. Had he been? He preferred not to know.

She didn't seem to want to talk about it and dropped the subject by asking, "Any place you'd like to go?"

He shrugged. "I'd rather not go where gangs of kids hang out after school."

"Motion seconded," Ms. R. said. "There's a little

place I like that serves wonderful cappuccino, and they have soda and ice cream and pastries. I used to go there with . . .''

She stopped, as if she had just recalled something painful, and her expression of sadness made him blurt out, "Is that coffee with cinnamon?"

What a dumb question! He knew what cappuccino was.

It was clear that she was trying to control herself. For an instant he was afraid that she might burst into tears. But she said, "Mmm, you've had it?"

"My mother likes it. She and my . . . dad used to go to Greenwich Village to find places that made it well. Sounds kind of nutty to me."

"Forget about trying to figure out parents," Ms. R. said, smiling at him, adding, "or teenagers."

The coffee place was on a side street in Manhasset. It was all white, with hanging plants and small trees throughout the room. The tables were ovals of what looked like marble, and the chairs resembled ice cream parlor chairs with padded seats. There were only two other people in the place—a man and a woman, sitting off to one side, deep in conversation.

After they ordered, cappuccino for her and a large Coke for him, he felt groggy. Maybe the Coke would wake him up. Then she began to talk.

"I'm imposing on you, Doug, by practically kidnapping you, but I care about you. If there's anything I can do to help you, I'm volunteering."

The thought was only half-formed in his head, but the words came out, and he was stunned when he heard himself say, "Six hundred dollars. I need six hundred dollars."

She didn't look shocked or dismayed or anything. She waited, seeming to expect him to say more.

"I owe Hoke six hundred bucks. Until I pay him, I can't get him off my back. I can't quit, not when the stuff's there for me, as much as I want. But the bill gets higher and higher."

"And you think if you pay him off, you may have a chance," she said quietly.

He nodded, turning his head so that she would not see the sudden tears in his eyes.

"Okay," she said.

"Okay?"

"I'll lend you the money, Doug, to be paid back when you're graduated from college or med school—if that's still in the cards—and have a job. How does that sound?"

He was silent, trying to understand. What did she want of him? Hoke needed a slave—What did *she* want?

She seemed to have read his thoughts. "No strings attached, Doug. None at all. You're not my student anymore. Last year when you broke your ankle, while the tutoring was going on, we became friends. I'm giving you the money to save your life."

"Lending," he said with the first tinge of self-respect he had felt in a long time. "I'll pay you back sooner than you said, though. You really mean it? You'll lend me that much money?"

She smiled. Then her face grew serious. "There's something I hope you'll agree to."

There, he thought, the condition. What did she want?

"It's important that I hand him the money myself. If you give it to him, by next week or so he'll pretend he never got it—that you were dreaming or stoned. He'll keep giving you more drugs and he'll talk you into believing him. He can't do that to me."

As she spoke, his heart sank. Her condition was impossible.

"I can't let you meet him, Ms. R. The places he tells me are secret. I don't even know where he'll be until he calls me and tells me."

He expected her to say, "I'm sorry, Doug, but I can't lend you the money under those circumstances."

Instead, she said, "I'm afraid I was being naive when I suggested it. When do you see him again?"

"Tomorrow night."

"Well then, suppose I drive over and give you the money right before you're due to meet him. How does that sound?"

"Are you sure you want to do this? Remember you said you thought he'd pretend I never gave it to him at all. Then your money would be lost."

"Doug," she said, leaning across the table and putting her hand on his arm. "You told me about this because you want to stop the drugs. If this is the only way, so be it. Edith Pierce is going to help get you into a program that will make the process possible. It's not something you can do on your own. But first, you've got to get free of that monster. I want to give you the money. When it's passed from your hands into his, I ask only that you call me and tell me that it's finally happened."

It was hard to believe that she was still willing, that she cared enough about him to stick her neck out like this.

"You really mean it, don't you?" The sudden lump in his throat made it hard to talk.

"With all my heart. Do I stop at your house some time tomorrow?"

"He'll call me by three-thirty, I guess, so if you want to come by about then . . ."

"Fine. On my way home from school. I can even take you home if you'd like a lift."

He hesitated. "Better not. He could be snooping around. Anyway, I'll be leaving school before you do."

"Okay. I'll see you at three-thirty."

"Did I say thank you?" he asked, hearing himself sound like a small boy.

Leaning over again, smiling a lovely smile, she kissed his cheek. "I think so. Now let me drive you home."

In the car he told her something he had never revealed to another living being. "You know, sometimes I've thought it would be easier just to quit . . . to put an end to the whole thing."

He regretted the confidence as soon as the words left his lips.

She looked horrified. ''No, Doug! You can't ever think that way! It was because you've been so desperate—but we're going to get you out of this. You'll see.''

Was it possible? he wondered. Maybe it was.

That night he actually tried to eat dinner. His mother, who had appeared not to notice his lack of appetite in recent weeks—as if by not noticing, any problem would immediately disappear—smiled when she saw him put some macaroni on his plate. ''I knew you'd start feeling better soon,'' she said.

It was hard to eat after that. Shit! he thought. Why don't you look at me! Did you go blind when Dad died? Ms. R. sees what's happening to me. Why don't *you!* Immediately he felt remorseful.

She had been his father's darling, and when he died so suddenly she had lost her anchor. For the first time in twenty years, she had gone to work. She was a receptionist in a law office. It was all she could do to keep herself together. How could he expect any help from her? If his dad were alive . . . he would never have met Hoke, and if he had, his father would have taken care of him. Ms. R. was his last hope.

Once in his room, though, a wave of foreboding swept over him. Was it possible that Hoke would let him go? He had as good as promised Ms. R. that he was quitting. Tomorrow, when he gave Hoke the money, he definitely would.

Swallowing the little green pill in his hand, he thought, This may be the last one.

❧ ❧ ❧
CHAPTER THIRTY-ONE

May 26

When Liz pulled into the driveway of Doug's house, she saw the window blind move. He must have been watching for her. In an instant the door opened, and Doug stepped out.

"Right on time," he said, sounding like the Doug she used to know. "I'm meeting him at four. Do you . . . want a Coke or coffee?"

"Maybe a quick Coke," she said. "I'm always thirsty after my last period. It's probably because I talk too much. Remember?"

He laughed, and her own mood lifted amazingly. In the kitchen, they sat at the butcher block table and drank their Cokes. Liz saw Doug's eyes go to his watch every few minutes. As the time passed, he seemed to grow agitated. It was time to leave, she decided.

Handing him the money in twenties, she said, "Good luck! I hope this is the key to getting that bastard off your back. Tomorrow, you and I are going to see Edith Pierce and get moving on a plan."

"Thanks, Ms. R. It doesn't seem enough just to say 'Thanks,' does it?"

"Quite enough!" She smiled up at him. "I'll run along now, Doug. Suppose I call you later to find out how it went?"

"Sure. Any time. I'm giving him the money and then I'm out of there as fast as I can. He has no idea that he's getting all I owe him. Thanks, again."

As she drove away, Liz wished that she could move time forward and make it evening. When Doug had opened up to her in the café the thought of giving him the money had come to her almost automatically. Then, when she considered the possibility of handing over the money to Hoke herself, the next thought was of the police. She could alert them, lead them to the drug dealer, and by evening he would be in police custody.

In retrospect, the scenario she had worked out sounded like Hollywood. Life had strange ways of dealing with the best laid plans, but even if she could not be instrumental in landing Hoke for the police, she could do something to rescue Doug. She hoped that things would go smoothly. Sometimes things did. . . . Now she could admit to herself how terrified she would have been to confront Hoke.

Be brave, Doug, she thought. Please be brave!

Doug was relieved that Ms. R. had not suggested driving him to where he was supposed to meet Hoke. He would have had to refuse, and it would have been difficult. She had given him six hundred dollars, demanding nothing from him, not even an I.O.U. How could she have possibly understood his refusal? he wondered, glad not to have been put in this position.

Now, sitting in the booth at the back of the restaurant, Doug glanced at his watch. It was five after four. Hoke, whenever they'd met before, had never been even one minute late. "When I say we're meeting at four, that's what I mean. I may give you five minutes margin, but that's all! If you want what I can give you, make sure you're there, kid!"

And Doug had been, each time, often at least ten minutes early, eager and waiting, breathing freely only when Hoke appeared punctually at four.

"Four o'clock!" Hoke had barked on the phone earlier today, and immediately afterwards the line was dead. The angry tone was not unusual. Hoke often had a short fuse, but each time Doug heard the hostility his heart began to race and he wished desperately that he didn't crave what Hoke could provide him with.

After this meeting he would no longer need to be afraid. If, as Ms. R. had said, Hoke would take the money and pretend never to have received it, Ms. R. was his witness. After today, maybe his life could once again become his own. He knew it wouldn't be easy. At least twice before he had tried to stop and had gone through hell, until his savior appeared once more, cajoling him, comforting him, telling him not to worry about money. He was his friend, and he wanted him to have what Doug could no longer live without. No, after today, he would be free.

The next time he glanced at his watch it was ten after four. He put his head in his hands, anxiety churning his insides. Where was he!

Then, at four-thirty, a waiter came over to the booth. "You Doug Williams?" he asked.

Doug nodded, his throat so dry he could hardly trust himself to speak.

"Call for you in that booth in the back."

Doug's legs shook as he ran to the phone booth. "Hello," he said, clearing his throat.

"I can't trust you, kid," Hoke said sadly.

"What do you mean? What did I do?"

"I saw you get into your teacher's car yesterday and go off for a little drive. I told you that I didn't want you to be in touch with her!"

"She just wanted to talk to me. Don't you remember I told you she was so nice to me when I broke my ankle. . . ?"

"This is where I came in. When I tell you to do something or forbid you to do something, that's it. You don't do it and then give me a stupid reason for having done it! Am I making myself clear?"

"It doesn't matter anymore. I can pay you what I owe you, and then I want to quit. When are you coming to Marco's?"

The silence seemed interminable. Finally, Doug heard Hoke laugh, a humorless laugh. "You think it's that easy, kid? You're wrong. I call the shots, not you, not your fucking teacher!"

The phone clicked. Doug sat there, holding the receiver in his hand. Hoke was not coming, and he still owed him six hundred dollars.

The day of the funeral, when his father lay in the closed casket, Doug recalled stories of people wanting to throw themselves into the grave with their dead loved ones. Crazy, he had thought, but as his father's body was lowered into the grave, he had finally understood.

This was the beginning of his suicide obsession. He began to view it as the only possible end to pain, but this solution both fascinated and terrified him.

Nobody in his family was religious, and he didn't know whether he believed in God or not. But since his father's death, he had increasingly come to feel that one day he would see his father again. This was what had carried him through the first weeks. Then Hoke had appeared.

The intense pain of separation had been diluted . . . for a while. Then it took more and more of whatever Hoke chose to give him to make insulation possible.

He remembered how optimistic he had been when Ms. R. was making her plans. "I'll give him the money, and then I'm out of there." What an idiot he'd been to think that Hoke would let go so easily. And still he had waited another full hour, hoping that Hoke would appear. He left Marco's at six and walked aimlessly, almost stopping at Ms. R.'s house to return the money, but he didn't want to talk to Ms. R. or anyone.

His mother had a dinner date and then a bridge game that evening. That was a big relief. Pretending to be cheerful so that his mother wouldn't get upset was beyond him right now.

When the phone rang, hoping that it would be Hoke, he picked up the receiver.

"Doug," Ms. R. said, "I've been calling and calling. Is something wrong?"

"Everything. He didn't show up." He didn't add that he had aroused Hoke's anger because of her. It wasn't her fault that he had allowed himself to become Hoke's slave. "I'm kind of busy, Ms. R. I'll give you your money tomorrow."

Because there was nothing more to say, he hung up.

But the phone rang again immediately. This time she said, "I'm not giving up, Doug. You can't either. You can stop accepting drugs from him. He can't force you to take them. After a while—when he realizes you're serious—he may decide to accept the money and back off. In any case, tomorrow I'll talk to Edith Pierce and see what kind of program we can get you into." Now she sounded like a teacher. "I'll meet you in Edith's office at eight-thirty— she gets in about eight-fifteen—and we can get started. How does that sound to you?"

"Sound? Oh, fine, fine. See you tomorrow, Ms. R." He added as an obvious afterthought, "Thanks. Thanks for all your trouble." The forced cheerfulness in his own voice disgusted him.

"Forget it, Doug. See you at eight-thirty, then. Good night."

"Yeah, sure. Good night."

"Doug . . ."

He had been about to hang up the receiver. Stifling an exclamation of impatience, he waited.

"If you want to talk later . . . just remember, I'm here. You can call me any time. My number is unlisted now, but I'll give it to you. Promise me you won't give it to anyone else."

"Sure—I promise."

Anything to get her off the line. He half-heard her rattle off the number. The digits didn't register. She must have assumed that he was writing it down. He didn't want her number. What he wanted was oblivion. He had agreed to meet her at Ms. Pierce's office. She couldn't know that he would have agreed to anything she suggested. He couldn't just say, "Forget it and leave me alone. There's no way I can get free of him."

Suddenly the solution had appeared, dazzling in its brilliance. There *was* one way. And it would be permanent. He smiled at the thought of Ms. R.'s number, glad that he hadn't taken it down. Where he was headed, there probably weren't any phones.

Doug knew that he had plenty of time. After his mother's bridge game they always had coffee. She wouldn't be home until after eleven at least. By then it would all be over.

Assuming he was asleep as usual, she would not find him until the morning. An unexpected flash of empathy brought tears to his eyes. It would be hard for her, but she had survived his father's death, and she would survive his. Maybe she would even marry again. Odd that the thought could still hurt, but soon nothing she did would affect him.

With his own cache of pills, his mother's sleeping pills, and the pills the doctor had given him for pain when he fractured his ankle, he had more than enough to kill two people. No danger of his surviving to become a vegetable.

After setting the various bottles out on his desk he poured out the pills, aware that for the first time he could mix them in any order he chose. Then he thought of Ms. R. and her money. He had almost forgotten, but he knew he didn't want to die and have her think he was a thief.

Quickly, taking the envelope from his pocket, he wrote her name on it and added, "Thank you. Sorry it didn't work out. Love, Doug."

Now there was nothing to wait for. Still, he hesitated for at least a moment. Then stifling a pang of pure regret, he placed the first yellow pill in his mouth and with a sip of water, he swallowed it.

❀ ❀ ❀

CHAPTER
THIRTY-TWO

May 28

The conversation with Doug had left Liz in a turmoil. He had said little, not expressing his disappointment, seeming to have removed himself from the situation.

Although he had agreed to meet her at Edith's office the next morning, when, she assumed, he would also return her money, she couldn't help wondering if he had any intention of appearing. He had successfully avoided her for weeks, and she feared that any progress they had made in the last day was now destroyed. How stupid she had been to think that Hoke would make it easy for him to break away.

She had been startled when Doug hung up so abruptly, and desperation had made her try again. The second time he had sounded a bit more like himself, but she could tell that he was impatient to get off the phone. Only her uneasiness had made her ask him to call her if he wanted to talk. Somehow she knew that he would not.

Television, which usually put her to sleep, had the opposite effect tonight. A prey to her own anxiety, she dialed his number, but after fifteen rings she had hung up.

Why am I imagining the worst? she asked herself. Determined not to give in, she began to think of places he might be. Doug's friends seemed to have given him up. A movie . . . maybe, but not alone.

With six hundred dollars in his possession, he could find someone else to sell him drugs if Hoke chose to make himself scarce. Maybe that's where he was—out there somewhere, looking for a fix.

She had to call again and keep calling. At some point his mother would return and, she hoped, would tell her something that might be helpful.

But there was no answer. After twenty rings she gave up and tried to read.

Instead of distracting herself, she kept returning to the words Doug had said to her yesterday in the café in Manhasset, the words now haunting her. *I could put an end to the whole thing.*

This is stupid, she thought, furious with herself and her too vivid imagination. I'm painting the whole world black. Again she replayed the possible scenario, aware that she was repeating her thoughts of a few moments earlier. What does a kid do in the evening—especially if nobody is home?

Hoke? Could he be with Hoke? Maybe he did know how to reach Hoke when he needed him. Wasn't it possible that he had no intention of returning her money? Or ever had?

Finally, she reached a decision. If it turned out that she was overdramatizing the situation, she would take a solemn vow to mind her own business. But if minding her own business meant leaving Doug to flounder and destroy himself, it was no solution. If there was even a remote chance that she was right, she could not sit back and do nothing. I'll try once more, just once more, she thought.

This time she let the phone ring twenty-five times.

At 10:45 she showered and dressed, and by 11:15 she had driven up to Doug's house. Ringing the doorbell and knocking as hard as she could, she stood and waited, feeling more and more desperate, hoping that her imagination was just running wild.

Then, when she was about to knock at a neighbor's door so that she could get to a phone to call 911, Ann Williams drove up in her car.

Explaining as quickly as she could, Liz followed her into the house and raced up the stairs to Doug's room, his mother following behind her. She seemed not to have heard a word she said, saying over and over, "He's asleep, Ms. Ransome. Doug has always been a sound sleeper."

Doug lay on his back, empty bottles—the kind pills came in—on the bed near him. At first glance she thought he was dead, but there was a pulse. There was no awakening him, though. He must be in a coma, she thought, the horror of it washing over her.

His mother seemed to be in shock, gazing at Doug, touching him but seemingly unable to speak.

Liz dialed 911 and within minutes the police were there and had taken charge. Doug's mother was weeping softly. The only thing Liz heard her say was, "I'm going in the ambulance with him."

"Yes, of course," was the police officer's reply. Then he turned to Liz and said, "There's room enough if you want to ride along too."

"I'll take my car," Liz said. It was better, she thought, to let Doug's mother be alone with him.

She followed the ambulance almost all the way, and got to North Shore Hospital within minutes. In the Emergency Room, she was surprised to see Doug's mother, sitting on a lounge, her head in her hands, weeping.

When she sensed that someone had sat down beside her, she lifted her head. "They've just taken him up. I'm waiting down here to give them the information they want about insurance. Someone will come down to tell me how . . . he is." It was evident that she was holding on to every bit of control she had.

"If you give me the policy number, I can do that," Liz said. "They may send word for you to come upstairs."

Doug's mother handed her the Blue Cross/Blue Shield card. "Thank you," she said, adding, "Before you go, would you tell me what happened—how you knew anything was wrong?"

Liz nodded, struggling with her own tears. She told her the sequence of events as succinctly as she could. Then quickly, she went to the Admitting Office and took care of the details. On her way back to the waiting room, she saw a tired-looking young man in green heading for Doug's mother.

"Mrs. Williams?" he said.

Ann Williams nodded, rising and moving forward. Her face was ashen. "Is he . . . ?" she began, then stopped.

"He's alive, Mrs. Williams. We can't tell you much more than that right now. He's lucky you found him when you did."

"No," she said. "No, I didn't do anything. She . . ." She looked up and saw Liz standing behind the doctor. "She, Ms. Ransome—Doug's teacher—she was worried about him. He didn't answer the phone, and she got scared. She drove over. If she hadn't, I would have tried to wake him in the morning for school. But I would have been too late." She began to sob again, helplessly. "My son would have been dead. . . ."

"Mrs. Williams, try to hold on. We'll know more in a few hours. Why don't you and your friend come upstairs to the fourth floor. There's a waiting room there too, and we'll tell you as soon as we know more."

Liz had not prayed for a long time. Now she closed her eyes and silently begged, Oh dear God, please, please!

May 29

As the night wore on with no word, Liz decided to go home. Sleepless for hours, she had finally drifted off towards morning and had overslept. Before calling the school, she knew that she must call the hospital. But the floor nurse's line was busy, and Liz was too impatient to wait.

Now on her way to North Shore hospital, Liz prayed that Doug had made it through the night.

She had reached Dotty, reported an emergency that she needed to take care of, and said that she would be in touch with Edith Pierce as soon as it was possible.

Traffic was heavy, and for a few minutes at a time she was able to suspend her thoughts to focus on the traffic, able only briefly to erase the pictures that insisted on invading her brain.

As the light turned red, a shudder passed through her body. If Doug's mother had not returned just when she did . . .

All her movements seemed to be on automatic—from the time she parked the car to her arrival at the admitting desk. "My name is Elizabeth Ransome. Douglas Williams came in last night on an emergency. . . . I'm a close friend of the family."

The speed with which she was dispatched unnerved her even further. Once on the floor, she finally dared to ask the nurse on duty the question that was haunting her. "Did he make it through the night?"

"He was lucky," the nurse said quietly, "very, very lucky. You'll see for yourself."

Liz knew that she would never forget that first sight of Doug in the narrow hospital bed, his face pale, his lips still blue. Then, after a long time, his eyes opened and alighted on her. His voice was low and rough. "I screwed up again, didn't I? I couldn't even do that right." And then his eyes closed, and he seemed to be asleep.

In an obvious panic, his mother turned to the nurse. "Is he all right? Should he be sleeping now?"

"His body has suffered a severe trauma. I think he'll be sleeping a great deal now, off and on. It's good for him to sleep."

And awaken to what? Liz thought. Suddenly she knew what she must do. "Where is the nearest phone?" she whispered to the nurse.

The nurse gave her directions, and Liz turned to Doug's mother. "I'll be back in a few minutes."

Edith sounded horrified and shaken when Liz told her what had happened.

"He can't go home again," Liz said. "I'll talk to his mother, but if you have a place for him to go right after he's discharged from the hospital, he may have a chance."

"There are places, and this is an emergency." Edith was obviously thinking aloud. "Explain to his mother, Liz, and give me a ring about two. I should know something by then."

When Liz came back Doug's mother was sitting at his bedside, her eyes on his face. He seemed to be sleeping more easily.

For an instant Liz was afraid that she had overstepped any authority she might reasonably have. After all, Doug had a mother and it was she who must agree to whatever solution Edith could come up with.

"Can we step outside for a couple of minutes, Mrs. Williams?" Liz asked, adding, "It's important."

She nodded and rose, following Liz out. They stood in the corridor outside the room and Liz told her as succinctly as she could about her call to Edith Pierce and why she thought that Doug must not re-enter the environment that had led to his suicide attempt.

Mrs. Williams listened, her pale face expressionless. Finally, she said, "I'm his mother, and you and Ms. Pierce know so much more about Doug than I do. I feel so guilty, so stupid and guilty and ashamed. My poor boy—what hell he's been through."

"I realize," Liz began softly "that I've taken matters into my own hands and that I didn't have any right to. But he's unusually vulnerable now. . . . If that bastard Hoke gets hold of him, it will start all over again."

"And next time we may not be so lucky." Ann Williams reached out for Liz's hand. "You saved his life, Ms. Ransome, and I'll be grateful to you for the rest of mine. I'll do anything you and Ms. Pierce suggest—anything."

Impulsively Liz kissed her cheek. "That's wonderful!"

She looked at the pale face and lips, the bloodshot eyes, and exclaimed, "You haven't eaten, have you? I'll bet you haven't eaten since last night."

Doug's mother smiled a wan smile. "I would have choked if I had tried to eat. The nurse brought me coffee . . . it was hard to swallow even that. Can we go back in now?"

She didn't wait for an answer but headed for the room. Liz followed.

And, as if he knew that they had returned, Doug opened his eyes once more.

Edith Pierce couldn't have acted more quickly had she been dealing with a personal emergency. When Liz phoned her at two, the arrangements—except for getting Mrs. Williams' signature—were complete.

"What kind of place is it?" Liz asked, aware of her own doubts and fears.

"It's upstate, a renovated old farmhouse as living quarters and other buildings on the premises for classes and recreation. I know the place because I checked it out for another student a few months ago. The best thing about it is that they'll accept Doug as soon as he's released. I've been corresponding with the student who is there. You may know him—Tom Klein. He's doing very well and expects to come home before school starts again in the fall. He's been able to keep up with his school work—they've got good tutors there. I have some pictures of the facility and the staff . . . you can take them to Doug. They may make the whole idea easier for him to accept."

"Edith . . . I can't thank you enough! You may be saving his life."

"You've saved his life, Liz. I'm moving the process a step further."

They made plans for Liz to drive Mrs. Williams over to the school at three. Now, the next step would be to tell Doug.

When Liz entered the hospital room again, having given Doug's mother some time alone with him, Mrs. Williams was standing near the bed, looking down at him. Apparently they had been talking about something disturbing to Doug. His expression was tight and drawn.

"I'm sorry," Liz began. "I didn't mean to interrupt, but I've spoken to Edith Pierce, and it's all worked out."

"What's worked out, Mrs. R.?" Doug demanded, sounding annoyed. "Am I going to be sent to some booby hatch for people who try to commit suicide? I'm not going anywhere!"

Liz hadn't reckoned on this, but neither had she reckoned on what Doug's mother would say next.

"You have no choice, Douglas." She spoke calmly but with a strength she had not shown until now. "If it weren't for Ms. Ransome's quick thinking, you would be dead. I couldn't help losing your father, but I'm not going to lose you! It sounds as though Ms. Pierce has found a good place for you, and that's where you're going as soon as you're well enough to leave here."

She kissed his forehead and went back to her chair.

Liz had never heard her speak so strongly, and perhaps Doug hadn't either. He was staring at his mother as if he couldn't believe what he had just heard.

"Doug," Liz said softly, "we knew you couldn't go home and resume your life as it had been. Hoke would never let you go. But he can't follow you to the mountains. That's where you'll be staying for a while, with other people who have gone through what you have. Edith Pierce says it's a wonderful place with a very high success rate. Kids leave there and go on to resume their lives. You'll even be able to complete this semester there and graduate with your class."

Doug was eying her warily but his expression had changed. "You mean that, Ms. R.? Are you being straight with me?"

Liz nodded. "I've always been 'straight' with you, Doug. I'm not about to stop now."

"I've got to hear more about this 'great place.' Is Ms. Pierce the only one who knows anything about it?" Doug asked, for an instant sounding like the boy Liz remembered from the pre-drug days.

"Your mother and I are going over to school at three to learn as much as we can and to register you so that you can go there as soon as you're released. And," Liz added, "there are some pictures of the place that Edith will lend us.

Three hours later Liz stood beside Doug's bed, handing him the photographs one by one. He examined them carefully, at first with suspicion; then as he continued to look, his expression grew more absorbed, his interest more apparent.

At one point he said, "I think I know that guy—he was on the basketball team. Is he still there?"

"That's something you can ask Ms. Pierce. She'll give you a rundown when she comes to see you tomorrow."

"She's coming to see *me?*" Doug asked incredulously.

"Of course she is. She's the one who worked all this out, and she knew you might have some questions."

For the first time, a look of peace came over Doug's face. "I feel sleepy again," he said.

"That's the best thing you can do, sweetheart," his mother said. "Sweet dreams."

Doug was in the hospital for two days longer—time enough for the doctors to determine that no permanent damage had been done. A day after that he and his mother were enroute to the Catskills, where she would see him settled in.

When Liz said goodbye to Doug that last day in the hospital, he said quietly, "Watch out for Hoke, Ms. R. He was always asking things about you, and I know I told

him stuff . . . but I can't remember what. I'm so sorry!''
Suddenly his face grew worried. "Did you get your money
back?''

"Your mother gave it to me yesterday. I can't get over
your putting it in an envelope for me when you were . . .''
She stopped, unable to go on.

But Doug was still talking about Hoke. "Ms. R, please
be careful. He can be vicious!''

Suddenly her own horror—in abeyance for the last couple of days—surfaced once more. She longed to tell Doug
and his mother what she had been enduring, but she knew
that she could not inflict this on either of them.

She was, she struggled to remind herself, a grown
woman. Whom somebody wanted dead.

❦ ❦ ❦
CHAPTER
THIRTY-THREE

May 31

The phone calls had become more frequent, at least once a day now. But a few moments ago, there had been an ominous difference, a terrifying variation.

Just before she had slammed down the receiver, she heard the words delivered in a chilling monotone. "You know that I am going to kill you, Elizabeth Ransome. And now I'll tell you when. In twenty-eight days you will be dead!"

Her hand seemed suddenly to have ceased to function, and the telephone clattered to the floor. She stared at it, unable to move. Then propelled into frenzied activity, she dialed the phone company and heard herself report the most recent event, first to the operator and then to a special operator. For an instant, even the operator seemed to have lost her metallic confidence. "I'll report this immediately. Where can we reach you?"

She told her and replaced the receiver.

Then she phoned the police and asked for Detective Levin. He wasn't in, but she left a message on his private tape. He knew the story. There was no point in reporting everything to someone new.

Abruptly her frenzied activity ceased. She was sitting on a stool at the kitchen snack bar, staring at nothing, when Loren ran into the kitchen—how much later she had no idea. She had even forgotten he was out jogging.

"What's the matter, Liz? What happened?"

Her muscles felt frozen. From a distance she heard, "Liz, wake up! What happened?"

The sharp concern in his voice registered. "There was another call," she said dully. "This time it said . . ." She repeated the seven words that seemed to have engraved themselves on her brain.

"How long ago?"

"Fifteen minutes or so, I guess. I've lost track of time."

"When I was out jogging. Sometimes I wonder if that creep doesn't know all *my* movements too."

"I did call the phone company and then the police."

"And?"

"And nothing. I'll probably get a call from Detective Levin when he gets in."

"Liz," he said gently, "you sound as if you've given up."

"Sometimes I want to, Lor. As long as I'm alive, the calls will keep coming. The police are doing what they can, but the calls go on. Sometimes I wonder if they think I'm a kook who's imagining all of this. The person who's making these calls is crazy! Right now, I think I'm going crazy too!"

His eyebrows lifted. "New York is full of crazies, Liz. The cops are used to crazy people, but not all crazy people act on their threats. They can't think you're imagining the packages you've received or the calls. They've taken it seriously enough to monitor Dad's line."

"I know . . . I'm not being fair. But the kind of crazy that threatens to kill someone is a dangerous kind of crazy. I'm petrified, Loren."

"How could you not be." He put his arm around her, squeezing her shoulder. "But maybe this—this nut has done this kind of thing before to other people. If he—or she—has, the police will find out, but it takes time. Tell me, why haven't you let me in on how scared you've been? Why have you carried this all by yourself?"

You haven't been around, she thought, unwilling to say

it, unwilling to spoil their mood of closeness. Even you haven't taken it seriously enough. I didn't think you wanted to know what I've been going through.

But he seemed to have sensed what she was thinking and not saying. "I guess," he said slowly, "I haven't been there for you, or you may have thought that. I've been self-absorbed—as usual." He gave a deprecating little laugh. "But I'm here now, Liz, and I do want to help."

It wasn't like him to speak so positively. Her terror was easing its icy grip, and she could begin to think more rationally again. "Thank you," she said, adding, "Having you around helps."

"Thank God for little miracles. I'm good for something after all. Damn it, Liz, I wish I had been here to pick up that phone."

"It wouldn't have mattered, Lor. It would have been a wrong number. Don't you remember trying that soon after the calls started?"

His face sobered. "I wasn't taking it as seriously then. I'm sorry."

"Thanks." She forced herself to smile at him, grateful that for now at least, he was there.

June 3

It was something Loren did periodically—to check it out once again, he told himself. But he was aware that the checking was no longer necessary, and that unless something extraordinary happened, this would be the last time.

The bar was ordinary-looking—a horseshoe shape with dishes of peanuts and pretzels, brightly glistening glasses, and stools occupied by men.

It was dark but not so dark that one couldn't see that the young men who sat at the bar or who lounged against the stools, were the most beautiful men in New York City—perhaps even in the world.

In the past he had succumbed and gone off with one or another of them. Hell, he thought in sudden disgust, what was he doing here anyway? He might look like them, but he was not one of them.

How comforting it would be—no, would have been, to discover that he truly was one of them and that the agony and self-doubting might be over. Even now as he thought about it, the faintest vestige of a doubt appeared for an instant.

He sat alone at a table where he had taken his Scotch and water and surveyed the scene. Ah, the signals—the subtle and not so subtle games that must be played.

The dark-haired man standing at the side of the bar was discreetly signaling his sexual preference by means of a simple leather keycase strap placed in his left-hand shirt pocket. Left was dominant, right submissive.

Loren concealed a smile. Another young man, with a full head of curly platinum hair, wore his badge with less subtlety. He had a green handkerchief sticking out of his right pocket. A submissive hustler. How convenient it all was. And how much time it saved. So different from the straight world where the only signals were indirect ones that could very well be mistaken and lead to havoc.

A voice at the table directly next to his said, "May I buy you another drink?"

Loren looked up. The speaker was a well-built man, probably in his mid-forties. His brown hair was just beginning to gray, and his eyes were alert and intelligent.

"Another drink?" A glance at his almost-empty glass made him realize that he had been sipping without realizing it. What the hell, he thought, give it one last shot. "Thanks," he said, smiling. "I'm drinking Scotch."

"May I join you?"

"Sure."

The man rose—he was close to six feet and moved easily and well. As he turned his chair to face Loren's table, he said, "Bob Jones," and held out his hand.

His grip was powerful, and Loren's interest quickened at the same time he was thinking, Jones . . . Okay. I can play too. "Bill Smith," he said.

For an instant their eyes met, their mutual wariness obvious to both of them, and they began to laugh at the ludicrous aspect of the situation.

Music with a strong disco beat was blaring from a tape deck, and a few couples were dancing, some close, some moving individually to the music's rhythm.

Bob Jones called to the waiter, "Two Scotches over here." Then to Loren, "Feel like dancing . . . Bill?"

He was here, wasn't he? Why had he come if not to be one of them, to appear one of them, to do what they did. "Okay," he said, adding, "I'm not a great dancer."

"You look as if you'd be a beautiful dancer. You're so light, and I like the way you move."

"You haven't seen me move," Loren said.

"I spotted you as soon as you walked in. I repeat . . . I like the way you move."

There was a poise, an assurance in his manner that was very visible. Bob Jones needed no key-chain signal to assert what he preferred. He reached for Loren's hand and pulled him up. "Come on, let's try."

"I feel like a fool." Loren was unaware that he had spoken aloud until Bob, putting a casual arm around his shoulders, said, "At least you admit it. Most of us don't."

"I mean . . . I'm really not a dancer. My sister is. That's why I know the difference. There's a looseness in good dancers. . . . I just don't have it."

"Let's try. Just watch me for a few seconds and do what I do. If you're uncomfortable, we'll stop."

Loren allowed himself to be pulled out onto the crowded dance floor. His mood, mellowed by the Scotch, made him feel much less tense, more adventurous. Nobody was watching anybody, and this gave him courage. The dancers, each doing his own individual dance, gyrated, pranced, swayed, some with eyes closed.

He watched Bob Jones dance. His body was beautifully coordinated, and he did a combination of steps, obviously improvising as he went along. He smiled at Loren, and Loren found himself smiling back. Then he began to dance too, at first emulating Bob as closely as he could, then, as he grew freer, inventing his own steps and body movements.

When the music ended, he felt exhilarated, and when Bob Jones said, "Let's go back to my place for some coffee," it seemed the most natural thing in the world to agree.

The cab ride was short—there was little traffic—and upon entering the lobby of a large, obviously expensive apartment house on East Fifty-second Street, Loren knew that he had accidentally hit it rich. The tiny lurking doubt that had vanished now reappeared, allowing him to think, maybe. Just maybe.

The apartment overlooked the East River. It was expensively if casually furnished and seemed the right background for this person who called himself Bob Jones.

"Is coffee all right, or would you like a drink?" he asked as he settled himself in a soft leather chair, facing Loren who was perched on the couch.

"Coffee, thanks," Loren said. "Teaching math with a hangover has too many strikes against it."

The older man laughed. "So you're a teacher. I suspected something of the kind. Excuse me for a couple of minutes while I plug in the coffeepot."

Loren glanced around, still fuzzy from all the alcohol. The walls were stark white; one was burnt orange. The paintings were of abstract geometric figures, the furniture low and modern, the white shag rug thick and luxurious. Beyond the living room, a shut door probably led into the bedroom.

Bedroom! Loren became aware with sudden sharp discomfort that his hands were sweating and that part of him, the cool detached part that often sat in judgment of him, was saying, Shit! So it's a bedroom! What are you doing here if that's not what you want? Stop coming on like a poor little virgin about to be seduced!

Sometimes that part of him sounded like his father, or at least the father he had known as a child, and he was tempted to salute with an "Aye, aye, sir," that implied "Fuck you, sir!"

Bob Jones was carrying a tray with two mugs of coffee, a pitcher of cream, and a bowl of sugar. "Hungry?" he asked. "I've got some salami and cheese I can rustle up."

"No, no, thanks. Coffee will be fine." As Loren reached for the coffeepot, he noticed that his hand was trembling.

"Bill," Bob Jones began, but Loren was still gazing at his own hand. "You're new to the scene, aren't you?"

Why was he calling him Bill? Loren wondered for an instant before he remembered. He nodded. "Is it that obvious?"

"Only to someone perceptive. Most of those guys are so full of themselves, preening and acting like caricatures, they don't seem to know there's anyone else in the room.

"So you're a teacher," Bob Jones went on. "Got any idea of what I do?"

"You're not a teacher." Loren smiled. "That was apparent as soon as I walked into this building."

"I'm an attorney in a corporate law firm, and of course my name isn't Bob Jones any more than yours is Bill Smith, but we can let that ride for a while. There's plenty of time to get to know each other, and I'm in no hurry."

He moved to the sofa and motioned to Loren. "Sit closer," he said, adding, in a voice that was barely audible, "baby."

What am I doing here? whispered a voice in Loren's head, while the other one, the detached one, said scornfully, You ass! This is a better setup than you deserve. Fuck your honor and integrity—you know what you can do with them! This guy is no fag off the street. He's intelligent, attractive, and very masculine! He's made to order . . . for now. "Fuck off," Loren thought, and realized from the expression on Bob's face that he had said it aloud.

"Is something the matter?" he asked.

"No, I'm sorry. I was talking to myself."

"That's okay. I thought maybe you were bothered by something. Come on . . . sit beside me."

Loren moved closer to him on the couch. For a few moments they sat there quietly, Bob's arm around him, one hand stroking his hair.

Then, almost automatically, they rose and headed for the closed door.

❧ ❧ ❧

CHAPTER
THIRTY-FIVE

June 3

Slowly, almost imperceptibly, Liz's world had grown smaller. First, her mother, then her father, then Mike. She had been desperate in her struggle to hold onto her father.

On three separate occasions Liz had driven to the sanitarium. But each time, as she had waited at the desk, she had heard the same words from the pleasant-looking, gray-haired receptionist. "He isn't seeing any visitors, Ms. Ransome."

"But . . . if you tell him it's his daughter," she had protested and listened again to the painful reply. "He knows. His instructions are 'No Visitors.' I am sorry."

Now sitting on her father's favorite lounge chair in the living room, with Duke asleep at her feet, she thought, I still have Loren . . . sometimes. Yes, Loren was still there, and from time to time—as had happened a few days earlier—he had removed the wall he had built around himself and, for that day and a couple of others, he had seemed interested in and sympathetic to what was happening to her.

But then on the next night he hadn't come home at all, and on Thursday, he went to Mike's directly from school. Dinners with Mike and his children had become a weekly occurrence.

Liz tried not to be envious, but her longing to see Mike, to touch him, to be held by him, was often so strong that the longing became an ache. Why had he not phoned her?

She had told him she was wrong about Donna. What was keeping him away from her now?

She looked down at the furry bundle near her feet. "You're all I have, Duke," she said softly.

The sound of his name, coupled with the shrill noise of an automobile horn outside, must have awakened him. He shook himself and ran to the window, uttering low growling barks at whoever was out there.

"Silly Duke," Liz said fondly. "I'm impressed. Now you can go back to sleep."

When the street became quiet again, Duke apparently decided to follow her suggestion. After a brief detour into the kitchen for what she assumed was a drink, he returned to his position at her feet, looked up at her with eyes almost hidden by the fur around his eyes, and settled down to resume his nap.

The touch of his fur against her ankles was comforting.

At five o'clock she took the phone off the hook and knew an instant of triumph at having beaten her enemy to it—if only for the moment.

June 6

The days were getting longer, and Duke seemed so happy running about the yard that Liz decided to leave him outside until nine or so when she would walk him.

She took out the elaborate chicken salad Bertha had left for her and tried to eat some of it, but she could only nibble. Fatigue had settled over her like a heavy cloak. A short nap might make her feel better, she thought, and went upstairs to her room. The bed was so crisply made, it seemed a pity to disturb it. Removing her shoes, she lay down on the bed and closed her eyes.

Sometime later—it was dark outside—she was awakened by a sound, the sound of a door opening and closing. "Loren," she called sharply, but there was no answer.

It couldn't be Loren! It was Thursday.

If someone had broken in, the alarm system at the front door would have been activated unless . . .

Slowly, she walked down the stairs. The living room was dark. She had left a lamp on—or had she? Confusion made her head feel heavy, disoriented. Maybe Steve Rosner was right to feel skeptical about her teaching ability now.

As she stepped into the living room to light the lamp, a hand grabbed her wrist.

She screamed, and a voice said softly, "Be quiet. I'd rather not hurt you!"

Then, in the shadows, she saw him—Hoke—his long slender face, sinister, frightening. How had he entered her house? It sounded as if he had come in through the front door. But how . . . ?

Desperately she clutched at a courage she knew she didn't possess. "What do you want?" she demanded.

"A little talk. Sit down beside me." He pulled her down, one hand on her waist, the other close to her mouth. "Don't scream again, Elizabeth!"

She didn't. Her mouth was dry, and as in a nightmare, she knew that her throat was paralyzed and that no sound could emerge. Horrified, she realized that the hand on her mouth was wearing a leather glove.

"What do you want of me?" she whispered.

His hands in the leather gloves became insistent now and intimate, stroking, touching, caressing, almost strangely appealing. Evil—he was evil! she reminded herself. He had almost destroyed Doug, and yet his hands seemed to exist apart from him. She had not been held like this by anyone for a long time.

She fought against the sensations beginning in her body, when suddenly he said harshly, "You asked what I want with you, Elizabeth? You owe me!"

Now he was holding her too tightly, and she struggled to move, but his grip was like a vise. She forced herself to reply. "Owe you?"

"Owe me! Doug thought he could take a powder and make a fool out of Hoke. No way, Elizabeth! No way!"

It was as sobering as a slap in the face. She pulled away to face him, and although his hands still held her, she had created her own distance, and succeeded in freeing one of her hands. Her dormant brain had finally begun to work again. Her voice had returned too. "You still haven't told me what you want with *me.*"

Her fingers were groping along the edge of the table near the lamp. Damn! Where was it!

"You are going to tell me where that damn student of yours is and how I can contact him without anybody knowing about it."

Talk, she told herself, her fingers continuing to grope. Keep talking.

"He almost died to get away from you. Why can't you leave him alone!"

"My friend Doug and I understand each other. He needs what I've got, and I want him to have it. I'm his friend. Now, are you going to tell me where he is or do I have to persuade you?"

The way he uttered the word *persuade* made a shiver go down her spine. And then an idea came to her, an idea that should have appeared much earlier. Slowly, she thought, let him try to persuade me.

"You think it's hard for him to be . . . without drugs?" she asked, trying to sound naive enough to convince him.

She caught his surprise, as self-controlled as he was. "Hard? Yes, it's hard! Without them, he's probably climbing the walls. Talk about killing himself—now's the time he could try it and make it—for real. Then think of how you'll feel. You'll be as guilty as if you had given him cyanide to swallow."

She appeared to be thinking, considering. If she could light the lamp for one instant, she could locate the alarm.

"I wish I could be sure," she murmured, still stalling.

His hand reached up to stroke her neck. "Your time is running out, Elizabeth!"

"What do you mean?"

"If you don't tell me where Doug Williams is right now, I wouldn't mind in the least settling for you and then maybe breaking that sweet little neck. Or maybe in the reverse order. I've never tried that."

She forced her lips to stop trembling. Suddenly, as if it had been on the sidelines watching and listening, her brain took over. "What guarantee do I have that you won't do . . . what you said after I tell you?"

"Guarantee?" He snorted in derision. "She wants a guarantee. No guarantees in this business, Ms. Ransome. The truth is your best guarantee. If you give me the wrong information, then I'm up a tree, but so are you. Don't forget that!"

"I've got the address in the desk . . . over there. I'll get it."

"You don't know Doug's address?" he said suspiciously.

"It's in New Jersey. I didn't memorize it. Put the light on," she said, adding, "please."

"Okay, but make it quick." He lit the lamp at the same instant that her fingers found the alarm.

"Get it," he commanded, taking his hands off her.

She turned to face him. To her amazement, her words came out slowly and evenly. "You have one second to get out of here," she said, and there must have been something in her tone that ruffled his composure.

"What the hell are you talking about?" he snarled.

"One press of my finger and the house alarm goes off. The police will surround this place. They'd love to get their hands on you."

Where was she getting this—not courage—more like hubris?

There was a sharp crack as his palm struck her face. His expression was ugly and menacing. "I can't take a chance that you're bluffing, you goddamn bitch!'' he hissed as he darted from the room.

She heard the slam of the door. Now she ran to the door and locked it. Then, steeling herself against the cacophony that would follow, she pressed the alarm button.

Nothing! She pressed again and again before realizing that she had turned off the alarm before Bertha's arrival that morning. Bertha was always afraid of setting it off by accident.

Hysterical now, she called the police, but it was some time before she was coherent enough to report what had happened. They would be there in minutes, the dispatcher promised, to investigate and file a report.

Hoke tried to calm down on the ride back to his hotel, but memories of the fiasco continued to enrage him.

Getting into the Ransome house so easily must have made him careless—he had forgotten all about the alarm system a house like that would be sure to have. But the fact that he had a key had undoubtedly given him a false sense of security.

Stupid! Idiot! he railed at himself, even as he realized that he was not a common thief or burglar who should be expected to know about alarm systems.

What irked him most was that the princess had gotten the upper hand. Another few seconds, and she would have been at his mercy.

Elizabeth Ransome had dared to interfere—to take Doug away from him—and in a sudden burst of clarity, he saw that she had bested him in a game of wits.

Why had the alarm not gone off as he was running out the door? Why hadn't he heard police sirens until some minutes later?

Because she was lying! She had been defenseless all along, and he, stupid fool that he was, had fallen for her ruse.

"You'll get yours, my lady!'' he said aloud, his penis throbbing at the thought of what he would do to her.

CHAPTER THIRTY-SIX

June 10

Caren no longer asked Ken why he got up so early, nor why he left the house often by six. As soon as her pregnancy had been confirmed—she had insisted on two tests, not believing the first when it proved positive—her behavior changed drastically.

She began to eat again and to sleep, and her face began slowly to fill out. Now she had the look of a hopeful, expectant young mother. Elinor had looked like that once.

Only last evening she had said, "Ken, I don't cry for Ellie every day anymore. It's not that I miss her less—but it's almost as though we're being given another chance. I mean . . ."

"Don't analyze it, Caren," he broke in, more harshly than he intended, and then to make amends, had patted her shoulder and kissed her cheek.

The prospect of the new baby had absolutely no reality for him. Unlike Caren who was now sleeping through the night, he hardly slept; he went to his job at the paper, and he had even made some attempts at working on the novel, but his laughing little girl continued to live in his head.

He heard her voice when his key turned in the lock at night. When he drifted off for a few moments of sleep, the sound of her voice asking for a drink of water awakened him.

At night he would walk into her room and sit down on her bed. Sometimes he held her old teddy bear in his arms—the smell of the freshly bathed child still seemed to cling to the bear, to the room itself.

When Caren had spoken of readying the room for the new baby, she had seemed puzzled and hurt by his angry reaction. "I don't want you to touch it! Leave it alone!"

The pregnancy had undeniably given her new courage. She had faced him steadily, and although her voice quivered, she said, "Ken, be reasonable. Where will we put the baby's crib?"

It was apparent to him that she had moved beyond him, and his fury frightened him. By now, she had obviously accepted Ellie's death, and her thoughts were only on the coming child. For an instant, he wanted to hit her, to hurt her as she had hurt him. He looked down at his clenched fists. Striving for control, he had said as gently as possible, "I'll take care of everything later on—we have months and months ahead of us."

Her relief shone in her eyes. "Thank you, Ken." She was grateful for so little, he thought, wishing that he could respond honestly, hating himself for what he was doing to her and unable to act any differently.

Two evenings later she knocked on the door of his study, and without waiting for an invitation, had opened the door. "Ken, Dr. Sabot—my obstetrician—says that I can have an amniocentesis or a newer procedure—it's called a chorionic villus, and I can have that much sooner. But there's a little more risk!"

"Why for God's sake are you considering either? You're only twenty-eight. I thought thirty-five is when they recommend those tests."

"The tests tell the doctor if there is any abnormality. I can have the chorionic pretty soon, but they don't do the amnio until around the sixteenth week."

"I still don't understand why you want to have it done at all."

She had gazed at him in disbelief. "I can't have an

abnormal child—not after losing Ellie. I couldn't survive it.''

"Then, if the baby is abnormal . . ." he began, and she finished the sentence harshly.

"God forbid! They'll do an abortion."

"Okay," he said quietly, "if that's what you want."

"One other thing," she added quietly, "it takes some of the surprise away, but they can tell the sex of the child."

Suddenly he wanted to hear no more about "the child."

"Excuse me, I have work to do," he said rising and gently pushing her toward the door.

To his amazement, she jerked away from him. Her face was ugly in her torment. "I know you don't give a damn about this baby. You never wanted it in the first place. It would serve you right if . . ." She burst into heavy racking sobs.

Rigidly controlling himself, he said, "I'm sorry if I hurt you, Caren. I didn't mean to."

Misinterpreting him—deliberately—he felt, she cried, "Then you do want the baby! Say it! If you don't, it will be abnormal. I know it doesn't make sense to you, but that's the way I feel. I couldn't lose another child!"

God forgive me, he thought, and said what she wanted to hear.

❧❧❧
CHAPTER
THIRTY-SEVEN

June 11

Liz's car was already in the driveway as Loren drove up. His briefcase in one hand, books under the other arm, he rang the bell instead of fumbling for his keys, aware of the new bolt.

He heard the bell ring, but when the door was not opened, he pressed down harder. Still no answer. Liz was probably upstairs, he thought, and proceeded to rummage through his trouser pocket for his new key.

Finally negotiating the complex business of getting into the house, he entered the hall and saw Liz sitting on the stairs, staring straight ahead. There was a package on the step beside her.

"Why didn't you answer the door?" he demanded.

She appeared not to have heard him, appeared almost unaware that he was talking to her. He did notice that a muscle in her cheek had tightened. Obviously she had heard him and for some reason was choosing not to speak to him. It was startling because this was not Liz's way. Actually, it was the kind of thing he might have done to get her goat.

His eyes went back to the package, and the puzzle seemed easier to solve now. "Liz," he said gently. "What's in that? Have you opened it?"

She nodded.

"What's in it?"

There was no immediate response, but he waited.

Finally she spoke in a whisper that he had to strain to

hear. "I was going to take it to the police . . . but I couldn't make myself even touch it again."

"Liz," he said gently, "let me see it, and then we can take it together. Is that okay?"

A long, shuddering sigh preceded her nod. He sensed that she was watching every movement of his, the removal of the brown paper to reveal an ordinary white box, and then the lifting off of the cover.

He gasped. On a mound of newspaper lay a knife, the blade covered with dried blood. "Jesus Christ!" he said and rapidly moved the box away from her, replacing the cover. "Get your jacket. We're going to the station!"

Officer James was on duty at the front desk, drinking a cup of coffee, a box of donuts from Dunkin' Donuts at his elbow. He nodded to them pleasantly. "Good afternoon. Anything I can do for you today or do you want to see Detective Levin?"

"Please," Liz said quietly.

Officer James got him on the phone, and in a couple of minutes, Detective Levin came out to greet her. When Liz introduced Loren to him, he said, "I think I'd know you were her twin brother if I saw you on the street. It isn't usual for fraternal twins to look so much alike, is it?"

Loren shook his head. "Not common, but it exists. My sister got another package," he added, hearing the tension in his own voice.

"Another one? From one of her nutty students?" Detective Levin frowned. "Let's have it," he said.

As he looked at the bloodied knife, his frown deepened. "Looks sharp," he commented. "I'll send this over to the lab. See if they can tell us something."

"Thank you," Liz said coolly.

Loren recognized the steely tone in her voice and was not surprised when she turned to the detective. "I don't have any nutty students! None of my students would do anything as bizarre as this. After what's been happening to me, why would you even think it's any of my students?''

"Okay, Ms. Ransome, I'm sorry. I was half kidding, but I know it's not something you can kid about. I guess you're sure it's this guy you suspect of dealing drugs, the one who got into your house. But we have no information on him—no last name, no address. No car ownership. Nothing. He's our invisible man.''

Opening his top desk drawer, the detective scanned the file folders, pulled one out and glanced at it, reading quickly. "What got him out of your house? The report doesn't mention that.''

"I used my head," Liz said and told him about the alarm system.

Loren detected a change in his manner. Good for her!

When he spoke, the detective sounded troubled. "By the time our guys got there, he was gone. The report says they were there in less than five minutes. Is that right?''

"Yes. I got to the window, but it was so dark I couldn't see his license number. By then I was hysterical!''

"Small wonder. No point in blaming yourself, Ms. Ransome. Is there any way of finding out this creep's last name?''

Liz shook her head. "Nobody knows it. The only thing I'm sure of is that he deals drugs. One of my students almost died because of him, but I got in his way and he's out to get me. I feel it!''

"We need more to go on. This Hoke you refer to is a skilled bastard. He left no fingerprints in your house. None! When he calls you, it's always from a pay phone. But, Ms. Ransome," he said softly, "professional drug dealers do not indulge in the kinds of idiotic pranks that are being directed at you. I'm not playing them down by calling them pranks, but experienced drug dealers don't waste their time doing stupid things like trying to scare people. When they want to kill someone, they go to it so fast there's no time for the victim to get scared. That's why I'm not ruling out one of your students. There are plenty of crazy kids in this world. Their parents don't know it, and their teachers probably don't either.''

"There's only one kid . . ." Abruptly Liz stopped, her hand over her mouth in a childlike gesture Loren had not seen for years.

"What kid?" the detective asked, his tone brisk, his attention apparently seized.

"Nobody," she said quickly. "It was just a thought, but I was wrong."

"Look, if the kid is innocent, nobody is going to hurt him. The best way of making sure is to check him out."

It's not a he, Loren thought. Liz had been about to mention Donna's name. He knew it as surely as if he had been able to read her mind.

She had shut her lips tightly as if to make sure that this name would not escape. "No," she said, "I was wrong. I'm sorry."

Detective Levin was trying hard not to show his exasperation, but Loren could hear it in his overly polite tone when he said, "Ms. Ransome, I'd appreciate your doing whatever you can to get that guy's last name."

On the way home, they sat quietly, not talking at all.

"Let's have a cup of coffee," Loren said as they passed a diner on Middle Neck Road.

Later as they sat at a table, two cups of coffee in front of them, he said, "Why didn't you want to tell the cop Donna's name?"

She didn't seem surprised that he had guessed, but she turned to him almost angrily. "In the first place, I don't see even Donna sending me a bloody knife. In the second, how can you even think that I'd want to hurt Mike this way!"

"Sorry, Liz. I wasn't thinking. You still love him, don't you?"

There was no answer. She had picked up the cup and was drinking her coffee.

❦ ❦ ❦
CHAPTER
THIRTY-EIGHT

June 12

When Liz made the appointment with Dr. Annette Matthews, a psychiatrist recommended by her father's friend Bill Reiser, she was asked to come half an hour early so that she could fill out a questionnaire.

She sat in the air-conditioned reception room of the psychiatrist's office, writing busily. When she had completed the form, it was taken into Dr. Matthews' office by the auburn-haired young receptionist. Ten minutes later, she was called into her first meeting with Dr. Annette Matthews.

Dr. Matthews was a bright-eyed, attractive woman with a head of frizzy dark hair that reminded Liz of Colette.

She listened patiently to Liz's recital. It was clear that she was reacting with horror to what Liz had been enduring. At the mention of the bloody knife, the color left her face.

"Then the police are looking for this drug dealer?"

Liz shrugged wearily. "I guess so, but there's so little to go on. The man I spoke to, Detective Levin, thinks this is some kind of childish prank. He seems convinced it's one of my students. I know I sound cynical, and I realize the police are trying to find Hoke, but it may be impossible. The kids claim nobody knows his last name. I contacted all the kids Doug knew. Sometimes, when I'm feeling especially hopeless, I wonder if the police think I'm sending these ghastly things to myself!"

"Try not to worry about what they may be thinking—

for now at least. Are there other tensions in your life, Ms. Ransome?''

Without any warning, Liz began to cry.

Dr. Matthews pushed a box of tissues towards her.

''I'm sorry.'' Liz tried to speak through her tears.

''No, no, you need to let it out.''

At ninety dollars for fifty minutes, this thought made Liz half smile. Dr. Matthews must have taken this as an encouraging sign and was now obviously waiting for her to continue.

It all came out—the events concerning her father, Mike and Donna, her mother, Doug, and even the last meeting with the principal. ''He said, in effect, that if things don't change soon, he's going to have to act. Principals don't like irate parents. I guess some of my kids have noticed that I'm distraught most of the time now, and their parents have called my boss.''

Suddenly, Liz glanced at her watch and was appalled to discover that only five minutes of her time remained.

''You're getting a bit more than your share, aren't you?''

The sympathy in this stranger's voice made tears come to her eyes again.

''From this one meeting, I think that the strain you've been experiencing has taken its toll and that you are probably overreacting to a situation you might normally take much more in stride.''

''Do you think I'm being paranoid?''

The woman shook her head. ''I dislike labels. Real things are happening to you and terrifying you. The threat that someone wants to kill you would be enough to upset anyone. You are *not* sending these things to yourself. I know you're not—based on a number of questions you've answered.''

She smiled apologetically as she added, ''I'm sorry. We're out of time. I would suggest that we continue. If you agree, you can make an appointment with my receptionist.''

Unable to evaluate or make an assessment, Liz obeyed and came away with an appointment reminder on a small white card. Five o'clock, Wednesday. She wasn't sure that she would keep it, but at this moment she wasn't sure of anything—except that crying had been a release. Instinctively, she knew that she trusted Dr. Matthews.

❦❦❦

CHAPTER
THIRTY-NINE

June 13

An inch taller, and I could model, Loren thought, absorbed with his mirror image. Half wistful, half amused at himself, he realized that one of the things he especially liked about David's apartment were all the mirrors. The walls of the three bathrooms were all mirrored; the bedroom they shared had floor-to-ceiling mirrors on three walls.

When he had first been given a tour of the apartment, he had said teasingly, "You don't look like a narcissist, David."

David had laughed and affectionately touched Loren's cheek. "I'm not, my dear. The people who rented the apartment before me did the decorating, and I'm too lazy to change anything. You may enjoy it. If I looked like you, I certainly should."

The naked desire in the dark eyes focused on him had made Loren wish he could respond honestly.

Now, he continued to gaze at himself. The full, flowered skirt swished about his calves. The lavender blouse open at the neck showed the slender gold chain that David had given him as a first present. He moved easily in the flattering high-heeled sandals. Yes, he did have nice legs. Liz was always saying that it was unfair that his legs were so beautifully shaped while hers just looked skinny.

His hair was a touch too short, but a silk lavender scarf covered it, and the long gold earrings were perfect. Slip-

ping a white silk stole over his shoulders, he joined David
in the living room.

David had a drink in his hand, and clearly from the flush
on his cheeks, this was not the first of the evening. Damn,
Loren thought, I know he hates this, but it's something I
want. He promised!

"What would you like?" David asked, the words a bit
slurred.

"Let's have cocktails in the restaurant," Loren said,
assuming a light cheerful tone.

"Of course, darling, but that has nothing to do with
what we're having here."

Loren suppressed a sigh. "Cinzano, then, David, but
just one. I'd really like to go soon."

He saw that David was looking at him coolly, with rare
dispassion.

"My dear," he said, "I'm giving in to you, but that
doesn't mean I must like it."

Don't spoil it, Loren wailed inwardly. Christ, don't spoil
it! He steeled himself to say calmly, "Look, I'm ready to
go. If you don't want to have dinner and go dancing as
you promised, then fuck it, we'll forget the whole thing."

It was a test of wills, and Loren was fully aware of it.
He stood there quietly, waiting. Finally David took a last
gulp of his Scotch and said, "You win, my love. Let it
never be said that I failed to keep a promise."

The temptation to say, Screw you, you fag, was strong,
but Loren fought it successfully.

He was wearing clothes he had coveted for a long time,
and he was soon to be wearing them in public with a man
as his escort. From time to time, of course, he wore the
beautiful clothes stashed away in that miserable room on
Twenty-third Street, but he was always uneasy.

Now he was in a good neighborhood with a wealthy
man, soon to be going out in a cab. There was little danger
of being mugged and beaten on Sutton Place with David
as an escort. And if he wished that David were less stoned

and were happier about taking him out as a woman, believing in the fairy tale had been done with a long time ago.

David set down his drink and visibly straightened up. "Where do you want to go?" he asked.

"There's a place I've heard of . . . my sister mentioned it once. Roma di Notte. Have you been there?"

"Probably. There aren't many places I haven't been. It's the one with the intimate little caves . . . yes, I've been there." He sounded tired, disenchanted, and for an instant, Loren felt sorry for him.

"I'd better make a reservation."

David made the call and Loren was once more impressed by his authority and self-assurance. Money and power did that for you, he thought. Money was something he had grown up with, yet he doubted that he would ever possess even half of David's assurance.

True, there wasn't an overabundance of money now—teachers were rarely wealthy. He recalled his father's scorn of the occupations he and Liz had chosen, and sometimes he speculated: Had he chosen law or medicine, would his father have been less contemptuous?

Anyway, one day when the old man died, there would be money, plenty of it. But power . . . that was a foreign concept. Or was it?

David opened the door, but instead of holding it for him, he walked out first. A bit uneasy, Loren followed him.

In the cab, David sat stiff and withdrawn. Loren reached over and touched his arm. "David," he said, "please . . . this means so much to me."

"I'm going along with this . . . masquerade . . . because I love you!" The last words were whispered.

"I know," Loren said softly.

"But for God's sake, don't expect me to like it!" He turned away again, and they didn't speak for the rest of the drive.

Loren curbed the desire to look at himself in the small mirror of his compact. He recalled David's disgusted reminiscences of his former wife. Had she applied lipstick in public? Yes, now that he thought of it, he was almost sure she had.

The taxi drew up before the restaurant, and David paid the driver and got out of the cab. Loren noted that he did not help him out, did not even look in his direction.

It was not an auspicious beginning, but Loren was determined not to let David spoil this evening to which he had looked forward for such a long time . . . forever, it seemed.

As they were about to enter the restaurant, Loren took David's hand and squeezed it gently. David hesitated, then returned the pressure and put his arm around Loren's shoulder. "Okay, baby," he said sounding more like himself, "let's go."

The headwaiter, starched and impeccably groomed, greeted them cordially. "Have you a reservation, sir?"

"Yes, David Martin. We'd like a cave if that's possible."

The man's careful smile seemed weary. "I'm sorry, sir. There are no caves free. They are usually reserved in advance."

Loren waited for David's hand to slip into his pocket and emerge with bills that he would discreetly fold into the waiter's hand. To his amazement, David's hand remained where it was.

"Show us what you have, then," he said brusquely.

The waiter's shrug was barely discernible. Loren pushed his nail into the fleshy part of his palm. Fury at David permeated his body, but the pain of the pressing nail kept his mouth shut. So far, he had dared and won, but he must not underestimate David. Still, there was a challenge to daring.

The waiter led them to a table against the wall. This room was lighter than the intimate caves they passed. At the table directly opposite, a tall brown-haired man stared at Loren with obvious interest.

Loren's annoyance with David was steadily increasing. He took a mirror out of his small bag and proceeded to touch up his lipstick. As he carefully re-applied the color— Mauve Mist—a subtle lavender pink, he wondered why he was doing this. He had always detested women who applied makeup in public. Of course it gave his hands something to do. Since he had almost stopped smoking, he realized how often his hands had automatically lit a cigarette. Now, of course, he was doing this out of pure malice. If David wanted to act like a grouchy fuck, he could damn well take the consequences.

"Jesus!" The voice sounded strangled.

Loren raised his eyes innocently. "I'm sorry, David," he murmured.

One waiter had taken their drink order, and now another waiter appeared at the table to take their order for dinner. Suddenly David seemed more affable. "What do you suggest?" he asked.

"We have a veal speciality with wine and herbs, some prosciutto and mozzarella."

To David's inquiring look, Loren nodded. "Two orders of the veal, then," David said.

Now the man at the other table was frankly staring. His companion, whose face Loren couldn't see, seemed to be talking in a constant stream of words. From time to time, the man nodded.

Abruptly, Loren felt charged as if by a spurt of adrenaline. That he was beautiful was evident, but even more important was that this stranger was reacting to him as if he were a beautiful woman!

David had launched into a long account of a merger his company was planning. Loren was occasionally interested in David's cases, and he respected David's intelligence. Actually, law had interested him briefly as a possible career until his father had grudgingly approved of it. "At least,'' he had said, ''you'll have a profession at which you can make a decent income. I won't be around forever, you know.''

David was still talking, and the man at the opposite table seemed unable to take his eyes off Loren. Titillated, Loren raised his head boldly and met the eyes that were fastened on him.

A sharp exclamation of disgust cut through Loren's reverie and brought him back to awareness that David had turned his head to see whom or what he was staring at. The man at the other table reddened and lowered his eyes.

An odd expression had flitted across David's face. ''Have you been taking notes all this time?'' he asked sarcastically.

''Notes?'' Loren asked blankly. ''What are you talking about?''

''In my stupider moments, I told you all about Jill, about the things she did that drove me up a wall. This evening you've gone through her entire repertoire. It can't be coincidental.''

''I don't know what you're talking about,'' Loren said, more or less honestly.

''You're a very beautiful woman, my love,'' David said, and now venom edged his sarcasm.

Loren's insulation was beginning to wear thin. He rose. ''Excuse me,'' he said, ''I'm going to the john.''

''Which one?'' David said, too loudly.

Loren's teeth were clenched. ''The powder room,'' he hissed, draping his stole over the back of his chair.

David, the boor, didn't even have the grace to go through the motions of rising. Loren, head high, swept away from the table.

As he passed the brown-haired man, whose eyes were following his every movement, he allowed one glove to drop at his feet.

Hastily retrieving it, the man rose and handed it to Loren.

"Thank you," Loren said softly.

Staring at him, the man seemed mesmerized.

The powder room was empty—not that he particularly cared, but it was easier to assess his makeup with the attention he chose to give it. He applied no more color to his cheeks—the flush of excitement was rouge enough—just a touch more mascara to lengthen the naturally long eyelashes and a dab of musk on his wrists and at his throat.

When after some time Loren returned to the table, he was startled to see that David was standing, tapping his foot impatiently. On the table were a few scattered bills.

"What's that matter?" he whispered. People, he realized, were staring.

"We're leaving," David said loudly. The flush on his face told Loren clearly that he was drunk.

"But our dinners . . ."

"Screw our dinners!"

There were a few faint titters. Loren's face felt hot. His throat constricted as if he were choking. Through the corner of his eye he saw a pitying look on the face of the man who had been staring at him.

Suddenly he knew that he had to get out of there before he was violently sick. The walk out of the dining room was nothing like the entrance. Intent on negotiating the length of the room in his high heels, Loren made no effort to hold his head high or to walk gracefully. Getting out of there without further disgracing himself was all he could hope for.

Outside David hailed a cab. As one stopped, Loren shook his head. "I'm walking," he said unsteadily.

"Like hell you are!" David pushed him into the cab.

I could scream, Loren thought, and then as a feeling of doomed helplessness settled over him, he gave up and even moved over so that David could get in.

There was no conversation during the drive, nor on the elevator riding up to the forty-fifth floor. When they got into the apartment, David methodically locked and double-locked the door. Then without a word, he proceeded to rip off Loren's clothes and rape him.

At the sight of his beautiful lavender blouse lying torn on the floor, Loren uttered an animal howl of pain, but that was the only sound he made.

Wiry and tough as he knew he was, he knew, too, that he was no match for a David gone wild. If he tried to fight back, he could be badly beaten.

And then, miraculously, the insulation was back and Loren's body was no longer part of him. Do what you want, you fucking bastard, he thought. You're not even touching me!

When he was finished, David said, not looking at him, "I'm going out—for a couple of hours—and when I get back, I want you out of here. You and everything that belongs to you!" Then, facing him directly, his eyes bright with pain, he said, "I worshipped you, you know. But if I wanted a woman, I'd get myself a real one!"

To Loren's amazement, the insulation was solid and held. You can't touch me, he thought jubilantly. You poor bastard, you can't touch me!

Later, a cab took Loren and his suitcase to the apartment downtown on Twenty-third Street. As he climbed the dirty stairs, he congratulated himself on having had the foresight to continue paying his rent.

❦ ❦ ❦
CHAPTER FORTY

June 13

Ken blinked several times to erase the mirage, conspicuously enough for Caren to notice. "What's the matter, Ken? Do you have something in your eye?"

"A . . . cinder, I think," he murmured, taking out his handkerchief and touching it to his eye.

"In the restaurant?" She sounded dubious, then added, "It probably happened in the street."

"Probably," he agreed, continuing to observe the vision that appeared real, actually sitting at the table directly in front of him.

She had obviously been made aware of his staring, and now she glanced at him overtly, a tiny smile hovering at the edge of her mouth.

Going to school in her skirts or slacks, Elizabeth Ransome always looked lovely, but now in the soft light of the lamps hanging above each table, there was an exquisiteness about her that made Ken catch his breath. In that lavender outfit, the scarf around her hair, she seemed more beautiful, more desirable, then he had ever seen her. There was a subtle difference that he could not identify. He found himself envying the man she was with.

"Ken!" Caren's voice betrayed a shade of impatience. "Did you say something?"

"The waiter has been standing here, waiting to take our drink orders."

"Sorry," he murmured, glancing up. Indeed he was,

a tall, slim young man standing patiently, with just the right air of deference.

"Dewars and water for me. Sherry for you, Caren?"

She looked shocked. "Ken! I'm pregnant. I haven't had a drink since the doctor told me the test results." To the waiter, she said, "Just ginger ale, please . . . with a touch of lime."

When the waiter had written down the order and gone off, she said softly, having apparently decided not to make an issue of his not remembering, "This is the first time we've been out since . . ."

"I know."

"Do you feel guilty . . . as if we shouldn't be doing this?"

His voice sounded harsher than he intended. "Don't, Caren, please, don't."

"I'm sorry, Ken. It's just . . . we never talk about her. She seems so far away—each day, farther and farther away."

With deliberate calmness, forcing himself away from his absorption in the young woman facing him, he said, "We're celebrating, Caren. This is our wedding anniversary, you're going to have a . . . baby, and we're taking a night out on the town. Let's not spoil it . . . please!"

She reached across the table and pressed his hand.

He concentrated on appearing attentive. It was a trick he had cultivated, of seeming to listen with interest, when in reality he was totally absorbed in his own thoughts.

Caren had begun to talk of something or other when he allowed himself to shift slightly so that he had a better view of Elizabeth Ransome.

Now she was frowning, and her magnificent eyes had filled with tears. He could only see the back of her escort, a tailored, expensively dressed back. Obviously whatever they were discussing was upsetting her.

His heart began to hammer; he was aware of skipped

beats. She had risen and was passing his table, staring down at him, the traces of tears still on her eyelashes.

As she passed him, one of her gloves dropped almost at his feet. He picked it up and handed it to her. "Thank you," she said, in a whisper.

Breathing in her fragrance as she moved past him, he had a sudden sense of disorientation. Something was wrong. The picture was out of focus.

Her perfume was a gardenia-like scent. This was musk! The one who wore the musk was the twin brother—Ken had passed him while jogging one day, and the scent of musk had remained in his awareness for some time. Why was Elizabeth wearing her brother's cologne? He wasn't hallucinating—not on one Scotch.

"Ken, where are you? You look peculiar! Are you sick?" Caren's voice had risen, probably from trying to get his attention.

"I just got a little dizzy," he said, closing his eyes for an instant. "I'll be okay. Just let me be quiet for a few minutes, Caren."

Caren watched him anxiously as he kept his eyes on the woman who had just walked past. After a few minutes he smelled the musk perfume again and turned, watching the woman walk back to her table, conscious that there was a difference in the walk.

The woman glanced at him, then quickly averted her eyes. There was something alien about her presence. He realized it now. Her jaw was clenched, and the eyes were smoldering. It was as though an artist had subtly modified a sketch.

And then it struck him. This exquisite young woman was not Elizabeth Ransome! For some reason the twin, Loren Ransome, was dressed like a woman. The excitement that always pulsed in him when he watched her, or even thought about her, was gone. He felt dull, leaden, and more than vaguely troubled.

Caren was staring at him oddly. "If you're sick, honey, let's leave."

What a bastard I am, he thought, remorse filling him. He turned to her, and with a tenderness that had been absent for a long time, he said, "No, no, sweetheart! We're celebrating. The waiter is coming back. Let's order."

Ken drove home in an odd, bemused state, hardly hearing what Caren said, responding in monosyllables.

Maybe there had been some crazy mistake. He had always prided himself on his perception. This was one of his qualities as a newspaperman and as a writer. Of course, he wasn't much of a writer anymore . . . his perception might have disappeared too.

Tomorrow . . . no, on Monday, he would know.

June 16

He was up before dawn. The night had been one of fitful sleeping—dreaming desire-laden dreams of her, then watching her transformation into a man with a beard.

Shuddering, glad to have the night behind him, he showered quickly, shaved, and gulped a cup of black coffee, the bitterness invigorating, shaking him into full wakefulness.

Today he drove closer to the house than ever before. The brother came out first, moving mechanically, his face drawn and sad. He headed for his car, but instead of starting it instantly as he was wont to do, he sat there for a long time, apparently thinking. Poor guy, Ken thought, recalling his beauty and radiance only two nights earlier.

Later, when he thought about it, Ken pinpointed this moment as the one when his resolve to avenge Ellie's death vanished. He must have been insane to think he could actually *kill* Elizabeth Ransome . . . that he could kill anyone.

And of course he had been insane—insane with grief.

The grief, at first a boiling cauldron inside of him, had changed its character and had become part of his life.

When Elinor was killed, his determination to avenge what he still thought of as murder by a drunken driver had driven him to follow the woman, carefully plan how he would kill her, and then this resolution had dissipated into an overwhelming sadness.

One morning he had awakened, knowing that he could never carry out this kind of vengeance.

And now it was happening again.

When he thought of Ellie, the soft plump cheek pressed close to his, the tinkling laugh, the delicious powdery smell of her, he ached—at times fiercely. But destroying Elizabeth Ransome or even Dr. Ransome himself, would do nothing to assuage the grief. At times, he welcomed the grief. It was his tie with Ellie. But the zombie days of wanting oblivion were over.

He experienced a strange sense of finality—as if something were over. Now his trips here could stop.

But something wasn't right. Was he trying to find a reason for his desire to see *her* again? No, he was honest enough with himself to know that he would miss these almost daily visits—part of him would—but there was something more, something that troubled him. He decided that he would return—just once or twice more.

CHAPTER
FORTY-ONE

June 17

Fifteen minutes before the lunch period was to end, the phone rang in the Teachers' Room. Liz cringed. The sound of the phone had become an abomination, one that often made her feel physically ill.

"Yes, she's here. Just a moment," Lia Faye said. "Liz, it's for you."

This was the one place that had been a sanctuary, and now it had followed her here. She rose automatically. "Who is it?" she asked and was surprised to hear, "Bertha Towers. She said she was sorry to bother you, but it was important."

Bertha! She rarely phoned the school. There had to be an emergency of some sort for her to make a call like this. Something had happened! But relief that her caller was not the faceless phantom who had been stalking her made Liz's voice almost cheerful as she said, "Hello, Bertha. What's up?"

"I'm so sorry, Lizzie, to bother you at school, but"—Bertha's voice cracked—"Duke isn't in the backyard."

"Duke . . . but I put him there myself, this morning. I know I did! And I locked the gate. I'm almost sure I did. It was such a nice day that I thought he'd enjoy the exercise. Are you positive?"

"He wasn't there when I got here this morning, so I thought maybe you had taken him to the vet. Well, I waited a while—I know about how long it takes—and then I phoned Dr. Nickson, but his nurse said you hadn't been there and weren't expected until next month. I went back out in the yard and checked again. The lock wasn't fastened.''

''That means . . . No, I couldn't have! I always lock the gate. Someone must have taken him right after I left for school. I'll call the police from here. Oh, Bertha, what could have happened to him!''

''Lizzie, don't panic yet. He's a valuable dog, and someone may want money for him. You'll probably be hearing something soon if that's it.''

''I'll call you at home if I hear something,'' Liz said, trying to control her voice. ''Thank you . . . I'll phone the police now.''

When the bell rang she had just completed her phone call to the Sixth Precinct, and after providing a complete description of Duke, was told that they would be on the lookout for him. If he turned up at home, they would appreciate a call from her.

Fortunately there were only two periods left in the afternoon. She gave one class a quiz and the other a group work session. To assume that there was a connection between her caller and the person who had taken Duke was madness, but the thought persisted. If only it were somebody who wanted money, she would pay it gladly—no matter what the amount.

This hypothesis buoyed her up and made it possible for her to drive home, planning her actions minutely. She would offer a reward and ask the post office to place the note in a prominent place. Then she would phone the local paper as well as *The Pennysaver* and take out ads offering a reward in return for any information about Duke. There would be no questions asked.

The image of the bulky brown furry body made tears come to her eyes. ''Oh Dukey, be safe, baby, please!'' she whispered aloud.

As she drove up Bayview Avenue, her spirits sank, and

she was made aware by the loud blast of someone's horn that she was driving too slowly.

The thought came to her that maybe it was all a terrible mistake. Maybe Loren had taken him—where she could not imagine—but maybe he was back in the yard now and all her fears were groundless.

She set her things down in the hall and ran to the back door, opening it, praying that she would hear that beloved bark as soon as she stepped into the yard.

There was no sound except for the chirping of some starlings nearby. Slowly she headed for the doghouse, hardly daring to hope that he had crawled inside to sleep. He often did that, she told herself, walking more and more slowly as she approached the kennel.

She uttered a cry of joy as she saw the furry body inside. "Dukey," she cried, but there was no welcoming bark. He's ill, she thought, bending down to look in.

The sight that met her eyes made her heart plummet. Duke lay curled up in an odd position. His eyes were closed; his throat had been neatly slit.

❀ ❀ ❀
CHAPTER
FORTY-TWO

June 20

Losing Duke was more than Liz could bear. Awake for most of the night, at seven-thirty the next morning, she dragged herself to the phone to call the school office.

On the phone with Dotty, she burst into tears. "We've had a death," she finally managed to get out. When Dotty asked if she would be in the following day, she said, "I don't know," and quickly hung up.

This was not the first death she had experienced, but except for her grandmother's when she was sixteen, it was the first one so close to her. She had never known her maternal grandfather nor her paternal grandparents. She had wept for days at the time of her grandmother's death. The sense of loss persisted—she had adored her.

How could she compare losing a dog to the loss of her beloved grandmother? But except for Loren, Duke was all she had left.

She had actively observed Duke's growth from a rambunctious puppy to a responsible, devoted watch dog. With Duke, she was safe. Without him, she was bereft.

This morning, before leaving, Loren had patted her head and kissed her forehead. "Take it easy. I wish I could stay home, but I'm giving tests all day. I'll see you later. Liz—" He paused, a sad little smile hovering about his lips. "Think about Duke being with Grandma. She loved him too. Remember?"

And he was off, reminding her subtly that she still had him.

She had set herself a few tasks. One was to inform the police about Duke's murder. Another was to write a letter to Steve Rosner, trying to explain why she had been behaving so oddly. Her aim was to convince him that she was a good and conscientious teacher, but this proved difficult. And she made a number of starts, dissatisfied with the way her letter was taking shape.

Her head felt muddled. Maybe it would be better to go back to bed and try to sleep for a while. She had never functioned well without enough sleep.

But the dreams and nightmares were intolerable. June 28th was only eight days away.

Lying there, with images of Duke sprawled beside her bed, she caught that last image of the bloody gashed neck. The horror of it pushed her out of bed.

Maybe some breakfast and a cup of coffee . . . but when she got downstairs and sat down at the snack bar, all she could swallow were a few bites of toast and the coffee that Loren had left for her on its warming tray.

A sharp longing for her mother came over her. When she had been sick as a child, her mother was always there, ready with a cool cloth for a feverish head, some jello for a sore throat, and when she wanted something but didn't know what, there were freshly baked oatmeal cookies and a cold glass of milk.

At this moment, she felt as vulnerable—maybe more vulnerable—than she had ever felt as a child. If only she could *speak* to her mother.

Captivated by the tiny puppy in the elegant Great Neck pet store, her mother had been unable to resist buying Duke for her and Loren. "Fortunately," she had said more than once, "your birthday was only a week away."

Liz's mind brought back the playful contests among the three of them as to who should walk Duke. Yes, her mother was entitled to know what had happened to him. She would *want* to know.

Just hearing her mother's voice would bring her closer,

and maybe Liz could steel herself to ask why she was not answering any of the questions in her letters and why she had so distanced herself.

The only thing that made her hesitate was the memory of a conversation with Loren several days earlier when she had mentioned her strong desire to reach her mother.

She recalled his pained expression when he said, "She's given us up, Liz. Why is this so difficult for you to understand and accept?"

"I don't know, but it is. I keep telling myself that just because she fell in love with Leopold Chernik doesn't mean she's given us up."

"Hasn't she? How much satisfaction do her letters give you? I could see her running away from her husband, but not cutting herself off from us."

"Maybe she hasn't. Maybe she'll be glad to hear from me. . . . I can't believe she's changed so much."

This thought continued to sustain her and increased her determination to track her down.

In spite of Loren's disapproval, she decided to try to reach her mother through Leopold Chernik. It might not be easy to track them down, but she would persist. Once her mother became aware of how much Liz and Loren missed her, surely she would change her mind about the instructions in her letters. Maybe they could even fly out to see her.

If Liz were successful, Loren would forgive her for flouting his advice. Now was the time. Definitely, while she had the courage.

Too fidgety to consult the telephone book, Liz decided to try Directory Assistance. The operator gave her eight Manhattan listings that began with "Concert."

On a pad she wrote down what she wanted to ask, and was about to dial when a sudden inspiration seized her. She raced upstairs to her desk where she rummaged in her Memento file until she located what she was hoping to find—a program of one of Leopold Chernik's concerts that her mother had given her shortly after Liz's meeting with him.

There it was—*Concert Bureau of Allied Artists* printed in small letters on the bottom of the program.

She dialed the number, her heart beating erratically. The prospect of getting at least one step closer to reaching her mother and actually hearing her voice had, for an instant, raised her spirits, but on the heels of that a wave of anxiety was sweeping over her.

Certain that only an emergency would enable her to reach Leopold Chernik, she realized that Duke's murder was that emergency. Her right eye had begun to twitch, and as she uttered, "I must get in touch with Leopold Chernik," her voice trembled.

"That's impossible, I'm afraid. Who is this?" a male voice asked.

Liz gave her name, adding, "My mother is a close friend of Mr. Chernik's. Please contact him and have him call me at this number. Please, it's urgent!"

Why had she added that? Because, she rationalized, her own urgency was driving her crazy.

"This may take some time. I'll do my best."

There was nothing more to do except to wait, and waiting had never been easy. Her head began to throb. I'm going to pieces, she thought. Nothing so far—not the sinister phone calls, not even Mike's leaving her—had made her break down. Duke's death seemed to have become the catalyst to the kind of despair she had never before known. What was the matter with her! Was she going to fall apart now?

Liz didn't know how long she sat there, in her room, just staring at the phone.

At three—she heard the chiming of the clock downstairs—the phone rang. She recognized the heavily accented baritone voice that said, "This is Leopold Chernik. I am returning the call that was made to me about an emergency. To whom am I speaking, please?'' He sounded stiff, and yet she thought she detected a thread of anxiety in his voice.

"Mr. Chernik! This is Elizabeth Ransome, Thea's daughter. I haven't heard from my mother in a long time, and . . . I've been worried about her, but now something terrible has happened. My dog . . . Duke was murdered. Would you . . . could you ask her to call me, please?''

"I am sorry about your dog, but I don't understand, Miss Ransome, why you would call me.''

What was he talking about!

"Because she's with you, and you are the only person who knows where she is. I'm sorry if I'm bothering you, or interfering with something, but . . .''

He interrupted with, ''Your interfering with something is of little consequence, but I have no idea what you are talking about. Is this some kind of cruel joke?''

She felt as if she were surrounded by heavy fog. "My mother left letters for us saying that she would be traveling with you and she would contact us but that we mustn't try to contact her. I didn't understand, but I was glad she was happy. May I speak to my mother, please, or can you have her call me?''

Liz could feel her teeth begin to chatter. Why did he sound so cold and detached? Was he trying to protect her mother from her?

He didn't speak immediately. It was as if he were trying to digest what she had just said. Then he said slowly, "I cannot continue with this conversation. Perhaps you do not know your mother as well as you think you do. Please, Miss Ransome, do not try to contact me again.''

"No," Liz protested, "not yet, please! I got letters from her. Not often, but some were postmarked from California . . . some were from Texas. She told us to write to a post office box number, but she never answered any of our questions, mine or my brother's. That seemed so peculiar, not like her at all. Weren't you in California and Texas and . . . ?''

''And in Arizona and Oregon and Washington and Hawaii. What has this to do with anything?'' His tone had grown icy.

Afraid that Chernik would terminate the conversation, she said again, ''Please tell me how to reach my mother.''

''I cannot accomplish the impossible.'' There was a pause and then a sharp click.

The confusion she felt now was paralyzing. What was the matter with him! Was this the charming, debonaire Leopold Chernik she had met in her own home?

And then she had another terrifying thought. Maybe her mother was ill—too ill to come to the phone, and he was trying to spare her.

But he had not sounded worried or solicitous. His voice had been angry, glacial. Maybe they had quarreled just before the phone call. Maybe her mother had gone out to walk it off. She had often done that after an argument with her husband. If Leopold were hurt, perhaps furious, that could account for his manner. The last person he'd want to talk to was a member of the Ransome family.

Maybe she had threatened to leave him. . . . Maybe Chernik even thought that she had been in touch with her family and that this was some kind of malicious joke on Liz's part to get even with the man who had taken away her mother. After all, he had only met her once. He didn't know her at all.

This cold stranger was not the man she remembered meeting. But her mother had fallen in love with the man Liz *had* met, the one who had brought a glow to her mother's face when his name was mentioned—as if she came to life at the mere thought of him. But people change. Perhaps her mother was the one who had changed.

And I don't even know where they are, Liz realized. He had been so careful not to tell her. They could be in Europe, even in New Zealand.

In any case, quarrel or not, it was apparent from his manner that Leopold Chernik would not help her locate her mother. It was up to her mother now, and she felt utterly powerless.

When Loren came home from school, Liz told him about the call to Chernik. He frowned. The mere mention of the violinist's name seemed anathema to him.

"What can we do?" Liz said.

He gave a mirthless little laugh. "You could call the police, but Mother and Chernik haven't broken any law. There's no law—as far as I know—that prohibits an adult woman from going off with her lover."

"Didn't you hear what I said? Leopold Chernik acted as if he didn't know what I was talking about. He asked if this was some joke—I think he said, 'cruel' joke. When I asked to speak to Mother, he said he couldn't accomplish the impossible. What did that mean?"

"One of a number of things. Either that he didn't want you to speak to her or that *she* didn't want to speak to you. Or, as you suspect, that they had a fight and she was walking it off. It sounds pretty simple. That was a habit of hers, I recall. Do you remember the time she left Dad and us for two days? Bertha took care of us then. Maybe she walked out on Chernik, too, and when she's ready, she'll come back."

"But why would he be so distant, so unfriendly? Why didn't he just tell me?"

"You're being naive, Liz. It's in his interests to keep her to himself, away from her family. But it has to be what she wants, too. If she did walk out for a few days, why didn't she get in touch with us? You've gotten letters from her—more than I have because I didn't answer the ones I did get. In a couple of the early letters I asked questions, but she never answered them. What was the point of writing? She made it clear that she didn't want to be in any close contact with us. We can't blame only him. Obviously, she has changed. We can't figure out why.''

Often Loren was much more astute than she. Her confusion began to lift, but the ache was still there.

''Maybe nobody really knows anybody else,'' she said slowly. ''I had a picture of Dad in my mind that turned out to be unrealistic—not in all ways but in some pretty crucial ones. And,'' she added, ''I thought I knew Mike.''

''I'm sorry, Liz,'' Loren said gently. Then, ''I came home to see if you were okay, but it's getting late. I'd better take my shower.''

''Oh . . . it's Thursday!''

''Do I detect an edge in your voice? Come with me to Mike's. I'm sure nobody would mind.''

Nobody? Of course, Donna and Jimmy. Wryly she said, ''Thanks, but no thanks. I'm in mourning.''

''Do you want me to stay with you. I can call this off.''

She knew that he meant it, and it moved her enough to say, ''No, no, Loren. But . . . thank you.''

He gave her a quizzical look, then loped into his room, and soon she could hear his shower going.

After he had left, Liz continued her speculations, going over the conversation with Leopold again and again. The only thing that made sense was that Leopold and her mother had quarreled, and that he was still smarting from the quarrel. Surely this would account for his sounding so unfriendly—even hostile. It would also account for what he had said about the impossible. Maybe, several hours later, the quarrel was over and if she called now, her mother would be able to speak to her.

On the verge of picking up the phone again, she stopped. Leopold Chernik would have left instructions with the Concert Bureau never again to respond to any calls from Elizabeth Ransome.

The trail had ended—unless her mother had a change of heart. Maybe when he cooled off, Leopold would even tell her that Liz had called and wanted to hear from her.

She could almost hear Loren's voice chiding her. *More fairy tales, Liz? It's time to stop believing that every story has a happy ending.*

The confusion was returning. After the call to Leopold her first impulse had been to report the odd conversation to Detective Levin, but she would feel like a fool if as a result the police began to harass her mother and Leopold—if they could find them.

She knew she was being unfair, and she knew that Detective Levin and Officer James had taken her seriously, but she couldn't help thinking about what Levin had said about childish pranks. He was an experienced police officer, and he must wonder why following all the threats and packages no attempt had been made to actually harm her. Even when the car with the blazing headlights had come straight at her, she had not been hit. Why, when the calls continued and the packages kept coming, might they not think there was something peculiar about this whole thing? If she were a cop, might she not think that Elizabeth Ransome was some kind of nut? And the alleged drug dealer whom nobody could catch up with. "Our invisible man," Detective Levin had called him.

Only she knew that she was in danger, and she was growing more and more convinced that the police could not take her seriously until that voice on the phone did what it threatened—murdered her as it had Duke.

When she did phone the police station a few minutes later, she summoned up all her courage to report Duke's murder.

❀ ❀ ❀

CHAPTER
FORTY-THREE

June 20

A fit of coughing racked his body. The homeless man sank down on a bench, holding the newspaper tightly in his hands until the paroxysm passed. He felt hot and feverish. Maybe he would head for a shelter tonight. If he collapsed, someone might get him to a hospital.

He was dying—he knew it—and it didn't matter much where *he* died, but somehow it seemed more fitting to die in a bed.

Now the coughing spell had abated, and he leaned forward, the better to see the short squib at the bottom of the first page. As he read, a rush of heat flooded his face. *His* call had resulted in this.

Squinting, he read:

> Woman's body found in abandoned shack in the Ramapos, near Pleasantville, New York. In response to an anonymous 911 call, police discovered the decomposed body of a Caucasian female under the floorboards of a shack near the railroad tracks. No identification of any kind was found, and the police are asking anybody with information concerning a missing person in the area, to come forward. At present, there are no leads or clues of any kind. The number to call is (914) COP CALL.

Knowing that he was close to death, the homeless man felt a strange affinity towards this unknown woman.

"Rest in peace," he thought and was startled to realize that he had said the words aloud.

🙛 🙛 🙛
CHAPTER
FORTY-FOUR

June 21

A slender white envelope addressed to Elizabeth Ransome was on the hall table with the rest of the mail waiting for her when she came downstairs at noon. She had awakened at the usual time, had been in the midst of showering when she remembered: no longer did she have a job. Bed seemed her only refuge.

The message inside was on a sheet of white paper. On it were pasted sixteen words, cut from newspaper headlines.

HOW DOES IT FEEL, ELIZABETH RANSOME, TO KNOW THAT IN ONE WEEK YOU WILL BE DEAD?

Automatically, she picked up the envelope and placed the sheet back inside. There was no point in phoning the police. She would show it to them. . . .

The anguish she still felt over Duke's murder dissipated any feeling of terror she might have had at any other time. It had never been her caller's intention to make her death easy to face.

There seemed no purpose to her life now. Eating had become a chore, and Liz decided that her vitamin pills had all the nutrients she needed. Two days after Duke's death she had fallen apart in her second-period class, screaming at a student, and then storming out of the room.

That evening, Steve Rosner had called. He sounded regretful, even sad when he said, ''I want you to go on sick leave immediately, Liz. Come in tomorrow and leave your roll book in the office. You must get some kind of help before you return in the fall.''

"Steve, I don't want—'' she began, but he cut her off. "It's what *I* want, Liz. You're a damn good teacher, but I've had more calls about you in the last two months than in all the years you've been teaching here. We don't have a choice. If you come back in the fall, I expect you to be functioning normally—as you always have.''

She had done as he ordered, had returned her roll book, and turned in her various keys early the next morning so that she avoided seeing any of the teachers.

This morning Loren had said he would be home for dinner. She wondered if it was because she had, to all intents and purposes, lost her job. Maybe she would fix some kind of meal for them both. But it was hard to focus. Normally, when she was in the kitchen, Duke was nearby in one of his favorite spots—near his red food dish or at the window, looking out, occasionally barking if a squirrel ventured too close.

She mourned Duke as she mourned the lost members of her family . . . and Mike. Everyone was gone—everyone except Loren.

While she stood in the kitchen, looking around her as if this were some foreign territory, Loren came in and gave her a jovial pat on the shoulder. "What are you doing, kid?''

"I . . . was thinking about Duke.''

Now the hold on her shoulder became gentle, and he pulled her close to him so that her head was next to his. "I know. I haven't been able to get him out of my mind either. But you do have to eat, as Bertha would say, 'to keep your strength up.' I'll go out and get us some pizza and a salad, and then I'll stop at the liquor store for some red wine. You set the table. I'll be right back.''

Loren was trying to make her feel better, she thought gratefully. He must have sensed her feeling of disorientation.

She set the table with a red-checked cloth and took out two wine glasses. Tempted to use paper plates, she overcame the temptation and used the white china. For some reason, Loren hated paper plates. She even took out the espresso maker and two demitasse cups and proceeded to make the coffee. Then she scoured the fruit bin and found a lemon that she peeled for the espresso.

Loren, for his part, had brought back a pizza with everything on it and seemed delighted with her efforts to make the meal a festive one. Her own dormant appetite awakened briefly, and she found herself eating half a slice of pizza.

Every so often, Liz became aware of Loren's affection for her—as now, when he was gazing at her with pleasure and approval. "You're really eating! I thought the pizza would do it." His jovial expression gave way to one of boyish eagerness. He looks about twelve, Liz thought.

"Liz, do you remember when we were kids—how we always wanted to run away?"

"Every other week, as I recall."

"Do you ever think of that now?" It was not a flippant question. He was as serious as when he had spoken, several weeks earlier, of disappearing forever.

"Of running away? You mean for real?"

"For real. From all of this—from whoever it is who's hounding you . . . from jobs and . . . people."

Her face must have shadowed.

"You're thinking of Mike?" he said gently.

She nodded, her eyes lowered. "I'm a fool," she said. "It's over. . . . I haven't even spoken to him on the phone."

"Liz." Loren's eyes shone with excitement. "Let's do it. We have nothing here . . . anymore."

"Dad?" she said tentatively.

He snorted. "When he gets out of that plush nuthouse, he'll go right back to where he started. Then finally, they'll take away his license to practice. Even doctors can't go around killing people."

"He didn't kill anybody!"

"Not that last time he didn't. They stopped him. When you drink as much as he did, your brain gets like tissue paper. If I had a dollar for every time he's operated drunk, I'd have as much money as he does. Liz . . . let's take off! You look like hell. I see how you jump when the door opens or the phone rings. You cry with no provocation. The cops don't seem to be able to make an arrest. Has your shrink helped at all?"

Yes, she thought, but then realized that she wasn't sure. Dr. Matthews was gentle, kind, sympathetic, but what could *she* do? It was comforting to talk to her, but now, time was running out.

Instead of answering Loren's question, she said, "Money? What do we do for it?"

"We use our inheritance."

"You mean Grandma's money?"

"Is there something sacred about it? We've been letting it gather interest since we were twenty-one. She left it for us to use, Liz. She'd like to think we were using it for something that would make us happy. You remember Grandma."

Yes, she did, and her eyes filled with tears. Her grandmother had loved both her and Loren unreservedly. And they had worshipped her. She brushed a hand over her eyes and tried to control her voice. "I know why it would be good for me to get away—I don't even have a job anymore, but why do you want to? Do you hate *your* job that much? Anyway . . ." She paused, wondering how to phrase it delicately enough. "Aren't you involved with someone?"

Surprisingly Loren didn't even frown. All he said was, "One question at a time, okay?"

"Okay."

"Yes, I do hate my job that much . . . and my idiot students and our esteemed father and my whole goddamn life!"

His face twisted into a grimace of pain that cut through her. "And I'm no longer 'involved,' as you put it, with anyone."

She thought that she had never loved him as much as at this moment when he had revealed himself to her without any attempt at subterfuge.

For some time now she had been living without purpose, drifting through her days, waiting for some new catastrophe to happen. And the catastrophes continued to happen. Duke's murder was the most vicious of all. Nothing mattered anymore. Why not do this for Loren?

"Where?" she asked.

"Anywhere . . . Europe, Asia, India, Mexico. Who cares, Liz. You mean it? You really will go with me!"

She nodded. To her amazement he grabbed her around the waist and swung her in the air. For a moment they were the Liz and Loren of her childhood. Together, the two of them were magic. Nothing bad could ever happen to either of them when they were together.

"When are we going?" she asked when he finally set her down.

He laughed. "That's the spirit. That's my old twin. I can't stand what's been happening to you, kid."

"You're really doing this for me, aren't you?"

"Wouldn't you do it for me?"

Of course he knew that she would do anything for him, but she had not always been as certain of him. She had lost Mike, but if she regained Loren, maybe her life was worth something after all.

"One thing, Liz, no goodbyes."

"Not to Dad . . . or to Mike?"

"Write them notes. That's how I plan to resign—a note to everybody. It's you and me against the world, Liz. Hasn't it always been that way since we were kids?"

Yes, she thought, it had. The closeness between them had always lessened when other people intruded.

"Loren," she said, "seriously now, where are we going?"

He shook his head. The years fell away, and here again was the Loren of her childhood, with the look that told her he knew something that she did not. "It's a surprise. You'll find out at the airport."

She smiled—it seemed to her for the first time in weeks. "If we're going where it's warm, remember to pack the suntan lotion. I prefer Bain de Soleil."

He laughed joyously. She hadn't seen him so happy for a long time.

They cleared away together, and then Loren brought out a quart of Haagen Dazs coffee ice cream that he'd hidden in the freezer. As they were eating it, he said, suddenly looking reflective, "Remember the fun we used to have up at the cabin?"

She nodded. Abruptly she remembered the smell of the woodsmoke, the crackling log fires that took away the evening chill and made them cozily warm, the ghost stories, her mother's cheerfulness, the informality of their meals— her father had come only on the weekends.

Sitting up straight in her chair, she said, hearing the urgency in her own voice, "Loren, let's go!"

"I haven't finished my ice cream."

"No, silly. I mean before we're off to see the world, let's go up to the cabin for a weekend."

His brows puckered as they often did when he was seriously thinking.

"Please, Loren!"

"I'm way ahead of you, kid. I was thinking about when."

"Why not today or tomorrow?"

He hesitated. "You know me, Mr. Fusspot. Let's get the chores out of the way. We've got to sell my car—the weekend is the best time for that . . . take care of our money, checking accounts, things like that. Then, when that's all taken care of, we can go just before we leave for good. How does that strike you?''

She was embarrassed at her childish letdown feeling, and did not want him to see how disappointed she felt. "I guess it's okay. It's just . . . now that it's a fact, I want to get out of here—away from that maniac. I told you—he's threatening to kill me, Loren! Only one week left." She was having trouble controlling the sudden hysteria that threatened to overwhelm her.

"He's not going to kill you. Okay . . . this is Friday. We'll attend to everything within the next week—write our letters of resignation, and turn them in the last day of the term, and go up to the country Friday morning. Is that better?''

She took a deep breath. "Much! You know I feel as if you've given my life back to me.''

"You even *look* better. I wish I had thought of this sooner.''

"Maybe," she said slowly, "things happen when they're supposed to. If Mike and I weren't finished, I couldn't have left him.''

An expression she couldn't fathom had crossed Loren's face. Softly she said, "You care about him too. I've been so selfish I forgot he's your best friend.''

He shook his head. "You're my best friend, Liz, and I guess I'm yours too.''

"I guess," she said.

June 22

The good feeling lasted an entire day for Liz, and then, the next morning, doubts began to subtly filter in. What if she were being precipitous? She loved Mike—even after all these weeks of hearing nothing from him, the thought of him, his smile, his laugh, the memory of his touch, made her ache inside.

What if in a month or two he decided to give her another chance? The thought made her frown. I sound like a beggar! Fine feminist I am. But she knew that she would give her life for that chance.

I can't go, she thought, not without telling Mike. Maybe the prospect of her leaving would make him realize how idiotic this whole thing was. Should she call him?

A feeling of extreme weariness came over her. She hadn't slept much last night. If she tried to sleep for a while, the day would seem to pass more quickly, and then maybe, if she could summon up the courage, she would phone Mike.

She slept fitfully, awakening with a start when she realized that her father's phone was ringing. Her thoughts had been so full of Mike that she hurried to answer it, irrationally certain that it must be he.

Instead it was that voice—the flat voice that said, "Your days are numbered, Elizabeth Ransome." And then the pause that preceded the inevitable click of finality—"Counting today, only seven to go!"

She forced herself to go downstairs and take in the mail. Depositing the letters and magazines on the hall table, she saw that there was a bulky letter for her—no return address. When her shaking fingers managed to get it open, she found an envelope and tore it, spilling the contents on the table—six capsules and a note with letters taken from a newspaper. "Why not take these and make it easier for yourself?"

The immediate thought that followed made her wince. Donna sometimes took pills to help her sleep. And then the words of the note began a hypnotic refrain in her head. Why not take these . . . why not take these?

Why not indeed! Gathering up the capsules and holding the envelope carefully, she walked upstairs like a sleep-walker and sat down on the edge of her bed. I'm so tired, she thought, so tired. What a delusion it had been to think that Mike would ever come back to her. Loren's idea of escape now seemed like an impossible fantasy.

It was odd, she realized, that she didn't feel sorry for herself at all. In a way, maybe this unseen enemy was doing her a favor.

She shook out the capsules and held them in her hand. But she would need water. Swallowing any kind of pill was always difficult for her—she didn't want to choke to death.

The ludicrousness of the situation struck her. At another time she would have howled with laughter. Now she merely smiled.

A sudden fatigue came over her once again, and she lay down, the pills still in her hand. Rest before the long rest. The permanent one, she thought, lying back on her pillow. One of the pills rolled out of her hand, but she would pick it up later.

"Liz!" A hand was shaking her vigorously. "Wake up!"

The panic in Loren's voice cut through her sleepy haze. "What's the matter?" she said, sitting upright.

"There's a pill on the floor . . . and you've got something in your hands! Liz, you . . . you haven't taken anything!"

"Not yet," she said quietly, now fully awake.

His face blanched as she showed him the note. He ripped it in half and was about to throw it in the wastebasket when he stopped. "The cops may want to see this. I'll Scotch tape it." Then he sat down on the bed beside her. "Liz, don't give up now. We'll be out of this by next Friday. Please hang on."

"It's a dream, Lor," she said softly, "a crazy fantasy. How long could it go on? Someday, we'd have to come back."

"Not ever—if you don't want to. There are villages in Spain, in Portugal, in Mexico, so cheap our income would last for years. The old man hasn't long to go—his liver can't be in good shape. We may never have to do a lick of work again. And if we do, we can always teach. Liz . . . I can't do this alone. And I feel as if I'm drowning!"

Again she was torn. He had known exactly what to say to her.

"Give me the pills," he said.

She shook her head. "No, let me keep them. It's a kind of insurance."

For the first time he grinned. "Okay, but promise me that you won't take them until you've told me first."

"And be talked out of it again?" she said half-facetiously.

But there was no answering smile on his face. "Yes," he said. "A hundred times if that's how long it takes, Liz. Something in nature went berserk with us. We were supposed to be identicals not fraternals. We're half of each other. You could probably survive without me, but without you, there would be nothing left of me. Promise me, Liz!"

"I promise," she said softly.

Dinner that night was almost cheerful. They opened a bottle of Moet that they had been saving for some time—for a real occasion—and toasted each other. He had sold his car at a good price, he told her, sounding elated.

Suddenly Liz remembered the garden behind the cabin. "Loren," she said urgently, "let's plant perennials . . . in memory of us."

"Behind the cabin." He followed her thoughts as if they were his own. "Great idea. Lilacs and azaleas and . . . She may come back to it someday."

"You mean . . . Mother?"

He nodded, but the lightness was gone, and they finished their dinner in silence.

CHAPTER
FORTY-SIX

June 22

The atmosphere in the apartment had undergone a change. Caren had withdrawn from Ken to the extent that they spoke only when it was necessary. She shopped and cooked now, was civil when he spoke to her, but his apparent lack of excitement over the baby had hurt her so deeply that as the time grew closer she simply chose to insulate herself from him.

The dependent, weeping Caren had disappeared. It was as if the fetus growing inside of her had given her an inner strength she had never before possessed. She had stopped talking about the coming baby, and she made her doctor's appointments when Ken was working.

Only last week, he had said, "Have you decided which test you're having done?"

She had looked up at him coolly, her expression one he was unable to read. "Why?" she asked.

"Because I'd like to go with you. I want to be there."

"That's a change of heart, isn't it? I'd just as soon not discuss the test with you."

She had turned and walked out of the room, leaving him surprised and chagrined.

No, he was not interested in the coming baby, and if Caren wanted to punish him for that, so be it. He could survive her coldness and withdrawal.

Something was happening to him that he had not foreseen. For days, the events he had experienced replayed themselves in his mind. As painful as they were, he had begun to make notes about what he remembered. This superseded the novel and stirred his imagination more deeply than the book he had so carefully outlined and which had engrossed him for almost a year.

One evening, sitting alone in his study after working for several hours, he realized that this new idea was now taking the place of his obsession with Liz.

It had been an engrossing preoccupation, but it was over.

He was coming to understand that he could continue to live if he refused to think about the future. There had been so many plans for things that would happen when Ellie was older. They had moved to this neighborhood in Queens because the school was reported to be unusually good. When she was five, they would enroll her at the New Dance Group in New York, and when she was seven they would start her with piano lessons. The piano had been his and Elinor's first big purchase after Ellie's birth.

He closed his eyes tightly. They were hot with tears.

Sometime later when he opened the door of his study and glanced into the living room, he saw that Caren was asleep on the couch. She had been watching television. He walked over and stood next to her. How young she looked, how vulnerable. One hand was flung across her chest.

He bent down and gently kissed her cheek, but she slept on. He was aware that the bitterness inside him had disappeared. He had saved a life instead of destroying one, and in the process, perhaps he had saved himself.

June 24

Ken was in the middle of typing a story for the three o'clock deadline when his phone rang. Without looking up from his computer, he called over to the man sitting at the desk next to his. "Would you take a message, Dennis, please? I've got to finish this."

"Ken . . . it's your wife. She said it was important."

He grabbed the phone from Dennis Stevens; his heart was pounding in an erratic rhythm. She's lost it, he thought, and was horrified at his own sense of desolation.

"Ken . . ." Her voice sounded excited. It was higher pitched than usual. "I know you hate to be called at work, but I had to tell someone!"

Anxiety made his voice harsh. "Caren, what are you talking about! What's happened? Where are you?"

"I'm at home, Ken. Dr. Sabot just got back from his vacation. That's why it took more time. He just phoned me about the chorionic villus."

"What do you mean? Are you taking the test soon?"

"I've had the test . . . almost two weeks ago, but he was away, and that's why he just called me."

It was taking some time for Ken to absorb all of this. When he did, he realized that she sounded happy. *Happy!* Heart still pounding, he finally got the words out. "Then you're . . . it's . . . you're *both* okay?"

"Ken, it's a boy! I'm going to have a boy!"

His throat seemed to close. Gratitude and joy were emotions he had not known for a long time. He didn't even care that Dennis Stevens was looking at him in alarm. He made no motion to stop the tears rolling down his cheeks.

Caren's voice came over the wire loudly. "Ken . . . did you hear me! I said . . ."

He interrupted her. "Sweetheart! I'll be through with this story in ten minutes. Then I'm coming home. We have to start thinking about a name for our kid."

Caren began to laugh, and he thought that he had never heard a lovelier sound.

❦ ❦ ❦
CHAPTER
FORTY-SEVEN

June 27

After a quick shower Ken set water to boil and made himself a cup of filtered coffee. The hot coffee furthered the awakening process and soon he was in his car, almost automatically headed for Bayview Avenue. There was a difference, however. A strong difference. The obsession was over, but the journalist in him needed to know what was happening so that the events had some kind of order, and ultimately an ending.

Signs of life began earlier this morning. The brother came out of the house and pulled the blue car out of the garage.

Through the binoculars, his face looked intense, serious, and the contrast between his appearance now and that evening in the restaurant, triggered vivid memories.

Even up close, wearing ordinary men's clothes, Loren Ransome looked amazingly like his sister. Small wonder, Ken thought, that he had been confused. The guy was gay, no doubt about that now, but the feeling of disquiet he was experiencing now bothered and puzzled him.

Certainly the disquiet had nothing to do with Loren's obvious homosexuality. Phil Adams, Ken's best friend all through high school had been gay—an incidental matter that had never interfered with their friendship. Sometimes Phil would joke about it—"You're not my type, old boy."

Ken would discuss his girlfriends, and Phil his boyfriends, and Ken was privy to information that most of the school community was ignorant of.

Still trying unsuccessfully to account for his uneasiness, Ken sat there, under the lush fir tree, waiting for Elizabeth to come out. When she did, she was wearing jeans and didn't seem to be going to school at all. Was school over for her? he wondered. Her mood seemed tense—as if she were wired up, and as Loren got into the blue car, she said, "Where's the shovel? Didn't you remember what we said about planting?"

"I'm sorry. I guess Mr. Organized isn't as organized as he thought."

"Never mind. I'll get it. Let's buy seeds along the way. Tomorrow." Without waiting for an answer, she ran into the garage and came out with a large shovel in her hands and a pair of gardening gloves which she placed in the trunk.

"There are lots of places along the road to buy seeds," she said. Abruptly, she clapped her hands. "Lor, I just had a great idea. Why don't we leave today—when you come home from school? My bag is packed." She spoke quickly, her voice tight and tense.

Ken saw that her face was flushed. She appeared different, somehow.

"Let's stick to our original plan," Loren said. "I'd rather drive when I'm rested. I didn't sleep well last night."

"Neither did I. I haven't since . . . Duke. The conversation with Chernik keeps going through my head, too. Tomorrow, then, but no later than seven. Okay?"

"Yes, Sergeant! Okay."

Maybe school was over for them both, and the brother was going on some kind of errand. By now Ken knew so much about them that any dramatic change in their lives disconcerted him. Where were they going and why was she showing signs of so much strain?

Maybe he'd learn more tomorrow.

Images of Elizabeth Ransome had pervaded Hoke's dreams since that night when he had been so close to success. Unable to resist the urge to see her again, he drove to Bayview Avenue and parked in a spot where he could watch her house unobserved.

Maybe he could follow her to school and cut her off. Just the thought of this possibility excited him.

Elizabeth and her brother soon emerged from the house, and Hoke's first glimpse of her twin astounded him. Doug had told him how much they looked alike, but he could not have imagined how close the resemblance actually was. The expressions on their faces were different, though. He looked preoccupied, a trifle sad. Elizabeth's movements were quick, but she seemed disturbed. Her eyes were red, as if she might have been crying.

There was a great deal of movement going on and packing of the blue car with assorted boxes and containers. Finally, the car seemed to be packed to their satisfaction, and the trunk was slammed shut.

A sharp stab of disappointment went through Hoke. They were going somewhere together. But it was a school day. No, school would be over about now. Then he realized that this was Friday and that they might be going off for the weekend.

Doug had told him about the family cabin in the Schunemonk Mountains where various family members often spent weekends. Maybe that's where they were headed.

Sometimes Hoke thought that his unusual intelligence gave him a sense of prescience. This sense was unusually strong now, and his disappointment evaporated. It didn't matter where they were going, he decided. He was certain that opportunities would arise that would get him what he wanted—Elizabeth Ransome.

The twin brother would be no match for him. Elizabeth

would struggle, but he was taller and bigger and stronger, and he would overpower her easily.

His excitement mounted as his thoughts raced on. He would follow them wherever they led. And then, God help her!

Abruptly the two got into the car, the brother in the driver's seat. Hoke heard the sound of the revving engine, and almost as soon as the car left the driveway, he started his newly rented car and drove off. He liked this one. It was a black Mazda.

June 28

Tomorrow had come quickly, and Ken was back at his post. It was clear that they were going on a trip of some sort. This would be *his* last trip to the Ransome house.

At the edge of his awareness, a perception was surfacing. A small black Mazda was parked across the street from the Ransome House; it, too, was partially concealed by a huge fir tree. Trying to be as unobtrusive as possible, Ken focused on the car window and spotted the driver—a dark young man who seemed intent on what he was watching. This was someone who was doing exactly what he was doing, observing the occupants of the house.

His journalist's instincts were aroused, and he felt a twinge of annoyance that someone was encroaching on his territory.

As the blue car left the driveway, the driver of the other car waited a second or two and then revved up his engine.

He's going to follow them, Ken thought uneasily. Based on nothing but instinct, he decided what his next move must be.

And almost instantly, he changed his mind. This was his last visit to the Ransome home. He had decided that yesterday.

It struck him forcibly that he owed Elizabeth Ransome a great deal. She had restored something vitally human in him. At first, he had been certain that Caren had become pregnant on the day he'd been aroused by the young woman he had determined to kill. Then, after the doctor estimated the due date, it was clear to both Ken and Caren that she had conceived before then, on that night a month after Ellie's death. Still, it was after the lovemaking that afternoon that the real Caren had begun her return to life. Unwittingly, Elizabeth Ransome had saved Caren for him.

Just the thought of his unborn son—this "unwanted" child—thrilled him in a way that he could never have anticipated.

The period of his craziness was over. There was no reason to follow either Elizabeth and Loren Ransome or the black Mazda. He could no longer rationalize the actions of the past months. But following Dr. Ransome, spying on his daughter, making insane plans had probably kept *him* from insanity, he realized now. It was time to go to work.

June 28

Finally in the car, knowing that they were at last on their way, Liz began to relax. The evening before had been spent in last-minute chores. At times Loren had been exasperating in his meticulous attention to details.

"Where is your letter?" he had asked.

"Which letter?"

"The resignation letter." She could still hear the barely concealed impatience in his voice.

"It's here—all typed and signed."

"Where? I don't see any letter."

"On my desk. Stop acting like a . . . like a . . ."

"Drill sergeant?" he supplied.

"Not exactly." She had begun to smile.

"A schoolmarm?" Now his eyes were twinkling.

"That's more what I meant. Now, Loren, stop it! I hate it when you're so super-organized." But she was laughing as she said it.

"I get carried away. This is such a disorganized household. Sometimes it's hard to resist trying to make some order out of the chaos."

"Try! Everything is in order. I'm all packed, Loren. I'm ready for . . ."

He had gazed at her intently. "For our new life?"

Nodding, she lifted an imaginary glass. "Our new life!"

"I'll drink to that." He appeared suddenly exuberant, his eyes sparkling, his face animated as he clinked his imaginary glass with hers and pretended to drink.

They were up at dawn and on the road by seven as Liz had stipulated. They both wore jeans, as if by prearrangement, and Loren wore his red Western kerchief around his neck. Hers was blue.

As they drove into the driveway of a diner that seemed to appear miraculously just when Liz thought she would starve if Loren drove past one more that didn't suit him, a flurry of fear made her say, "Lor, I thought I saw a black Mazda behind us."

"So?"

"I've seen Hoke drive a black Mazda."

"So do a million other people in New York." Loren got out of the car and walked around the lot. When he came back, he said, "No black Mazda in this lot. Relax, Liz. You're far away from that creep now. He can't hurt you. Nobody can."

Liz glanced down at her watch. "Nine hours to go," she said.

"Till what?"

"That's how many hours I may have left," Liz said, trying to get her voice to sound steady and almost succeeding. Her fear was slowly dissipating.

When the breakfast arrived, the orange juice was cold, the French toast brown and crusty, the coffee steaming and fragrant.

As Liz started on her second slice of the thick golden-brown toast, liberally soaked with maple syrup, she became aware that Loren was gazing at her and grinning.

"What's the matter?" she asked. "Do I have syrup on my nose?"

"Nope. I haven't seen you eat like this for weeks."

"I haven't been hungry in weeks. This morning before we left—it was so early—but somehow I thought the phone would ring any minute. Why do you think I was rushing you? I was afraid that somehow 'it' would know and stop us."

"It?" Loren repeated.

"That's how I think of . . . the voice. It's oddly flat. There's no way of telling what it is."

"Stop thinking about it. Go back to your French toast. Nobody has our cabin number, and once we're on our way, 'it' will never be able to bother you again."

"I feel as if you're saving my life," she said, and inexplicably, her eyes filled with tears.

"The waitress is looking at us. She probably thinks I've said something nasty and hurt your feelings. Go back to your food, Liz—she's looking daggers at me."

Glancing over at his plate, she saw that his French toast had barely been touched. "Why aren't you eating?" she demanded.

"Excitement—you know me. I can hardly believe this is really happening."

"Loren . . . isn't it time you told me where we're going after the weekend?"

"Nope. I promised you'd find out at the airport. That's the bargain." He looked elated with his secret, she thought.

"Have I ever been there before?" She wondered how she had been able to contain her curiosity until now. I'm better, she thought. I'm beginning to feel almost normal.

"You've never been there, and that's my last word on the subject," he said firmly.

"You sound like Dad—even the intonation," she observed with admiration.

"Please! Elizabeth! One more word, and I'll be forced to ask you to leave the table."

"Loren, stop! I don't want to remember . . . not now."

"Sorry," he said in his normal voice. "I got carried away. Liz, have you eaten enough?"

The impatience in his voice was audible. She laid down her fork, took a last sip of coffee, and said, "I can take a hint. Let's go."

Once on the Cross County Parkway with mountains in the distance and lush green foliage all around them, Liz

found herself relaxing even more. For an instant she closed
her eyes. She felt peaceful. "Do you mind if I snooze for
a little while? Are you wide awake or do you need me to
talk to you?"

"No, I'm fine. I know you haven't been sleeping much
lately. Sweet dreams."

She was in the state between sleep and wakefulness
when the neuter voice in her head intruded. *Your days are
numbered.* . . .

Abruptly a strange heat flooded her body, and she began
to count. Three days had passed since the last phone call.
One more—the rest of today—and she would feel safe.

Now on the Thruway the car was moving very fast.
Opening her eyes and focusing on the speedometer, she
saw that they were approaching eighty.

"Loren," she cried out, "slow down!"

Obviously startled, he swerved and then quickly
straightened the car.

"You scared the hell out of me!"

"I'm sorry . . . but we don't need a speeding ticket
now. We've got to start thinking about saving money."

"Okay," he said, beginning to decelerate. "The Thruway is so smooth—even in this car. For a little while there,
we were flying."

"We'll actually be flying soon enough, Loren."

"Now *you* sound like a schoolmarm," he observed.

"Touché!"

Soon they left the Thruway and turned down a small
country road. Evergreens stood in clusters like sentinels
guarding a dark and mysterious forest.

"I love the way the woods look," Liz said. "They remind me of those drawings in *Little Red Riding Hood*—
you know the ones by Elizabeth Orton Jones?"

"Big shot! I hated that book. Don't you remember what
I did with it?"

A dim memory surfaced. "You threw it in the wastebasket, didn't you?"

"Those pictures scared the hell out of me!"

"Now I remember . . . and Mommy rescued it and put it away in the closet."

He smiled, and she knew a momentary embarrassment at having used the childish name.

"Best of all, she didn't tell *him*. He would have had a field day. He thought I was the biggest coward alive. 'Your sister is a girl and she catches a ball better than you do. She doesn't run away from it!' "

The scene from childhood returned to Liz too vividly.

They drove quietly for fifteen minutes or so until they came to the big sign that said "Steep curve ahead. Slow." Liz felt her pulse begin to race. They were almost there—on their road.

And suddenly there it was. Hidden among the trees, off the road, the small cabin, creosote-treated for the rustic look that Thea Ransome had loved.

For a few moments they stood there quietly, just looking at it.

"I wonder how long it's been since anyone was here," Loren said.

"Mother said she was coming up here before she left," Liz said. A wave of sadness engulfed her at the thought that nothing would ever be the same again.

Loren nodded. "I know . . . I remember her saying that."

"Do you suppose . . . he came with her?"

"The virtuoso?" Loren's voice was contemptuous. "I'd rather not think about that if you don't mind, Liz."

Swiftly he changed the subject. "Let's get cracking. I'm starving. What shall we have for lunch?"

"Ham sandwiches. I packed them in the cooler. Let's have a festive meal tonight, though. I brought some steaks in the ice chest. Loren, did we bring charcoal?"

"There's some around—we always kept big bags of it in the back room closet."

Liz stepped across the threshold and snapped the light

switch. The blue and green living room was as trim and neat as though it had been recently used. She ran her fingers over the coffee table in front of the couch. "There's hardly any dust," she said. "Isn't that odd?"

"*He* may have used it before he went loco at the operation. As a matter of fact, he mentioned it during one of our rare bits of dialogue. He said something about having bought charcoal."

"Oh . . . okay. Want to choose for rooms?" Liz asked, uncomfortable at the way Loren spoke of their father.

"I can afford to be munificent for a weekend. You get first choice."

From the outside, the cabin appeared deceptively small, but it was in fact spacious. There were three bedrooms, and the couch in the living room slept two.

Liz opened the door to her favorite bedroom. Tiny sprigs of violet graced the papered walls, and the bedspread and drapes were of the same pattern. She felt a sharp jab of love for her mother, who knew that violet was her favorite color and had planned the room decor as a surprise for her.

It had turned out, though, that Loren preferred this room too, and rather than argue about it and subject him to their father's scorn, she had often let him have it without argument, especially when their father was around. His scathing contempt for what he called "Loren's girlish fancies" was as painful to her as she knew they were to Loren.

In the cupboard was a complete set of dishes and glasses, and there was also a supply of paper goods. They settled on paper in the interests of saving time, but Liz brewed real coffee.

They ate their ham sandwiches at the snack bar in the kitchen, Liz, hungrily, in spite of her hearty breakfast, while Loren nibbled as he had at breakfast. "What's the matter with you?" she asked. "You're hardly eating."

He yawned. "I'm tired. Don't forget I did the driving. I'll be okay after I've slept for a few hours. As a matter of fact, do you mind if I head for my bed right now?'' He stood up, waiting, she was sure, only as a polite gesture.

"Go ahead. I forgot I was snoozing while you drove. Sweet dreams," Liz called after him.

She felt so much better, she realized, only a few hours out of Great Neck and away from the terror that had been haunting her for weeks. The breeze that drifted in through the open kitchen window smelled of lilac from the flowering bushes in front of the cabin.

Unexpectedly, she yawned, a deep yawn. She must be sleepy too. Apparently the snooze in the car had not made up for the sleepless nights. The thought of her bed was suddenly irresistible and she quickly put the paper plates in the bag set aside for garbage, and the cutlery and cups in the sink.

The blinds in the lilac room were drawn, and the atmosphere was as serene and restful as she remembered. Slipping out of her loafers, she lay down on the bed and closed her eyes. Only six and a half hours to go, she thought.

Liz awakened to the sound of a Brahms quartet. It was one of their favorites. Loren and she had decided a number of years ago to keep duplicates of their favorite records in compact disks at the cabin. How luxurious it felt to awaken to it, to be able to stretch and yawn, and lie in bed with her eyes closed, just listening to the music.

When she glanced at her watch some time later, she saw that it was almost seven. How could she have slept away so many hours? There had always been periods in her life when she endured sleepless nights, she recalled, and when her body had chosen its own time to make up for the lost sleep.

"Your body knows what it's doing," her father had said on more than one occasion.

Sudden tears sprang to her eyes. She missed him and her mother and . . . Mike. If only, she mused, we could go back to wonderful periods in our lives whenever we choose. Maybe one day there would actually *be* a time machine—like the ones Asimov wrote about in his science fiction.

"Grow up, Liz," she said aloud. Even for Isaac Asimov, the concept was a fantasy. "There is no such thing as a time machine," Asimov had written somewhere in an article.

A shower, a brisk rubdown, and she'd be ready to accept the present, she decided. Loren had worked out their future, and only an ingrate would demand that the rosy hues of the past return.

As she was walking downstairs, the fragrance of brewing coffee wafted up to her. Loren was actually brewing coffee! Soon the smells of grilling steaks mingled with the savory ones of sauerkraut and beans and the fragrance of the Kona coffee drifted through the house.

The dining room was paneled in pine. When would they see this beloved place again, she wondered sadly, already nostalgic.

On the rare occasions when he cooked, Loren prided himself on synchronizing everything exactly, and by seven-thirty Liz and he sat facing each other across the wood table, the food on steaming platters in front of them.

In an abrupt movement, Loren rose. "Wait a minute . . . I almost forgot."

He went to the kitchen and brought in two glasses and a bottle of champagne. He seemed delighted at her surprise and anticipated her question. "I chilled it and hid it in the trunk in that styrofoam doohickey."

"Moet, again!" Liz raised her eyebrows.

"My last extravagant gesture," Loren said. "I promise."

He went to the window and drew the drapes.

"It feels cozier," he said. "I like being in here with the woods out there."

They ate and drank merrily. The food tasted marvelous.

Involuntarily, Liz raised her wrist and looked at her watch. "It's almost quarter of eight," she announced triumphantly.

"Who cares about the time?"

"A couple of minutes more, and I'm home free!"

"Great!" Suddenly his expression changed, and he cocked his head as if better to listen. "Do you hear anything peculiar?"

She concentrated. "Not a thing. It's the woods—you're always nervous here the first few hours. Let's drink to what's ahead!"

He repeated the words solemnly. "To the wonderful life ahead."

They drank deeply. Liz drained her glass thirstily. "More," she said.

He filled her glass again, then stood and moved away from the table.

The effect of the champagne was subtle and wonderful. She felt languorous and happy, and when she looked around for Loren, she was surprised to see him standing behind her.

His eyes were ice blue, as if they were made of glass. There was no expression on his face. She stared up at him, following the movements of his hands.

He had removed his neckerchief and was running his fingers over the cloth.

"Loren, what are you doing?"

"I am going to kill you, Elizabeth Ransome!"

That voice! The flat, neuter voice! With horror, she realized how she knew that voice.

The cloth was around her neck now. She pulled at it, trying to release herself at the same time she was screaming, "Loren! You're insane!"

But he was pulling the cloth tighter and tighter, holding her in a vise, and she was choking.

Desperate, frenzied, she was unable to make her body obey her. The champagne—two glasses of champagne! She flailed and kicked, but her breath grew more and more shallow. More and more dizzy, she felt the room revolve around her, and there was no way she could stop it.

She was choking.

Now he moved so that she could see his face. It was triumphant. He wants to kill me, she thought. He is killing me!

June 28

An overpowering desire to live flooded her, and she croaked the two words that had miraculously come to her mind. "See Same! See Same!"

The tightness around her throat eased. Liz stared up at him. The mask of cold hatred had been replaced by confusion and fear.

Darting out of his grasp, she ran to her purse and found the gun that she had been carrying around for weeks.

Later she could not imagine where she got the strength that enabled her to point the gun at him and hiss, "Sit down on that chair!"

Loren obeyed her blindly, whimpering as he had when they were small children.

With one eye on him, she lifted the receiver and dialed 911. Clearing her painful, hoarse throat repeatedly, she gave the operator directions to the cabin. The receiver was still in her hand when the enormity of what she had just done hit her.

I've just called the police to arrest Loren. Loren! And Loren wanted to _kill_ me! The thought was as bizarre as the events of the past four months.

For one crazy instant, she considered calling 911 back and canceling her request. What would she say? I didn't mean it? The cops would think she was crazy. They'd take her into custody and let Loren go.

An hysterical giggle rose to her lips, but there was no

sound. Instinctively she had covered her mouth with her free hand, her eyes flitting to Loren.

He had not stirred, seemingly unconscious although his eyes were wide open. She moved closer, the gun still pointed at him, to see if his chest was moving. He's dead, she thought, aware that an icy chill was pervading her body.

Approaching him slowly, she forced herself to touch his chest. He was breathing.

Then she tried to swallow. The pain was so intense, she wanted to scream, but only a harsh squawk came out. Loren had done this to her. Loren had tried to kill her.

Where are they? she demanded silently, desperately wanting them to be here. The police meant safety and sanity.

Conscious that she was still pointing the gun at Loren, she slipped it into her jacket pocket at the same instant she heard a sound and looked up. The door was opening.

The police, she thought gratefully, but the man who entered the room and closed the door was not wearing a uniform. He was holding a gun, and he was pointing it at her.

"Good evening, Elizabeth," he said, smiling. "I told you we'd meet again."

No, she screamed silently. No! It can't be Hoke. How did he get here? How did he know where I was?

It wasn't over. Somehow, she had known that there was more to come. Liz was facing him, but she turned just a fraction so that her jacket pocket was not visible.

Hoke's eyes were bright, his expression one of mild amusement. He seemed to be enjoying this—just as he had when he'd broken into her house that night and assumed she was finally in his power. Now she sensed that he was waiting for her to display her terror and give in to it.

What he didn't know was that she was devoid of feeling. His sudden appearance—almost at the exact moment she had begun to hope that she was finally safe—was another strange element in this drama. Loren had tried to kill her, and now Hoke had arrived to complete the job.

All this went through her mind while Hoke had been standing there, actively taking in the scene before him. He smiled again as he nodded to her. "No greeting, Elizabeth? I haven't had the pleasure of seeing you since the night of the alarm fiasco."

Pointing to her throat, she said in a hoarse whisper. "I've got a sore throat."

"What happened to him? The last I saw of you two, you were having a cozy lunch. I decided I'd have a more profitable afternoon elsewhere. When I came back a little while ago, the drapes were drawn, and I couldn't see anything."

Her head must remain clear, she warned herself. If she told him what Loren had tried to do, he would assume that she had called the police. And then he might go crazy and kill them both. Her best bet was to lie as creatively as she could.

She whispered, "I've got some kind of virus." Unexpectedly, she knew what she must say to convince him. "My brother has had psychotic episodes—all his life. He just lost his job—that must have triggered it. He hasn't had one of these in months. The medication controls it, but I guess he doesn't always take it. When we got here, he seemed fine, but then after we ate, he had an attack. I got scared. Once I gave him his pill, he calmed down. His eyes are open, but he's asleep."

She could see that Hoke was digesting this. A wary look came into his eyes. "What were you planning to do?"

"Nothing . . . now that he's back on the drug. I'm sure Loren will be fine when he wakes up."

"I have no reason to believe you, but we're getting out of here right now. And we'll take him with us. I think I can use him."

My God! She had thought she was devoid of feeling, but at the tone of his voice, terror seized her. *He'll* kill me and say that Loren was responsible. And he'll get away with it!

"Okay, Ms. Elizabeth, start moving, or do you want me to carry you?" This was his no nonsense tone. She was afraid of it. She was afraid of him.

Where are they? she railed at the same time she gave herself a sharp command. Keep talking . . . damn it . . . Keep talking! "Where are you taking us! Look, I know I haven't encouraged you, and I know you resented my attitude, but I was in another relationship. I really was engaged." She lowered her eyes, afraid that he would read the expression of loathing in them.

"My engagement is over, though. You were right—I've been interested since the beginning."

Look at him, she told herself. You're acting. You were in the drama society in school, and you acted in plays. Look sincere!

She touched her eyes, as if they were blurred, to erase the expression he must not fathom, then forced herself to look at him, but her ears were listening for any noise out of the ordinary.

Then she heard it—in the distance, a siren growing louder and shriller as it came closer.

"Goddamn you, you bitch!" Hoke hissed, but he was turning towards the door. Before she sensed what he was planning, he had opened it and was racing down the path.

As if on automatic pilot, Liz grabbed her gun and ran after him. "Please, God, please," she whispered, "don't let him get away again."

All of her jogging and running were paying off. She was gaining on him. Then to her horror, he turned and fired directly at her.

The sharp sting in her left shoulder told her that he had succeeded. "Damn you!" she shrieked, hardly making a sound. Before he could fire again, she aimed and shot, aware only of a fleeing figure, afraid that her shot would go wild but determined to stop him, somehow. She had never fired at a running target before.

Hardly able to believe the sight a short distance away, she saw that Hoke had crumpled to the ground. The bullet must have torn his leg. He was screaming in pain and blood was seeping through his trousers.

Quickly she continued down the path. The sting in her shoulder was more intense. As she tried to remove her jacket to press it down on the wound, she realized that it was stuck to her clothing.

Unexpectedly the screaming had stopped. He must have fainted. Trembling, suddenly cold all over, her legs seemed to give way, and when the police arrived, she was kneeling next to him, her gun beside her.

"He needs an ambulance," she barely managed to say.

"So do you," was the reply.

Later that evening

Within the hour, the ambulance had arrived and taken Hoke away and with him, Liz and a dazed, almost comatose Loren. Against her protests, the light-haired detective, who had introduced himself as Sergeant Harris, handcuffed him.

"Please," she pleaded, still hardly able to speak. "Don't. He won't hurt anyone, I promise."

"Rest now," the other detective said gently. "He's not in pain. You are." Miller was his name, she dimly recalled. "We'll talk to you in the hospital."

The bullet had grazed her shoulder, Liz learned later, surprised that the stinging was, at times, so intense.

In her hospital room, from which she would be discharged as soon as the police had interviewed her, Liz, speaking in fragmented sentences because of the trauma to her vocal chords, told the officers what she knew of the young man whose only name was Hoke and of his drug-dealing in the high school where she had taught. Then she had given them the address of Doug's facility in the Cat-skills.

"When he opened the door to the cottage, I was sure it was the police. He must have followed us from my home, and when we stopped at a diner, I thought I saw his car, but my brother went out to look and . . .

"He was planning to take us somewhere—just before you arrived. He got into my home a few weeks ago," she said, this time in a cracked voice but one that had begun to function. "The police department in Great Neck has a record of my call."

"You have a permit for this gun?" both detectives asked simultaneously.

"Yes." She hesitated. "And no. I've got two permits—one for my home and one for the rifle range. I couldn't get a carry permit. But my life was being threatened! I had to take my chances with the law. Are you arresting me?"

The light-haired detective held up his hand. "All in good time, Ms. Ransome. I'm getting confused, but I'll answer your question. We're not taking you to the pre-cinct, but you are guilty of a misdemeanor. I'm assuming this is a first offense, so you'll have to appear in court and pay a fine. Now let's get to the important stuff. First, tell us about the call we got. You say your brother tried to kill you?"

Liz's eyes drifted to Loren, who sat in a chair facing her bed. His eyes did not move.

"Ms. Ransome," Detective Miller said patiently, "your report stated that he was trying to kill you."

"He was," she said, suddenly drained as if the flood of adrenaline, now spent, had taken all of her energy. "I'll explain."

The explanations had taken a long time, but once the detectives were convinced that Liz did not want to press charges against her brother, they, Sergeant Harris, in particular, insisted that Loren be taken to a psychiatric hospital of some sort.

"Call his psychiatrist. Ask him what he wants done with him—where he wants him. Otherwise, we'll put your brother in one of our places."

"No, please! I'll call right now." She didn't say that she didn't know the name of Loren's psychiatrist. This was one area of his life that he had kept strictly private. Dr. Annette Matthews was the name that flashed into her mind, and if the cops thought she was Loren's doctor, what difference did it make?

Before the police left the hospital, Liz had phoned Dr. Matthews' office. She wasn't in, but her secretary assured Liz that her call would be returned in ten minutes. The police agreed to wait, in the meantime checking Loren's breathing, his pulse, his general demeanor, and conferring in low voices with each other. Liz wondered if they thought he might be faking.

Liz, still in shock, had spoken to Dr. Matthews on the phone. Within twenty minutes Dr. Matthews had given her the name of a colleague she highly respected. "Sit tight," she said. "I'll try to locate Miles Josephs. In any case, I'll call back."

Liz had followed her directions to sit near the phone and wait to hear from Dr. Josephs.

Not only did Dr. Matthews reach him, but she had explained the urgency of the situation and the necessity for immediate action. Dr. Josephs would meet Liz and Loren in his psychiatric hospital on Long Island in about three hours.

The detectives had not been willing to let Loren out of their sight. It was obvious that they did not understand Liz's unwillingness to press charges, even when she said, "Look at him. He hardly seems conscious."

"Okay," Detective Miller had said, "but this is still

our case, and if you want to ride in the police car, that's acceptable to us, but you've got to follow our rules. The captain will want to know why this guy isn't being booked.''

Liz, sitting in the front seat with Sergeant Harris, kept looking back at Detective Miller and Loren. Her pleas had kept them from handcuffing him.

They had made it clear that only their concern for her had made it possible for her to ride in the same car.

Her mind flitted from one event to another. Even now, she was unable to comprehend fully how Hoke had known where she and Loren were headed, until she realized that he must have followed them, but so cleverly that she had suspected the black Mazda only when Loren pulled into the diner. When the car disappeared, she had completely forgotten about it.

After they had driven a silent, almost motionless Loren to the psychiatric hospital, she had met Dr. Josephs, a tall, sensitive-looking man whose gentle manner reassured her. Dr. Matthews' recommendation had been enthusiastic, and Liz had forced herself to let go, to leave Loren in his care.

Leaving Loren in the hospital had been one of the most painful things she had ever been forced to do. Detective Miller had tried to make it easier by saying, ''You have no real choice, Ms. Ransome. It's either the hospital or a place the department sends him to. The fact is—he tried to kill you. You'd better keep that in mind.''

The detective's matter-of-fact tone helped more than she had realized at the moment. The Loren she loved was gone—for now at least—and fighting the reality would not help him but could break her heart.

To accept the fact that Loren—this twin brother for whom she would have given her life—had hated her enough to try to kill her, was an impossibility now. She didn't understand any of it. Her eyes were dry and burning. Even the ability to weep had deserted her.

Sergeant Harris called for an additional officer to drive Liz's car to her home.

It was past midnight by the time Loren was admitted to the hospital. There had been a brief meeting between Liz and Dr. Josephs, and finally the drive home by Sergeant Harris. As the sergeant walked Liz to the door and waited for her to unlock it, he asked, "Are your parents alive?"

She nodded, wanting to save her voice.

"I suggest that you contact them. They may be able to help your brother somehow . . . and you, of course."

How could she explain about her parents? Could she say, *My mother is traveling with her lover—I don't even know where—and my father is in a drying-out place?* It was all too incomprehensible for a stranger to grasp.

Finally, she said, "My mother is traveling, and my father is . . . ill. When I've spoken to the psychiatrist and have some idea of what he wants to do, I'll notify my father and try to get in touch with my mother."

After she had turned on the lights in the living room and hall, she ran upstairs to her room and saw that the red light of her phone answering machine was flashing. Rewinding the machine—the time it took indicated that a number of messages had been recorded—she began to listen.

❦❦❦

CHAPTER FIFTY

June 29

There was a message from Bertha. "I didn't understand your letter, honey. You're coming home on Sunday, and then you're going away again? Do you want me to come while you're gone? Call me when you get home, Liz, so we can talk."

I knew Bertha wouldn't understand that stupid note, Liz thought, annoyed that she had given in so easily at Loren's insistence. It was too late to phone tonight. She'd call her tomorrow morning.

Edith Pierce's voice came next. "What's the matter, Liz? Steve Rosner said you were ill—on an extended leave. What does that mean? I'm worried about you. Please call me as soon as you can."

Doug's mother's voice sounded more cheerful than the last time they had spoken. "I just wanted you to know that Doug is doing so well. He asked about you and made me promise to call you. Why, he's even gained some weight, and he's beginning to look more like himself. There are plenty of problems, and it will take time, but his therapist sounds very hopeful about him.

"I can never thank you enough—you and Ms. Pierce. I'd love to hear from you when you're not too busy. You have my number at work."

It was too late to phone Ann Williams tonight and tell her that she had shot Hoke and that he was in police custody. Jotting down a note under the other two, she waited, ready for the short beep that would indicate the completion of the messages.

She heard a click and was about to hang up and rewind again, when she heard something that made her heart begin to beat wildly.

"Liz . . . Liz, it's Mike. I've got to hear it from you. I don't give a damn whom you're seeing or what you've been doing. Ten times I've picked up this phone to call you, but I was afraid you'd hang up on me. Liz, darling Liz, please call me, even if you never want to see me again."

Oh, Mike! she thought, beginning to laugh and cry at the same time. Her watch told her it was past midnight. Too late to return her other calls, but not too late to return this one.

The number came to her fingers as if she had never stopped calling him. The phone rang once, twice, and then it was picked up.

"Hello," a sleepy voice answered.

"Mike," she tried to say, but the words did not come out. She tried to clear her throat over and over, and finally when she tried to say his name again, there was a sound, but hardly a voice. A whisper was the best she could do. "It's me, Mike. Liz."

"Who is this? I can hardly hear you."

"It's Liz, Mike . . . Liz!" The last "Liz" was no more than a whisper.

"Liz!"

❦ ❦ ❦

CHAPTER
FIFTY-ONE

July 5

A week later—was it only seven days since it had all happened?—Liz sat in the office of Dr. Miles Josephs.

Memories of the events of the past days overwhelmed her at times. A day after she had shot Hoke, Sergeant Harris had phoned Liz at home. "We checked on the young man you called Hoke, Ms. Ransome. He's been using an alias—his real name is Howard O. Kent. We determined that by checking his fingerprints.

"The police all over the country have been looking for him. He's a cool customer. There's much more to this case than you suspected. We'll tell you more when we're free to."

Two days after the first call, he phoned back with the news that the case against Howard O. Kent had been put in motion. The drug-dealing charge was a serious one, but the possibility of a first-degree murder charge brought by a wealthy oil executive in the West was what was making the papers.

The two officers had contacted Doug, and to Liz's surprise, Doug was willing to testify. He had even given the police the names of some of the kids he knew at the school. Two were in the same facility as he.

"Would *you* be willing to testify against him?" Sergeant Harris asked.

"If you need me, of course," she had said, wondering at her newly found courage. Loren, the brother she adored, had tried to kill her, and she had pointed a gun at him.

When Hoke's escape seemed imminent, she had run after him, been shot at, and then had shot him. *She* had *shot* him. Maybe when one's world fell apart, finding courage became easier.

Her eyes roamed the room. The walls were seafoam green, and the carpeting, almost identical in color, was thick and luxurious. It was a restful room with a Monet painting of the Grand Canal in Venice above a large bookcase.

On the bookcase stood a bust of Brahms that caught her attention. Was it exactly a week ago that she and Loren had listened to the Brahms quartet in the cabin? In these seven days her entire life had undergone an upheaval.

Deep in thought, she was aware that the doctor had entered the room only when he called her name.

"Ms. Ransome." Dr. Josephs crossed the room and extended his hand. "It's good to see you again. Your brother is, as you know, in my care. I wanted to meet with you to try to explain what has happened to him." He hesitated before adding, "You may be able to help me too."

"I don't understand . . . any of it," she said haltingly. "I feel so stupid, so inept. How could I not have sensed that something was terribly wrong?"

"Asking yourself how you *could* have sensed it is more realistic, I think," Dr. Josephs said quietly. "When you and the police brought him in, Loren seemed catatonic. After a few days, we tried a drug we've had some success with. The first words he uttered were that his name is Elizabeth Ransome and that his twin brother, Loren, is dead."

"My God," she whispered, horrified.

"Once he began to talk, he told us a great deal, not in sequence, of course, and obviously not realizing what he was saying. He is almost completely detached, except for moments when he seems to recall something painful. Then he stops and lapses into a semi-catatonic state—the kind you witnessed right after he attacked you and which lasted until we tried the drug. We stopped then—for a few hours or even a day or two. That's why it has taken so long to be able to give you any kind of picture . . . and why you may be able to help me.

"He told about the telephone calls and the careful planning of your murder. A grave behind the cabin in the woods had been carefully dug. He had even planned to use limestone so that there would never be a trace of the body. Then he would go to Mexico for the operation."

"The operation?" Liz repeated, bewildered.

"I'm sorry. I'm going too quickly. He was going to have a sex change."

"I don't understand. . . ." Her mind seemed enveloped in cotton wool.

"Your brother is what we call—for want of a better term—a transsexual. He was convinced that he was in the wrong body—this is not uncommon. You were twins, but, for some reason, he was convinced that there had been a genetic error. From that point, it's not too difficult to follow his perverted logic. Let me continue, and then you can ask all the questions that will undoubtedly come to your mind.

"In this country, there are preliminary procedures, but he had no time for those. He had planned your trip together very carefully, but of course, he would be the only one taking it. After the operation, he would assume your identity, return to the States, announce Loren's death, and marry the man he loved."

"The man he loved," she repeated. "There was a man he loved?" Even as she said the words, her heart sank.

"Mike is what he called him. 'Mike—Liz's lover.' You see, he slips in and out of his new identity. When he speaks of Liz, his tension is apparent. His face contorts, and his body becomes rigid. Then when he leaves the Loren identity, he seems to relax. We allow him to wear women's clothes, of course. He wanted his own . . . a member of my staff went to his apartment in Manhattan to get them."

His apartment in Manhattan!

At the look on her face, Dr. Josephs said, "I know you've gone through hell, but this had been building in him for a long time. He hates his father violently. He worships his mother, but he refers to her only when he speaks of his childhood. He had a male friend whom he loved, and then you took him away. When I say these things, I'm speaking from his viewpoint. The line between sanity and insanity is such a fragile one. Twins are so much closer than other siblings, and to make it worse, there was this incredible resemblance between you. Did you ever realize how desperately he wanted to be a woman?"

The cotton wool had become ice in which she was encased. It was hard to get the words out of her mouth.

"He was always talking about how nature had mixed us up. I should have been the boy, he said, because I was the stronger one. But he always laughed when he said it. He had a wicked sense of humor—we used to play things off each other. We'd spend hours together, just talking and laughing. We hardly ever needed anyone else. And then he met . . . Mike, and one night he felt sorry for me and asked me to come along and join them for dinner.

"That was the beginning for Mike and me. But Loren never said a word. He seemed to take it so well. . . ."

Abruptly she remembered the weekly dinners with Mike's children, which Loren had so loved and so subtly taunted her with. And who had told her about Donna's uncontrollable temper and how she had hated the new baby, Jimmy, and about the drugs she had taken, and her therapy? He had skillfully exacerbated her suspicions of Donna so that Mike and she would break up.

The horror of it, of the malevolent genius that had engineered this complicated plan, swept over her in a sickening rush.

She was afraid she would be sick and swallowed hard, breathing deeply.

After a while she became conscious that Dr. Josephs

was studying her, his eyes intent on her face. Finally he said with unusual gentleness, "You were putting things together, weren't you? Things you hadn't connected before?"

"I can't bear it." She could hardly manage to utter the words. There was a leaden weight inside her. "I've never lived in this world without Loren." Even in her desperation, she knew how childish she must sound.

"You've gone through hell—I said that before—but so has he. You have the advantage though, and he always knew you had it. You will survive."

"And he . . . will he survive too?"

Dr. Josephs raised his hands in a gesture of defeat. "His psychosis is in an advanced state, but who knows? I'm not God. Your family is wealthy—he'll have the best care possible. And if he chooses to live the rest of his life as 'Liz Ransome' in the small secluded world of this facility, this is survival too—for him. We'll be continuing to test him. There are elements in this that I still don't understand. Maybe you can help me."

On his desk was a tape recorder. As he inserted a cassette, he said, "I don't understand this—it's disjointed and fragmented, and after doing the taping, he was in a wretched state, unable to stop talking, suffering intensely as he spoke, as if the words were being forced out of him. We had to give him a shot to stop it. I was afraid of the possible consequences.

"This will be painful for you, but please bear with me."

She nodded, waiting.

At the first words, chills permeated her body. She had expected to hear Loren's voice, but the voice was hers! Only the venom in it did not reflect her.

"She didn't give a damn about me! She knew what she was doing!" Then, in a rush, "No time to plan . . . just do it. Not the cabin! A nice drive . . . the mountains . . . Floorboards loose enough . . . cover her. Not enough time. Her eyes, oh damn those eyes! Why is she still staring at me? Couldn't wait to leave me. 'Loren, what are you doing!' Unfaithful bitch . . . stop looking at me . . . leave me alone, damn you!''

Mesmerized, Liz heard the snap of the switch that shut off the machine. Tears that she was hardly conscious of rolled down her cheeks.

''I don't understand most of this,'' Dr. Josephs began. ''When the voice changed . . .'' He stopped, seeming abruptly to become aware of her.

In the past few days, Liz had had a recurrent nightmare. A horrifying suspicion had been haunting her since the night in the cabin. Her nightmare had just come true.

She felt dead inside. The words came out haltingly.

''It was . . . my mother's voice. Loren . . . killed my mother.''

EPILOGUE
THE SHOREHAVEN SANITARIUM

June 19—Two Years Later

A slender young person who called herself "Liz" looked out the window into the garden. The day was hazy—the weatherman had predicted a fifty percent chance of showers, but forecasts were often wrong.

The garden was such a lovely place in which to receive guests, especially now in June, and especially guests like Donna and Jimmy. How proud she was of them—of Donna, who at eighteen had completed her second year at Brown, and of Jimmy, wonderful, gentle boy, who had shot up so fast he was now as tall as a full-grown man.

A wave of sadness passed over her. She seldom saw Mike, but she understood why. With his new job he was forced to travel most of the time. At the moment she couldn't remember just what that new job was, but it didn't matter. Often he came to her at night when everyone was asleep. Those were the times that sustained her.

Loren, too, came at unexpected moments. It must have been Loren who had told Mike how to manage his unscheduled visits. Darling, clever Loren. She missed him so much. But twins were closer than other siblings. She had always known this, and when she most longed for Loren, he always came. Oh, the laughing and talking and reminiscing!

Sometimes she worried that they would awaken other guests in the hotel, but Loren said it was all right, and she believed him as she always had.

Her father came often too—she made sure that Loren

never visited on those days. What a pity that he didn't
know their father as she did.

Just an hour to wait now. It was time to choose her
outfit. She would dress for the garden event if the visit
took place in the guest lounge.

The long chiffon gown—her favorite—was soft and
filmy, a blue and lavender print on a white background.
Almost all her dresses had some lavender in them. Liz
loved lavender too.

A wave of pain shot through her skull. Why did she
think of herself in the third person? She tried to focus on
a memory, but it floated away from her. So many memories eluded her since the . . . breakdown.

One last look out the window. The sun was out. It was
a good omen. She headed for her favorite lawn chair and
settled down to wait. It was lovely here. The scent of
honeysuckle wafted toward her, bringing with it a wisp of
a memory that once again drifted away. But Dr. Josephs
had said it was to be expected. She trusted him.

Promptly at two, they arrived. Donna, walking quickly
towards her, fresh and elegant in a white tennis dress, and
then Jimmy, in jeans but wearing a new Madras shirt that
she had never seen.

She was drifting away . . . No, not now! It was an effort
to pull herself back. Donna was saying, "I've decided to
major in math."

"Liz" laughed. "You certainly don't take after me. I
passed Freshman Math by the skin of my teeth. My brother
was the math whiz in our family."

Donna looked at her oddly, and then "Liz" remembered. "Why would you take after me! Sometimes, darling, I forget that you and Jimmy aren't mine."

What a sweet smile Donna gave her.

And Jimmy took her hand and squeezed it.

Her love for them seemed to engulf her.

An instant later, a cloud shifted and hid the sun. She
shivered.

* * *

The waiting was never easy. At the beginning, Liz could not bear even thinking of Loren. Her mother's murder had destroyed something vital in her, and the fact that *he* had been responsible for taking her mother's life had wiped out in what seemed like a few seconds the close tie that had linked her to him.

"I'm empty," she often told Mike in those early dark days. "I lost my mother and my brother at almost the same moment."

"I know, love. And I feel helpless. God, how could I have been so stupid!"

Mike could hardly bear to have her out of his sight. In those first days they had talked and talked, but there was always more to talk about, more to question, more to try to understand,

He was still revealing fragments that Loren had slipped into their conversations about her. Each time Mike had spoken about phoning Liz, Loren had subtly but ingeniously dissuaded him, recounting incidents of the man Liz was seeing, someone she had known before she met Mike.

"He sounded so sympathetic, Liz, as if he wanted to keep me from being hurt. And I believed him. It never even occurred to me to check with you. I knew how deeply I had hurt you.

"Why wouldn't you start a relationship with someone you had known previously? My history was hardly a sterling one. I had made one stupid mistake when I got involved with Barbara and let it drag on for years. My confidence wasn't exactly in great shape at that point."

Liz recalled the twisted, sad little smile that had crossed Mike's lips when he told her this. He had taken her fingers to his lips and lingeringly kissed each one.

The strain on his face, around his mouth, had moved her unbearably.

A year after Liz and Mike were married, Liz abruptly

began to dream of Loren. Her body trembling, she would awaken to a sense of pervading loss.

When the dreams continued and showed no signs of abating, she began to perceive what had been happening. She *missed* Loren, she longed to be with him. She would miss him for the rest of her life, as she would her mother.

Taking firm root in her mind was the realization that the Loren she loved could not be the Loren who had killed her mother and had almost succeeded in killing her.

Then, as the longing to see him intensified, she thought, Maybe I can just see him through a glass window. And she had even gone up in the elevator as far as the lobby, where patients came to meet their guests. But swiftly she had turned and taken the elevator back down again.

No . . . if she didn't see him, she could picture him as he had been.

But the longing did not disappear, and over and over she had to push it away. How ironic that she was the only one who could not see him . . . except for Mike who had been forbidden, too.

Dr. Josephs had been adamant. "Seeing you could plunge him into a catatonic state that would probably be permanent. Your husband's relationship with Loren is Loren's fantasy. Even a glimmer of reality could be destructive."

But all the others went—Donna and Jimmy, faithfully every other week during the summer and as often as they could in the winter.

At times, Loren did not know them, but they continued to come. It was always possible, Dr. Josephs had warned Liz, that Loren's illness would overpower him and that the state would be permanent. But until that did happen, Donna and Jimmy would continue to come—as would the father whom Loren had detested.

Liz had been surprised when she learned that from the beginning her father had begun to visit Loren regularly. He had been sober for over two years, no longer practicing surgery but acting as a consultant and now teaching at Mt. Sinai.

Sober, he could face what his derisive attitude had contributed to his son's psychosis, and only Liz knew what it must have cost her father to see Loren this way. But he told Liz that he had forced himself to go that first time, and then again, and without conscious planning, the visits had become a habit.

And Liz suspected that her father was finding something in this son that he had never been willing to see before.

Recently, he had said to her, "If it weren't for you and . . . your mother, the chances are he would have succumbed to the psychosis much earlier."

The memory made tears come to her eyes, and when she looked up, she saw Donna and Jimmy coming down the path. Both looked cheerful.

"He's fine," Jimmy said.

Liz smiled through her tears. In the last year he had grown two inches taller than she.

"He looked so beautiful," Donna began. After a momentary hesitation, she went on. "We talked a lot—I told him about deciding to major in math. And then . . ." She stopped, looking stricken.

"And then," Liz said. "Please tell me—you know I want to hear everything.

Donna nodded. "I know. He said, 'You obviously don't take after me. I passed Freshman Math by the skin of my teeth.' He sounded just like *you*—it was as though he thought Jimmy and I were his `. . . and then he laughed and said he'd almost forgotten that we weren't."

Liz looked into the beautiful brown eyes that met hers. Was this beautiful, sensitive young woman the same girl she had suspected of wanting to kill her? She reached up to touch her cheek. "Most of the time," Liz said in a voice that was hard to control, "I forget too."

Donna's sudden grin was mischievous. "Who would ever have thought . . ."

"Yeah," Jimmy added, grinning too.

Their smiles were infectious. It struck Liz how dearly she loved them.

She had a sudden, whimsical thought. "How would you all like to stop at McDonald's?" she asked.

"Great," Donna and Jimmy said in unison.

Mike groaned.